Play...

I couldn't see what it was he had in his hands. Then I felt it. My wrists were clicked into two pairs of handcuffs. Before I knew it, each was fastened securely to loops set into the wall above the bed.

'What the hell are you doing?' I spluttered.

'Just teaching you a little restraint. You're too dominant for your own good.'

He stroked me – naked and wet – and once more I felt desperate to have him inside me. I suddenly felt excited. This was something new. I've done bondage before – who hasn't? But somehow this seemed different. He meant business.

Playing Hard

TINA TROY

BLACK
lace

Black Lace books contain sexual fantasies.
In real life always practise safe sex.

First published in 2001 by
Black Lace
Thames Wharf Studios,
Rainville Road, London W6 9HA

Copyright © Tina Troy 2001

The right of Tina Troy to be identified as the Author of
this Work has been asserted by her in accordance with
the Copyright, Designs and Patents Act 1988.

Typeset by SetSystems Ltd, Saffron Walden, Essex
Printed and bound by Mackays of Chatham PLC

ISBN 0 352 33617 X

Chapter One

The man lying beneath me groaned. I could see his erection bulging against his red satin boxer shorts. They're so obvious, these guys. Red satin. I ask you. He opened his eyes and gazed up at me, his expression all misty with his fulfilment. I clamped my legs around his middle and pulled them even tighter, till he groaned again.

'Oh God,' he managed to whisper. I grinned, but it was wasted as his eyes were closed. Ten more minutes to go, according to the clock. His cock was angry and straining. Should I lean down and finish him off with my mouth? It's not part of the agreement. He wants to feel the final, total submission in his own time. I wish he'd hurry up. He'd better come in the next ten minutes or he's out of luck. I wriggled slightly, letting him feel the strength in my legs. That's what they like, these men. My strength. Great. That did it. He's coming fast, panting and writhing. In my job, I don't even have to fake an orgasm to make my men happy. I love the power. The stain of his come spread over the red shorts. I

1

relaxed my hold and his body went completely limp. Safe sex? This has to be the ultimate.

'Lili, you are wonderful,' he murmured. 'Paradise.'

'Thanks,' I said, adding one of my special 'I know what you're thinking' grins. 'Shall I let you up or do you want me to restrain you for the last couple of minutes? Must give you your money's worth.'

'I think maybe I've had enough.'

'Too much for you, am I?' I said, predictably. The lines are getting hackneyed.

'I wouldn't say that. Next time, I'll make sure that you submit to me.'

'I won't be back here for a year.'

'That gives me plenty of time to train. Can I book you now? In anticipation?'

'You can talk to Dexi on your way out. I haven't booked any firm dates yet. If you like, you can put your name on the list and we'll get in touch.' I rose to my feet, towering over my client. I stretched an arm down to help him up. He groaned again, this time without any pleasure.

'I think you may have finished me off already,' he moaned.

'I thought that was what you wanted.' I pushed my long blonde hair back with a toss. Why does long hair always seem sexy to men? I suppose it's just one more thing to keep their fantasy going. His neck was tight. One heap of tension. I gripped his shoulders. My fingers stiffened and pressed hard into the knot of tension. I felt him squirming and pressed even harder.

'Ow!' he gasped. 'Are you made of steel instead of bone?'

I worked at his muscles more gently until he relaxed. When he stood up, I realised that we were exactly the same height. Six feet. I used to be self-conscious of my height at school. I towered over everyone else. Now I'm glad of it. I even wear heels, the higher the better, except when I'm actually fighting, of course. I enjoy being looked at. I work my body hard and use it to get exactly what I want out of life while I can. It's great when the clients are shorter than me. They're often much fatter and really fancy their chances against me. I'm too fit for them. Too good. The bigger their ego, the bigger the price they pay to win. My pride won't let me allow them to win and I'll never admit to feeling pain. It makes me strong inside as well as outside.

He lifted his arm, aiming towards my shoulders. I could so easily have thrown him down. It wasn't worth it.

'Lili,' he pleaded, 'can't we . . . I mean won't you . . . come for a drink with me? Please.'

'Sorry, I don't mix business and pleasure.'

'Call it business then, if it makes you feel better. I don't care. I like you. I'd like to get to know you.'

'If it's business you'd have to pay my usual hourly rates. I don't think you'd want to do that. Not just to have a drink with me. Besides, I'm moving on tomorrow. Now, maybe you'd like to make use of the bathroom? I think you'd better change before you leave.'

He glanced down at the stain on his underpants. 'You could be right. I could get arrested, appearing like this. Thanks again. It's been great fun.'

I smiled to acknowledge the compliment. My mind had moved on, focussing on the next appointment. God, I really need a drink, I thought, but I had to make do with a quick shower and a complete change of clothes. Mr Smith, or whatever his real name was, needed to get out of the apartment fast.

Dexi, my receptionist, secretary and close friend came in. I smiled at him. I nodded towards the bathroom and Dexi got the message.

'Your next keen client is waiting outside,' he told me. 'Champing at the bit.'

'He's early. I must shower and change before he comes in.'

'He's requested a special costume.'

'Oh God. Not one of those. What does he want?'

'Something very skimpy. He's a legs man, so none of the all-covering lycra body suit.'

'Great. Any colour specified?'

'Virginal white, preferably. And boots. He wants high, laced white boots. Best of luck. Hopefully he's unfit and thinks he's about to get cheap and kinky sex.'

'Nothing cheap about me. He knows my fees and it certainly does not include cheap sex. Most of these twerps are almost coming before I start working on them. Making them last the hour's more than I can do.'

The bathroom door opened and the fourth Mr Smith of the day came out. He was wearing a business suit and, apart from looking rather pink, showed no evidence of his exertions.

'Thanks again, Lili. Dexi, please keep in touch and let me know if you're ever in the area again. I can't wait for another session.'

'Sure, Mr Smith. I'll check your address and we'll send you a flyer next time we're here.' The six foot four of good-looking male that is Dexi, held the door open. He winked at me, leaving me to get ready for the next sucker.

God I was thirsty. I can never drink anything, not when I'm fighting. I sipped at a glass of iced water. Gulping it down, the way my body craved, would finish me off. I stepped out of the body suit, red lycra and all-enveloping. In the shower cubicle the high-pressure jet washed over me. I turned it to cold and it made my flesh tingle. The punishing spray helped wash away my weariness. My aching muscles felt refreshed. I thanked heaven it was my last client today. Six in one day is too much but, money aside, I hate disappointing anyone. I smiled, wondering where they said they'd be for the hour or more they're with me. I liked to think of their secretaries faces, if they were told the truth:

'I'm going to wrestle Lili for the next hour. Take my calls please, I'm not available!'

I sighed and took a deep breath, stretching my arms above my head. It's all very well for them, I thought. They fight for an hour and they feel exhausted. I lose count of how many there may have been in the day. Somerset tomorrow. Then it all starts over again. Another hotel room. Another collection of men needing my exclusive and somewhat unusual services. If it didn't pay so well, I'd jack it all in. I sighed again. Another year on the road and I may just be able to think about retiring and settling down. Something quiet and conventional, like the restaurant I've always dreamed of.

I scrubbed vigorously at my skin with the towel. I've got a good body. I could see every inch of me in the mirrors I like to have everywhere. Long, long thighs. I always take care to keep strong muscle tone but be free of body-builders' over-developed muscles. I felt my breasts, firm and well shaped. The nipples hardened as I fondled myself. Who needs a man? Wow! What am I saying? I need a man. It's always the same on the road. I want a man. I never give these guys a chance, not the ones I fight with, I mean. Most of them are so ... oh, I don't know.

5

They only want to come when I squeeze them between my thighs. Waste of good spunk, some may say. Pressure fetishists, all of them. Nothing wrong with it in its way, but it's not good, satisfying hard cock where it matters most.

As I stood gazing at myself in the mirror, just thinking, I'd become very wet. I pushed my fingers into my hot cleft and rubbed. Fast. Fast. Damn. Out of time. He's here. Mr Smith the nine hundredth. You'll have to wait, my girl, I told myself.

I looked in the mirrors again. Hard to miss looking in this place. Should I bleach my pubic hair? The dark triangle between my thighs proves chemical intervention elsewhere. Still, I'm picky about who views this particular part of my anatomy. Why bother? I've fought hard, literally, to get here. It's been a difficult journey.

I selected a white leotard. I keep a range of outfits to suit any requests: PVC, leather, lurex, whatever. The legs on this one were cut very high, revealing thigh almost to my waist. The top, high at the front, had a deep plunge at the back and short, tight sleeves. Just the thing for a legs man. I wriggled myself into the garment, pulling it tight over my body. No zips in case they cause injury. My nipples showed through the fabric, erect and dark beneath the shimmering surface. I pulled on a pair of soft, white kid boots and laced them tightly, right up my legs, almost to the knee. Everything was smooth and fluid. I always felt sexy in this particular outfit. I hoped he'd be worth it. The final touch. I brushed my hair. It shone in the bright lights. I twisted it into a ponytail high on my head. It was distinctly phallic and made me look even taller. I looked good, I knew it. The perfect picture of health and the epitome of male fantasy. What fools men could be. Fancy paying out three hundred and fifty pounds for less than an hour with me.

'Don't knock it, Lili,' I told myself. 'You'll soon be plain Penny Jackson. The brand new version. Another year or so and Lili can be buried forever.' I fixed my smile and opened the door.

Bill Davidson sat on the couch, opposite the door. He looked rather uncomfortable. His fingers twisted the handle of his sports bag. Hesitantly, he stood up.

'Miss, er ... Lili,' he stammered. My heart sank. He was yet another dork. He took a deep breath. 'I'm Bill Davidson. How do you do? Wow, you look absolutely stunning. Perfect.'

'Hi,' I drawled. I had to sound sexy for this man. He had a fantasy to live out and I needed to be ready to perform for him. 'Maybe you'd like to use the bathroom to change. Can I get you something to drink?'

'Oh, no thank you. I couldn't. I mean, I shouldn't, should I? I don't want alcohol to spoil anything.'

'I can get you a fruit juice or mineral water. You change and I'll fix us something to sip while we get to know each other a little, before the main event.'

'Great. Thanks. Ideal,' he said, sounding nervous as he rushed into the bathroom.

'Everything OK?' Dexi asked, popping his head round the door as usual. It lets the client know he's on hand, if there are any problems. He's big enough to provide the perfect insurance policy, though if anyone knew much about him, they would realise he's purely for show. But it's good to know he's there if ever I need assistance. A big, handsome, Rock Hudson type with much the same proclivities.

Bill came into the room. He was wearing the ubiquitous boxer shorts and nothing else. He was

7

barefooted. His body was firm and strong looking. Nice.

'I hope this is appropriate clothing. This is my first time with someone like you. I've always imagined what it might be like. I expect you think I'm rather strange.' Warning bells rang. He didn't sound exactly truthful to me. But it didn't bother me. Many of my clients get stage fright. I smiled reassuringly, hoping he didn't see through the act.

'Not at all. You sound like most of the men I meet. You'd be surprised how few have actually tried it for themselves. I guess there aren't all that many women around who are prepared to do what I do.'

'Too right.' His voice did make him seem quite tense. I watched his eyes as they travelled up and down my legs, showing zero tension. 'But you are gorgeous. Quite one of the loveliest women I have ever seen. Anywhere.' His eyes were still fixed on my legs. His voice sounded more confident by the minute.

'Why, thank you,' I replied politely, with the right amount of surprise in my voice. He had to believe he was saying something unique. As if he were the first man to tell me something I didn't already know. I always hate the chatty bit. I wanted to get down to the nitty gritty as soon as possible. That way, it's over sooner and I can relax. 'Now, perhaps you'll tell me exactly what you want me to do. We'll establish a few ground rules at the start.'

'May I touch you?' he asked suddenly. 'I want to feel your strength. May I stroke your lovely legs?' I stared at him, slightly confused for a moment. 'No, I'm sorry. Forget I said it. It was stupid of me.'

'Believe me, Bill –' Now why did I think that wasn't his name? He didn't look like a Bill '– you'll feel the power in my legs soon enough. They're my

8

main strength. Firstly, we need to establish a signal, for when both of us have had enough. A submission. I usually suggest a tap on my back. Or your back, of course.' Let him think he might win.

'Fine by me.'

'And your preferred holds? What do you want?'

'A head scissors. Body scissors. Anything that I can feel really gripping me. That's why I wanted your legs to be uncovered. I hope you don't mind.'

'Not at all. My own favourite holds. I gather you want to be overpowered rather than be the dominant player?' Fat chance of that, I thought. Me, not be dominant? Doesn't hurt to let them think they might have a choice.

'I think so, but let's see how it goes. I have a few ideas I'd like to try.'

'OK. Are you ready now?' He nodded. During the conversation, I had been summing him up. He was a couple of inches taller than me. His body looked wiry, rather than muscular. It probably meant he was strong. Made a change. Dexi's estimation was less than accurate.

The hotel room was virtually bare of furniture. The couch and a small table stood in the bay window and the main area was covered with my blue plastic wrestling mat. There were mirrors right along one wall, hiding the wardrobes. So many mirrors. The opportunity for people to watch themselves, whatever they're doing.

I adore the first moment at the start of a bout. We approached each other, knees slightly bent and arms hanging loosely. I watched his eyes. I was fully confident that he was about to be beaten by me. I'm powerful. Dominant. Men are inferior, whatever strength they think they own. I use their strength against them. The whole business of wrestling goes against everything they were taught about respecting women: 'You don't fight girls. You don't hit girls.' Fat chance. The way I look at it, I'm making things safer for their wives. I can look after myself all right.

We manoeuvred round the mat and I made the first move. I grabbed at him, flipped my legs beneath his and he hit the ground. Immediately, I threw myself on top of him to keep my advantage. Then began the slow business of gaining control. He made a huge effort and pushed himself up, dislodging my hold on him. He gained brief supremacy. He clamped my arms above my head, pressing them down on to the mat. I won't be beaten by this. I smiled up at him. It distracted him for the slightest fraction. I whipped my legs round his body and twisted. He was caught off balance and rolled to the mat. I clamped my legs together again and crossed my ankles. I squeezed him in my unbreakable grasp. He panted and a grin formed on his face. I gripped harder and felt his pulse beginning to throb beneath my thighs. He was easily pleased. I looked down at his cock. It was already fully erect and pressing hard against the thin fabric of his shorts.

'I think you'd better let go,' he cried hoarsely. 'It's too soon.'

I ignored him. He hadn't made the agreed signal.

'Please,' he gasped. He reached frantically for my back, trying to break my hold and relieve the pressure. I felt the agreed tap. Immediately, I released him.

'First blood to me, I believe,' I said. I moistened my lips. He looked at me with what I knew was desire. Here we go again, I thought. I hate worship of any kind. I love power but only when I've earned it, not just because of my looks or because someone fancies me.

'You were right. You have got amazing legs. Now I know what to look out for.' He took a sip of water from the tray on the table and turned back to me. He held out a hand, as if to shake hands. The oldest trick in the book. As if I'd fall for that one.

'Oh no. You don't catch me that way.'

'Can't blame me for trying.' He reached across me and grabbed my waist with both hands. I felt his long fingers almost encircle me. Suddenly, he snatched hard, trying to unbalance me. I let myself fall against him and once more used the strength in my legs to achieve dominance. He fell to the ground and I dropped on top of him. If I twisted my legs round his, I could force his legs apart with a grape-vine movement. A sort of splits. I felt myself sweating. This guy was tougher than he looked. I squeezed and gained the advantage. I'd got him powerless. After several seconds, he still didn't give the submit signal. Impasse. I let him go.

We both leapt to our feet. Almost monkey-like, we challenged each other, making short jabs towards each other and ducking away. He grabbed my arm and twisted his body. He'd got me. I needed to try a new strategy. I collapsed down to the ground. It was my only chance to break the hold. He fell with me. We locked together, rolling over and over. First me on top then him. He was still holding my arm in a gut-wrenching hold. I didn't dare let him see he was hurting me. I realised something. This bastard had done it before. Often.

Gradually, I worked my body round to relieve the pressure. I drew a deep breath to send more oxygen to my aching muscles. It had been a long day. A real competitor was the last thing I needed right now. I suddenly rolled in the opposite direction, unwound our bodies and quickly got into a winning position. I grabbed his arms and rolled over, twisting my legs round his head. I locked my ankles together. I'd got him. He was held firmly in a head scissors. No way could he get out of this one. I watched his face at each moment to make sure nothing went wrong. I could snap his neck with the slightest movement. Not good for business. He tapped my back and I released him.

'Was that what you wanted?' I asked conversationally. Must keep it light.

'It was, but I don't want that hold again. I didn't like the feeling. I was out of control.'

'But I wasn't. I'm very experienced. You need have no worries.'

'Maybe not. You're certainly good. I work out regularly but you have it over me every time.'

'Practice,' I replied. 'But you're good. Maybe not as used to wrestling as I am.' He's nice, I decided. A cut above the usual slobs who fancied themselves as amateur wrestlers.

'OK. I'm determined to win at least one hold,' he said. 'Are you ready, Madame Lili?'

'You'd better believe it. I didn't ask before – how do you want me to finish you off?'

'Pardon me.'

'I assume you'd like to climax in the usual way? I call it the final submission. Do you want to be held, if so where, and should I help?'

'Never thought about it. I damned nearly came when you had me in that body scissors grasp. Maybe another like that would be nice but maybe not quite so tight.'

'Wimp!' I challenged. His eyes flickered with something that looked like annoyance. He chased

12

me round the mat, bringing me crashing down, my face against the mat. I lay beneath him. I felt his dick pressing hard into my bum cleft. I felt the same old stirrings deep in my belly. He was powerful, not like most of the guys. He thought he had me. He rolled me over to face him. His arm pressed down across my chest. He realised he was crushing my breasts beneath one arm and relieved the pressure only slightly. One knee was pressing my arm down and he had the other arm beneath my body. Tricky.

'Now, something tells me you are in no position to tap my back. How are you going to let me know when you are ready to submit?'

I smiled back at him, licking my red lips.

'Maybe I won't. Submit, I mean.'

He leaned down until his mouth was almost covering my own. Before I knew it, he was pressing his mouth against mine. He was kissing me. Angrily, I fought back, trying to push him away. I was temporarily defenceless. Bastard. Gently, I drew my legs up until I could force them between my opponent's legs. With a quick flip, I sent him off balance and he crashed to the ground. Angrily, I pinned him flat and held him down with my full weight. I glared down at him.

'I don't do kissing,' I hissed. 'Only when and if I say so. You may have paid for the hour but I'm not some cheap tart you pay by the fuck.'

'Pardon me. I thought that was exactly what you do – hire yourself out by the hour, for physical recreation.'

His grin was beginning to irritate me. I raised myself and then slammed my body over his, knocking the air out of him. He gasped and, before he could recover, I gripped him between my thighs. I locked my ankles together and squeezed even harder. He was red in the face and he tried to tap my back. Unsportingly, I took no notice. I needed to punish him. I kept one eye on his breathing, just in case. I am a professional, after all. I do know exactly how far to go. I held him firm but with slightly less pressure. I daren't admit it but I knew exhaustion was sweeping over me. Every muscle was screaming out for a rest. This was the sixth client of the day and by far the most powerful. Most of them had been unfit types, wanting to try it for themselves. This character, Bill something or other, was different. Interestingly different.

'Please, Lili.' he gasped. 'Please, let me go. You can do no more for me.'

I felt the wet stickiness on my leg. I glanced down. His cock was flaccid and the inevitable stain had coloured a dark patch on his shorts. His semen was all over me as well.

'I think we both may need a shower,' he said, regaining his control. 'Dare I ask you to share it with me or would you construe that as being out of order?'

'Just get yourself in there. I'll wait, thank you very much.'

I sat on the couch and poured a glass of iced water. I smiled. My anger was totally feigned. I had enjoyed his kiss and, if I were truthful, I wanted more. Much more. The shower was running. I loosened the laces of the wrestling boots and pulled them off. Bliss. Once Bill had removed himself, Dexi could massage my aching limbs. Thank God we have a day off tomorrow, I thought. Even when we're travelling it's still a break. Dexi drove our van, with the huge mat, clothes and other equipment. The bathroom door opened and Bill came out, looking fresh and cool in a white silk shirt and beauti-

14

fully tailored slacks. He didn't look remotely like the gauche man who had come into the room only a short while before.

'Can I offer you dinner this evening?' he asked casually.

'Thanks, but I don't mix business and pleasure,' I replied automatically. I'd already turned one guy down.

'Oh, I wasn't thinking of business at all, so we wouldn't be mixing anything.' He was devastatingly good-looking, I realised. If he hadn't made that stupid attempt to kiss me, I might have accepted. On the other hand, if he hadn't, I wouldn't have wanted more of him. Dinner might be nice, after all, I thought. Dexi was going out for the evening. He'd arranged to meet up with one of his special friends. He has a collection of them, all over the country. A boy in every port, sort of thing.

'I promise I won't even insist on boots or white clothes or even anything that exposes your wonderful legs,' he said with a whimsical smile. 'I'm usually quite good company and I'd enjoy talking, getting to know you better.'

'I don't know.' What was the alternative? A solitary dinner in the hotel room? Packing my gear followed by an early night? This guy was a cut above the average, after all. It might be fun.

'Suit yourself.' Bill sounded impatient. 'I have to go now. I have a meeting.'

'OK. Thanks. I don't usually do this sort of thing but as we're leaving tomorrow anyway . . .'

'Call a cab around seven-thirty. Ask for the Green Dragon. Everyone knows it. I'll meet you there. I'd pick you up but, as I said, I have meeting. Don't know exactly when it will finish.' He pulled a slim leather wallet from his back pocket and extracted a ten pound note. 'That will cover your fare and tip. Till later then.' He hooked his sports bag over his shoulder and, with a brief smile, left the room.

I hoped I wasn't making a grave error. Dexi came in.

'Ready for a massage?' He pulled out the folding table and set it up. This is part of our own gear we carry with us in the van. You never know if there will be anything suitable where we are. Sometimes, when there isn't a suitable hotel in an area, we have to operate in village halls.

'I'm knackered.' I dropped my clothes to the floor and stretched out naked, on the towel. I lay there, waiting for the ministrations of the best masseur I have ever met. Dexi poured warm oil over my back and worked his fingers into the aching muscles. His hands were soft, firm and persuasive. He worked along my thighs, loosening tensed muscles and allowing his hands to slide sensuously all over me. His hands are magic. So sensitive. He turned me over and worked on my front. His hands slid up the inside of my thighs, past the dark triangle of hair and over the flat, taut belly. He circled my breasts, his thumb occasionally pressing round the hardening nipple. Although Dexi is outrageously gay, his gentle, sensuous hands always managed to drive me to orgasm.

'You know, darling, I wouldn't do this for any other woman but you.'

'I know, I know. But I adore your massages. You're one helluva talented guy.'

'Shame I can't enjoy you. Still, it's nice to know I'm appreciated.' He smiled as he worked his fingers into my cleft. He rubbed very gently at my clit, smiling again as he felt the nub harden between his fingers. I gasped as the first surges rushed through

16

my body. I felt my hips moving involuntarily, beating against the table. With a shudder, I felt the sticky wetness pumping out of me as my body floated off somewhere.

'Strange creatures, women,' Dexi mused, shaking his head. 'Especially you. You seem so cold to all your red-blooded clients, yet I can make you come and come ... can't I?' Once more, he pushed probing fingers into the slit between my thighs. I opened them wider, wanting the insistent fingers to plunge deeper and deeper inside. I wanted to be filled and if his cock wasn't available, I had to make do. Two fingers, three, four bunched together to fill the hot, needy passage. The thumb worked harder and harder against the nub of my centre and heat swept over my body in blistering intensity. I crested again, soaring and crashing my hips down in rushes of sheer relief and delight. At last, I got my breath back and stared at this Adonis.

'Thanks, Dexi. You are magic. You could earn a fortune with any woman.'

'Thanks, darling, but you and I both know what I like. I do it even better with men. Beautiful as you are, you simply don't do it for me. But you know that, so why bother to explain? Come on now, get yourself under the shower and I'll take your working togs down to the laundry. They'll be ready for the morning. What are you doing this evening? Do you want me to order something for you?'

'I'm going out to dinner, as it happens.' I waited for his reaction.

'With Bill, no doubt?'

'How d'you know?'

'Intuition. A different man came out of this room than went into it. I was also wrong about him not being fit, wasn't I? I think his nervousness was nothing more than a big act.'

'You're right. Am I being stupid, accepting his invitation?'

'You can look after yourself.'

'I guess so. I just need a break. I need to be a normal woman for once and be entertained. It's months since I had any sort of date, except for work. I guess it'll be all right. Just one problem. I don't have any idea of what to wear. I get the feeling it could be somewhere quite smart.'

'My, he did make an impression, didn't he? The hotel boutique is sure to have something. Take your shower and I'll pop in to see what they've got on my way back from the laundry. I'll bring something up for you.'

He always chooses things that are exactly right. Dexi has such good taste. What a strange mixture of a man. Everything about him looks so masculine, yet he's sensitive to every female trait. Maybe it's something to do with my being a female who specialises in wrestling men. Heterosexual wrestling, erotic wrestling, we call it. I am never short of clients, especially since the Internet has provided so many new opportunities. My website scores a huge number of hits. We do most of the booking through it now. It seems there are always more men in need than I have time for. And this is only the UK. The future is good.

Chapter Two

'*I*'ve brought a dress for you to try. In my opinion, it's the only one.' Dexi came into the room without knocking. He never even noticed that I was lying naked on the couch. We're too familiar with each other's bodies, purely professionally of course.

'Thanks.' He held out a long, dark navy dress that seems to have a slit practically all the way to the armpits. 'Mmm. Nice, but maybe a bit formal.'

'As you like. I don't know what sort of place you're going to.'

'Nor do I. But a bit of glamour wouldn't come amiss occasionally.'

I slipped on the soft blue dress. It clung like a second skin. The side slit almost reached the waist. I'd need very brief panties, even with the high cut legs I favour. Or none at all. For dinner with a man who liked looking at legs, it would seem perfect. On the other hand, I don't want to look too dressed up or look as if I was handing out some sort of invitation.

'Definitely,' Dexi spoke authoritatively.

'If you say so.'

'Makes you look very sexy, if you happen to like that sort of thing. Cover up as much as you can and reveal tempting glimpses of what lies beneath. I could almost fancy you myself.'

'Come on now, Dex. If I thought you meant it, I'd run, very fast.'

'And if I thought I meant it, I'd let you. You look gorgeous, sweetie. But I must be off or my own irresistible date will have given up on me. Have fun and do try to behave like a lady.'

'What, me? Don't I always?' I laughed as he left the room. I preened in front of the mirror. The dress was certainly a perfect fit. I felt good in it but I still wasn't sure if it was right. What the hell. I liked it. If it was too posh for him, Bill, or whatever he's called, would have to lump it. I put on some high-heeled, silver pumps. He'd had his fantasy for today but I felt like exaggerating everything. I twisted a slim silver chain round the exposed ankle, enjoying the effect. I left my hair hanging loose. It took away the formality of the dress and seemed to provide a few contradictions to my image.

The cab dropped me at the Green Dragon at precisely eight o'clock. It looked nothing at all like a restaurant from the outside. An imposing building that ought to be a bank. All the windows were heavily curtained and the only visible lights shone through the glass-panelled door. I pushed it open and blinked. The largest chandelier I had ever seen cast millions of diamond sparkles over the entrance hall. The mirror tiles everywhere reflected back, so it felt like stepping into spotlights. A Chinese woman wearing a beautiful emerald silk dress bowed her head gracefully.

'Good evening, madame. Whose party are you

with?' She spoke perfect English with just the right hint of an accent.

'I'm meeting Mr Davidson. Mr Bill Davidson. I believe he is expecting me.'

The woman frowned.

'I do not believe there is anyone of that name here this evening. I am sorry.'

'He must be here. Perhaps he's not yet arrived.' I began to feel uncomfortable. Silly. Just because I was not controlling the situation, I hated it.

'Lili,' called a vaguely familiar voice. 'I'm so sorry. I should have been here to greet you.'

I turned and saw Bill walking across the foyer, his arms stretched in greeting. I glanced back at the green lady, who smiled.

'I'm sorry, Mr Travers. I was not aware you were expecting the lady.'

'My fault entirely. I should have mentioned it. You look wonderful, darling. Perfect. We are in the Jasmin Suite. Come and join us.' I thought he looked wonderful too, in his dark dinner jacket. Very handsome. Eventually, I realised the implication of his words.

'Us?'

'A few business colleagues. I'm sorry but I had to invite them, after our meeting. To celebrate the deal. I do hope you won't mind too much.'

'I'm not sure. Maybe it would be better if I leave you to your celebrations. I know nothing about your business and I'm certain you wouldn't want them to know about our particular connection. Do you think they'd understand that you and I spent the afternoon wrestling?'

'They'd be very jealous, I expect.' He grinned. 'That dress looks as if it was poured over you. Perfect. I must make sure I sit on your left-hand side. I couldn't risk any of my colleagues being tempted by that glimpse of flawless thigh. Tell me something. Are you wearing anything at all underneath?'

'Hush. You're embarrassing me,' I said unconvincingly.

'I don't believe that for one minute.'

'Is your name really Bill, Mr Travers?'

'Sorry about that. William is my middle name. Most people call me James. I wasn't sure it was a good idea to use my real name, in case you recognised it.'

'James Travers. No, I don't think I've heard it.'

'You may be more familiar with JWT.'

'The building equipment company?' I'd noticed diggers with the initials on the side during our miles of motorway travel.

'The very same. Not very glamorous sounding. I'm sorry.'

'I'm not. It's good to know that the chairman or director, or whatever you are, of such a company was powerless between my thighs for several minutes this afternoon. Most amusing. Quite a turn on.' He smiled knowingly.

We walked along a dark, carpet-lined corridor and reached a heavy panelled door. He pushed it open. There was a murmur of conversation, which stopped as we entered the room. I was quite ready to turn round and go out as quickly as I could but Bill or James, whichever he was, blocked the way. He propelled me forward, holding my elbow in a vice-like grip, as if sensing my hesitation.

'Gentlemen, I'd like you to meet my good friend, Lili.' Murmurs of good evening were lost among the admiring whispers, which I couldn't help hearing. I wondered what they had been told about me and felt suddenly fearful. A lone woman, especially me, being invited to a business dinner did not sound too promising. I looked at James and saw the hint of a smile in his eyes. He's got green eyes, I noticed irrelevantly. He eased me into a chair at the head of the table, next to what was obviously his own empty chair. He placed a glass of champagne before me and a dish of savouries. I acknowledged him with a nod. There were eight other men seated round the table. They were the only occupants of the room, which was apparently kept for private parties. There was an open-work screen at one side of the room, through which I could see a serving hatch. The doors were closed and the serving table below it was set with spoons and plates. The lighting was dim and the fabric-lined walls were dark green. Beautiful Chinese silk-painted pictures were hanging on the walls, carefully lit by subtle overhead lights. The effect was very elegant and suggested a great deal of money and care had been taken to achieve the ambiance.

'I have taken the liberty of ordering our meal. I hope this is acceptable to everyone. This restaurant provides probably the best food this side of Beijing. I don't think you will have any complaints. Unless, of course, you do not like Chinese food.'

'I love it,' I assured him. I did not tell him that I usually ate it directly from foil cartons, shared with Dexi, usually while sitting in the van, on the way to another booking.

'Now, let me introduce my other guests,' James began. He reeled off the names and I knew at once that I would not remember a single one. Each of the men nodded as they were introduced and gave me smiles that could only be described as downright lecherous. They know, I thought. They know exactly

23

what I am. What I do. This bastard sitting next to me, with a hand already stroking my thigh, had told them everything. I felt myself blushing with shame and anger at being sucked into such a plan. How could he? Maybe I was expected to provide the entertainment for the evening. A bout with each in turn, no doubt, and all for the measly price of a meal. If that's what he thought, he was very much mistaken. To think, I had actually accepted the invitation because I wanted to be entertained for once. It proved my policy was right. Never try to mix business and pleasure.

'James, I need the ladies' room,' I whispered to him.

'I'll show you the way,' he said, a slight catch of excitement in his voice. 'Excuse us for a moment, gentlemen.' He stood and moved my chair out of the way, as I rose. 'This way, my dear.' He led me through the heavy oak door and into the corridor. 'You look flushed, Lili. Is everything all right?'

'You bet your arse it isn't right. How dare you? Do you think I haven't sussed your plan? Get her pissed and she'll perform for free. You can all have a go. She's wonderful. Strong thighs. The best. You'll never experience anyone better.' I paused for breath and he cut in.

'You certainly have a high opinion of yourself. You're good, but I'm not sure about the best.' I glared at him, gasping at his words.

'Only teasing you. You are the best. The best I have ever encountered anyway. And no, this evening is nothing at all like your vivid imagination is conjuring. It is a genuine business dinner. I told you I had a meeting after our bout. The deal was clinched much sooner than I anticipated. This celebration was to have been tomorrow, but there was no point in delaying it. It was too late to warn you. I did try to phone but you had already left the hotel. Now please, won't you come back and enjoy our meal? This is truly a wonderful restaurant. The food is unsurpassed.'

I hesitated. I hardly knew this man, so why should I believe him? If he was so successful and obviously rich, why choose me? There must be hundreds of women he could have asked. His wife, even. Maybe he was telling the truth. I had no way of knowing. Used to following my gut reaction, I made up my mind.

'OK. But one mention of wrestling, scissor holds or anything else and I'm right out of here. OK?'

'Understood. But I can't guarantee that your terms will be met exactly. Someone might genuinely have reason to talk about your taboo subjects. Grape scissors for example? Wrestling with accounts?'

I glared at him once more.

'And I haven't forgiven you for using a pseudonym. I felt very foolish back there in reception.'

'Don't your other clients ever use a different name?' I thought of the five Mr Smiths I had entertained already that day.

'I suppose,' I said, hesitantly.

'And were you really given the name Lili? Somehow it doesn't sound like the sort of name that parents like yours would have given to their only daughter. Not their sort of scene at all.'

'What do you know about my parents?' I gasped. 'They are dead, in any case. But how did you know I am an only child?'

'Maybe I'm good at guessing. Now, if you really want the ladies' room, you'd better go. Maybe I'll come with you. The cubicles are large enough here.'

'For what?'

'Use your imagination, woman. No. On second thoughts, I don't want to fuck you here, in such a hurry. I'd prefer to seduce you slowly.' He leaned over and kissed me again. However angry I may have felt, I simply kissed him back. He was one hell of a sexy guy, and getting more so by the minute. He took my hand and put it against his crotch. Now why hadn't I noticed just how large he was earlier? My groin started juicing immediately. Had I but known it, this evening was about to be a turning point in my life.

'Now, if you really want the loo, get on with it, and then we'll get back to our guests.'

'They're your guests. Nothing at all to do with me. And no, I don't really need the loo. I was making it an excuse to leave.'

'Relax, Lili. I promise there are no ulterior motives at all. Not here, at least. Later, we could be tempted to much more. Later, much later. Trust me.' For some reason, I did.

I felt myself growing hotter and wetter at his words. Whatever my logical thoughts may have been trying to tell me, every inch of my physical side was seriously turned on. The more I looked at him, the more certain I was that I fancied him rotten. I'd already seen most of him, almost naked, and felt distinctly excited at the prospects. *You don't do this, not with clients*, I tried to convince myself. But it seemed too long since I'd had real sex with anyone. Months and months. Well, apart from the odd encounter. If it hadn't been for Dexi's ministrations I'd never have survived. My vibrator may bring some relief but whoever could have an affair with a machine?

He led me back into the dining room and the meal began. Dish after dish of food was brought out.

Hotplates were placed round the table so that everyone could take small portions as they liked. He was right: it was all quite remarkable food and, for one evening, I gave up my usual diet. I did, however, keep a strict watch on the drinks. I needed to keep my wits, whatever James had said to reassure me.

At last, pale-green tea was served in tiny cups, bringing the meal to a conclusion. It had been a very pleasant evening, despite all my doubts. The men were intelligent and witty and almost every one found some reason to compliment me. Most of them were also pretty fuckable, given the right circumstances. How could I have helped but enjoy myself? When everyone was finally leaving, James took my arm, holding me back.

'I have an early start in the morning,' I protested, hoping he wasn't listening. After his hand had spent much of the evening clamped to my exposed thigh, I was well and truly hot for him. 'I should get back. Dexi will be worrying.' How I hoped he didn't take me seriously. The chances of Dexi being back before breakfast were almost zilch.

'The handsome hunk you keep in attendance?' I nodded. 'He isn't really a problem, is he?'

'What do you mean?'

'Well, for one thing I wouldn't have thought you were his type. I think I'd be at greater risk somehow.'

'I don't understand. He's my very good friend, manager, secretary, you name it.' I tried to play the innocent.

'But he's gay. Nothing wrong with that, of course, but he surely wouldn't be jealous, not of me?'

'No, of course not. He just looks out for me. How did you know he's gay by the way?'

'I just know. His assessment of me for a start. I had to put on a bit of a show for him.'

'He mentioned you were unconvincing. I guess I know what you mean.'

'Now, how about that drink? I'd like to take you back to my place and I'll guarantee that you'll be home in good time to make your early start.'

I considered him. He had conned me into being a guest at a business dinner and kept my interest going with unsubtle massage most of the evening. Now he was suggesting we went back to his place. I knew I wanted it, him, more than anything, despite the warning bells that were ringing. Had he done anything bad enough to stop me going home with him? His touch had been driving me slowly wild with desire. I'd even pressed myself against him on more than one occasion during the meal. He had responded, never actually looking at me. He even knew that I was wearing nothing beneath my dress. All the panties I owned had been visible, so there was no choice. I hoped I wasn't about to stain the fabric of the dress. Dexi was absolutely right. The more I covered my body, the sexier I felt and obviously looked. James was more than ready for me and me for him.

'You are sure you can risk coming with me?' James asked with a deep-throated chuckle. Throughout the taxi ride back, his hands wandered along my legs, while my own had slipped inside his pants. Our tongues had wrestled their way into new record books.

'Come on,' he said urgently when the taxi finally stopped.

'Try and stop me. I take it you live alone?' I muttered as we went inside.

'Apart from the harem and half a dozen servants,'

he replied. His eyes danced as he spoke and I returned the smile. I snatched off his jacket and tie, dropping them on the hall floor. He dragged me towards him and slid my dress forward, exposing my breasts with their taut, erect nipples. He leaned down and took one of them into his mouth. I felt myself soaring with desire and groped for the buttons at the front of his trousers. I tugged at them and then pushed the soft fabric of his pants out of the way.

'Not here,' he murmured. 'Come on.'

Not wanting to release him, I followed him, clasping his head close to my mouth. After several pauses, we went up a wide staircase and into a bedroom. The huge bed was covered with a silk counterpane, a rich red. He tugged away my dress and I stepped out, standing completely naked except for the high-heeled silver shoes and the ankle chain. He stopped trying to remove his own remaining clothes and stared. I watched him and followed his gaze to my triangle of dark hair. I pushed my fingers towards it and allowed the tips of them to disappear into myself. I flicked my tongue over red lips. I could see his arousal straining against the black silk boxer shorts. He stepped out of his trousers and shoes and slowly walked over to me. He pressed me face-down on to the bed and I felt the cool silk of his boxers slide against my back. He slowly pressed himself on top of me. Never had I felt so alive, so sensuous and so excited. What on earth was I doing here? What had this man got that made me give up all my usual principles? I'd had plenty of men before, but since my wrestling career took off, I had been almost celibate, apart from Dexi's services.

'Lili, Lili,' he whispered. 'Make love to me.'

'I thought this was just another fuck to you.'

'How can you think that? You are beautiful. Everything a man could want. This man in particular wants you right now.'

'Then follow your instincts.'

He slid down my body and began teasing me with quick darts of his tongue. I buried my face in the red silk, waiting to see where he was going. He rolled me over, pushing me down on my back. He did it roughly, as if he meant business. He pushed my legs apart and, pressing his face against my mound, stretched back with his hands to reach my ankles. Slowly, he slid his hands along my legs. Suddenly, with a swift movement, he pushed my swollen lips wide open. I stared up at the ceiling. A huge mirror showed the whole picture: my own body spread out with legs wide and welcoming, his dark head busily tonguing my deepest places. I felt the familiar surges of heat sweeping through my body. I was making no effort, no response and just lay, letting it happen. Just as I was about to climax, he lifted his head. His face was wet from me. My hips continued to rise and fall. Waiting. Waiting for the moment. Almost delirious with heightened desire, I hissed at him to get back to the right place. He wiped his face against my belly and shook his head.

'You have to earn it,' he whispered.

'You sod,' I moaned. 'Bastard man. Give it to me.'

'What? This?' he asked, holding out one of the biggest cocks I had ever seen. It was long, hard and more than ready to go. He bounced the glorious thing in his hand, taunting me with the sight of it.

'Yes. Go on. In me. Push it into me and fill me with it,' I begged.

'Sorry; you have to work for it.' He stood up and

I watched the enormous cock as it stood out in front of him. From a drawer beside the bed he drew something out. A condom? I couldn't see what he had. Then I felt it. My wrists were clicked into two pairs of handcuffs and before I realised it, each was fastened securely to loops set into the wall above the bed. This room was prepared for something I had not expected.

'What the hell are you doing?' I spluttered. My nerves began to tingle.

'Just teaching you a little restraint.' He laughed. 'You need a lesson or two. You are too dominant for your own good.' He stroked my naked wet pussy and, once more, despite everything, I felt myself desperate to have his cock inside me.

'Come on. I'm helpless. Put it inside me. Please.'

'Beg me.'

'I am begging. Get it inside me. Please.'

'You don't sound nearly contrite enough,' the bastard said. 'You need further restraint. Maybe I have to teach you a lesson.' I felt suddenly excited. This was something new. I've done bondage before, who hasn't? But somehow, this seemed different. He meant business. Gently but firmly, he took one of my feet, still in the high silver shoes, pushed my leg above my shoulders and clipped my ankle to the same loop as my wrist. The same treatment was given to the other leg. I saw the reflection above me. I was helpless. Trussed. My pussy was lying wide open, exposed, red and swollen.

'How does it feel to be dominated?' he asked.

'Out of control,' I managed to whisper. God, I was excited.

'Good. Now you'll have to beg, really beg.' I clamped my mouth shut. The truth was, I discovered I was loving the whole sensation. Me, the control freak, was suddenly meeting my match. He pushed long fingers into me, dancing his prick round the enormous hole that gaped before him. He teased me, again and again. His thumb touched my clit, barely moving at all but enough to make me know he was right there. The gentlest of touches kept me throbbing. I was beginning to sweat ... I could feel myself coming without even moving. I realised this must be something like the sensation my wrestling partners all enjoy. They come without doing anything themselves. I shuddered involuntarily as the thuds of orgasm rushed through me. He laughed. He slapped my backside with a flat hand. I gasped. He hit it again and again. I was trying to yell at him to stop but he was merciless.

'You're too greedy.' He laughed lasciviously. 'You like cock too much, don't you?'

'Bastard!' I cried out. My bum was stinging, showing red even in the mirror high above me. I couldn't take my eyes off the view of my upended arse with its reddening flesh. He leaned down, peering into the very deepest, most secret parts of me. Parts no one had ever seen before, not like this. He fingered me thoughtfully, as if he was surveying a piece of property. He smiled that smile again and I was lost. What the hell was I doing here, trussed up and helpless on a total stranger's bed? Yet, in spite of everything, I felt no fear. Not at all. All I knew was that I still longed to have my cunt filled with that glorious cock.

'Good girl. You have taken your punishment well. I am now ready to reward you. Say please, nicely.'

'Please nicely,' I yelled.

'Not good enough. I shall have to smack you again, I'm afraid. You don't learn, do you?'

As the first slap struck me, I realised to my

amazement, that I was already halfway to yet another orgasm. One hand still occupied my mound, the thumb pushed inside me, just where it mattered most. The second, third, fourth slaps and I was there. I cried out as my hips thrashed and my ankles pulled against their chains. The feel of the tight chains was so sexy. He was grinning at me all the time.

'I think you need a reward now.' To my utter joy, his cock pushed into my waiting hole. It sank in deeply, deeply, until I felt it couldn't go any deeper without splitting me. I sent a gush of hot liquid to greet it. I felt him pulsing into me, pumping and grinding into my body. Then at last he collapsed over me as he came. Heaven reached me. Maybe it got to him as well.

It seemed like hours later that he pulled out of me. I saw that, at some time, he had put a condom over his majestic tool. I was glad. I had given not one thought to our protection. Silently, he went into the bathroom to remove and dispose of it. He returned, standing to gaze at me, still lying helpless on his bed. Silently, he removed my restraints and I rubbed the sore places at wrists and ankles. I looked up at him. Bastard, I mouthed silently, again.

'But you loved every second of it, didn't you?' he asked.

'I won't commit myself,' I replied, but I could see that he knew the truth.

'Do you really have to leave in the morning?' he asked.

'Fraid so.'

'Why did we have to meet on your last day? I could have booked you solid for the entire week.'

'What! And deprive half the male population of Manchester of my services? What chaos you would

33

have caused. What frustration. Think of the mar-riages that might have suffered.'

'I'm not sure I want you wrestling with any Tom, Dick or Harry.'

'Oh I am very particular. I rarely wrestle with Dicks – they usually come quietly. Besides, you needn't think you own me. Not just anyone can afford me. And Dexi is always on hand if he's needed.'

'Ah yes. The redoubtable Dexi. Stay here, Lili, for just a few days. I'll pay double whatever you would earn. More, if necessary.'

'Thanks for the offer but I am committed. For the next three months at least. It would be unpro-fessional of me to renege. I hate to let anyone down. Besides, I don't like the thought of being paid for something other than wrestling.'

'But, Lili, surely that doesn't matter. You may be serving a need for many men. You'd be filling my needs. You'll have to stop your grand tour one day. Why not now?'

'I hardly know you. I only met you today. Now why on earth would I give up everything I've worked so hard for, just to stay with you for a few days?'

'Because I want you to. Because I think we could be good together. I like you a lot, Lili. Please, think about it.'

'Dream on, babe,' I said suddenly, rising from the bed. 'We had a good time together. That's it. End of story. Like I said, I don't mix business and pleasure. This was a pleasure. A one-off. I somehow managed to square my conscience about seeing a client out of work, as it were. I won't make the mistake again. I'm very well paid for doing what I do.'

'Don't try to sound like some cheap tart. You're better than that. OK, so you satisfy men for money.'

'So does any tart.'

'But you have skills.'

'So does a tart.'

'Special skills.'

'So does a tart.'

'Why do you put yourself down like this?'

'It's all I deserve. Yes, you've seen the bold, confident side of me. The me that is now. But I do have a history. I fought my way to the sort of status I have now. It took a lot of determination, I can tell you.'

'I'd like to hear about it. Why don't I get some wine? You can spend the rest of the night telling me all your guilty secrets.' He leapt off the bed and went out of the room. For a moment, I thought of pulling my clothes on again and making a dash for it. Warning signals were sounding, but not loudly enough. I knew I would regret staying. But something was holding me back. For some irrational reason, I didn't want to leave, not just yet. My own hesitation made the decision for me.

James came back into the room carrying a huge bottle, an ice bucket and two champagne flutes. He draped a red silk robe round my shoulders. It exactly matched the bed cover. With practised ease, he popped the cork and poured two glasses. He sat beside me. It was cosy, like any long-married couple sharing breakfast in bed.

'I shouldn't be doing this,' I protested, more to myself than him.

'I want you to. I want to know everything about you.'

'Why?'

'Here's to the past, the present and the future.'

35

We clinked glasses. Was there really a future for us? Maybe there was something, who could tell? I was already feeling something quite new to me. Love? Lili, having feelings? Never!

Chapter Three

'*I*'m flattered, James, of course, but you must realise I'm not going to hand over my entire earning
capacity on one whim.'

'Not a whim, sweetie. I'm deadly serious. You
have the potential to fulfil my every fantasy. I think
I can do a lot for you too.'

I opened my mouth to speak and he stuck a hand
over it. Why didn't I fight back? I didn't. I sat there
and let him.

'Don't even try to tell me you didn't love every
minute of what I did to you. There's plenty more
where that came from. One thing I do not lack is
imagination.'

Quite casually, I moved my mouth behind his
restraining hand and bit hard. His look of surprise
was more than worth it.

'Bitch,' he called out as I poured the last drop of
champagne over his cock. Sadly, it had warmed too
much to make the perfect shock. His expression
certainly gave me something to think about. In one
bound, he was on his feet, reaching for me. I dodged

round the bed, leaping over it and across the carpet. He made a flying tackle, more rugger than wrestling but effective enough to catch me and bring me down. Once I was back on my own turf it was easy to better him. Before he knew what had hit him, I had him in a headlock and he was helpless. If my calculations were right, he would be feeling a total loss of control. I looked forward to my punishment later. This could prove to be a very interesting relationship: he wanted to dominate, and I could easily dominate him. Point proved by his total submission to me at that very moment.

I released him and watched as he slowly rose to his feet.

'I'll make you very sorry you did that,' he mouthed. 'Very sorry indeed.'

The slight twitch at the corner of his eyes gave him away. He didn't mean a word of it and knew full well that I should revel in everything he wanted to give me. Interesting.

'I trust you are withdrawing your offer,' I asked wickedly.

'I shall bide my time. You'd better leave now. We'll catch up on our talk some other time. After all, your business is more important to you. You have commitments. Don't let me keep you.

I'm afraid your dress is a little the worse for wear. It somehow got torn. Don't worry, you can send me the bill. I'll get my chauffeur to take you home.'

I wasn't sure about being dismissed so casually. He'd been offering the moon one minute and now I was being packed off.

'Don't worry,' I snapped, 'I'm sure to catch a taxi.'

'Dressed like that, it's not all you'll catch.'

I'd pulled the tight dress over my head and was smoothing it down. Somehow, during our session, the side split had extended by several inches. It was no longer close fitting and covered precisely nothing except one tit on the side that was intact. I looked round for something to hold it together.

'A safety pin would be nice,' I said.

'I bet it would. Sorry. You'll have to go home like that. You can still change your mind, if you like.'

I glared at him. Six foot two of naked male standing in front of me. His erection was beginning to stretch in front of him again, like a mediaeval lance. Tempting enough. I might – no, I definitely knew I would enjoy his punishment. Instead, I stuck my head in the air, swung round to the door and flounced out – as much as half a dress allows one to flounce, that is. I slammed the door shut and strode off to the stairs. At least, I tried. I'd taken the wrong turning out of his room and ended up in a long corridor. I opened a couple of doors. More bedrooms, all sumptuous with deep-pile carpets and loads of mirrors. The next door was locked.

'Now, what's in there?' I murmured. I heard a slight sound and swung round.

'That's my special punishment room,' he said softly, with a hint of menace in his voice. I gave a small shudder. Anticipation? Fear? I couldn't tell. He was leaning casually against his door jamb, his robe hung over his shoulder. 'If you are really looking for the way out, you should try the other direction.'

'I'd worked that out, thanks.' I knew that it was now or never. If I didn't walk away at this very moment, I'd probably never leave. Dexi flashed into my mind. I couldn't do it to him. Maybe we'd slow down on bookings after this next tour and take it from there ... if James was still around and still making offers. I walked to the stairs and turned at the last moment, giving him a casual wave. I reached the main door and stood looking at it helplessly. There was the most complex series of locks I'd ever seen. Nobody could leave this place easily. A loud click and several whirring sounds later, the door opened automatically.

I stepped into the early, very early, morning air. The rain was falling heavily. I had no idea where I was. I could see nothing but trees and fields around us. In our haste to get down to business last night, I'd never looked out of the taxi once. I gave a shiver. This dress was certainly not made for all-weather activities, even before it fell apart. It didn't even seem like the sort of area where taxis cruised all night, looking for business. 'Shit, shit, shit,' I muttered. I realised that I didn't even have any money with me. Somewhere between now and leaving the hotel, I'd lost my little evening purse. I slumped down on his front step. The cold, wet marble practically froze my bare backside. I detested the thought of going back into the house and losing every last shred of pride, but what else could I do? Hell. I knew my rules of mixing work and play should never have been forgotten. I gritted my expensive crowns and stood up, ready to ring the doorbell. The sound of an engine purring gently behind me made me look round. A chauffeur, complete with immaculate peaked hat, was opening a door for me. He even gave a slight bow. I noticed his own lustful grin as he raised his head again. I hitched my dress round me, using it as a sort of sari-lookalike and climbed into the back seat. I tried to look as if I was in control but the goose bumps were beginning to make me look slightly leprous. I was also shivering quite noticeably. It was tough trying to look dignified.

'Thanks,' I spluttered.

'The address, madame?' he asked from his seat.

'Park Royal Hotel.'

'Thank you, madame. There's a flask of hot coffee if you would like it.' He pressed something and a door slid open silently in front of me. I poured coffee into a bone china cup and sipped the fragrant, most wonderful coffee. I felt the warmth spreading through me and driving the goose bumps away. I hoped it was a short journey. My soggy clothes were revolting.

'There is a towel in the cupboard below,' said a voice in my left ear. I swung round but it was only a loudspeaker set in the roof.

'Thanks,' I replied, hoping it was a two-way speaker. I pulled out a large soft towel and wrapped it round me, before removing the dress. I sat huddled in the seat for maybe half an hour. Surely it hadn't been such a long drive to James's house? I remembered how we'd occupied that particular journey. Doesn't time fly, I thought. Where on earth had we been? Not knowing Manchester at all, I had no idea even of the district we'd been in. Nor did I give any thought to the magical arrival of the chauffeur. The bastard James must have known I'd never find a taxi. So, where had this guy been all through our little confrontation? I hoped he hadn't been around to witness something so private as our bondage session. At last, we pulled up at the hotel. Even at five in the morning, a doorman stepped out to open my door.

'Thanks, er . . .'

'Davis, ma'm,' he said. 'You may take the towel, naturally.'

Can anyone imagine the utter idiot I must have looked? I sidled out of some great limo wearing nothing more than a large white towel and walked into the reception area of a rather posh hotel. I hadn't even got my swipe card to let me into my room and had to tackle the snooty-looking receptionist. She was giving me the sort of look that said she knew exactly what I was all about. I gave her a slow smile, hoping I was indicating that she was looking at one totally satisfied woman. Maybe she'd have looked less superior if she'd had a bit more of what I'd had. She did have the last laugh, as she ordered a security man to take me upstairs and let me into my own bedroom.

I took a hot shower and flopped down on the bed. I could have slept for a week. Instead, five minutes after I'd fallen asleep, or so it seemed, Dexi came in.

'Up you get, darling,' he said, opening the curtains to let in the horrible bright sunlight. 'My, don't you look the worse for wear? Good evening, was it? Or did it live up to the darker side we'd pictured?'

'It was fine. Good.' I knew I didn't want to talk about it to Dexi. Strange – I usually tell him everything. What was so special about this guy, James Travers?

'And how was Mr Davidson?'

'Travers. James William Travers. Some tycoon in building or something.'

'Not JWT?'

'I think it was. Why? You heard of them?'

'Big league, honey. Bet he's not short of the odd million or two. Cripes. Didn't he offer you diamonds or something less ostentatious, like a gold chastity belt?'

I stared at him.

'Maybe he offered the "or something". Needless to say, I refused.'

42

'Can't think why. Now, full breakfast, as usual? Here or downstairs?'

I always had the full works on rest days. Other times, I'd be sick if I ate anything cooked. I took the stay in bed option and waited for Dexi to organise it all for me. So, my host last night was indeed the very wealthy man I'd thought. Maybe I'd do well to keep in touch, somehow. Dexi kept records of bookings. James's address must be somewhere around.

'Did he ask to go on the database?' I asked casually.

'No. Said he'd make contact with us if he wanted a repeat bout.' I felt slightly disappointed but would never admit it, not even to Dexi.

Hours later, we arrived in Somerset, in a small market town that seemed to be in the middle of nowhere. The hotel had a fitness centre, which we had booked for our entire week's stay. The staff were immensely curious. They'd never experienced anything quite like our set-up but soon got used to the strings of clients. Five solid days, with five or six clients each day; I felt knackered. Dexi was his usual efficient self, though much less talkative than usual. I tried to draw him out but he said nothing. I decided he must be annoyed with me for my little dalliance with James: maybe he felt insecure about the future; maybe he was just plain jealous – not of my activities, but it could be that he fancied James himself. The man had made some comments about Dexi's sexuality, after all. I laughed at the thought. James certainly did not like other men. He was one hundred per cent heterosexual.

'You've got an hour,' Dexi said on the last afternoon. 'Want a massage?'

I nodded and he set up the table. I lay half dozing,

as he pulled and pushed my aching muscles. I wasn't in the mood for anything else and he worked away quietly. He gripped my ankles and began to stretch my legs. I held on to the top of the table and enjoyed the sensation. He pulled one leg out to the side, lifting it so I was doing a sort of splits while lying on my stomach. I remembered how I'd been laid open on James's bed and immediately felt myself growing wet.

'Think I'm in the mood for something more intimate,' I whispered huskily. Dutifully, Dexi rolled me over and began work on my more erogenous zones. I waited for something to happen but, try as he would, my orgasm did not come. Oh, it was all pleasant enough, but totally unfulfilling.

'Now, what's happened to you?' Dexi asked, looking marginally hurt.

'Not properly in the mood, I guess. Sorry.' He gave a shrug. He slapped my thighs and ordered me to get up and shower. He folded the table as I did so.

'What's next?' I asked.

'Anthony Vestrar, apparently. He's even provided the outfit.'

'Really? That's a first. Let's have a look.' He handed me a box, which he said had been delivered earlier. I unwrapped the tissue paper. It was a shiny black lycra body suit. Once I was inside that, my entire body would be covered.

'Just as well I'm not in the mood to show off more of the tempting bits of me.'

The suit even had a hood and a half mask. I pulled it on. The fine nylon zip was hidden down the back so, with Dexi's help, it closed and fitted like a second skin. I clipped the hood under my chin. I occasionally use a mask, so it was no problem to me.

'Very sinister,' Dexi remarked. 'You look a dead ringer for Seven of Nine. You know, *Startrek Voyager*?'

I didn't but I accepted his word. I thought I looked like an overgrown Barbie doll. Maybe Seven of what's her face does too. I was sleek and smooth all over. I left my feet bare, not wanting to disappoint the man by adding anything extra to his chosen outfit. I sat back on a chair, wondering who I was about to meet, here in rural Somerset. I sipped a glass of water and waited.

With a wicked grin, Dexi showed my last client of the week into the room.

He was six foot two and wore an almost identical suit to my own. He was also wearing a hood and a half mask. I was amused. He looked fit: broad shoulders and slim waist. I could hardly help noticing that he also looked well endowed in the crotch area.

'Mr ... may I call you Anthony? Is this your first bout ever or just your first with me?'

He shook his head but refused to speak. Odd. I felt a slight niggle hit me and nodded to Dexi.

'You'll be outside, as usual?' I said. He agreed and left the room. 'Any special requests?' I asked my client. Another shake of the head. Seemingly he wanted to omit the usual introduction rituals. 'You ready to go?' He nodded. I didn't like it. He was strange and I couldn't see his eyes behind the mask. I told him my rules for submission and we faced each other on the mat. Like two cats waiting to spring, we circled. Each of us darted our arms as if to touch and were fended off. I sprang at him, flicking my legs behind his in my usual moves to unbalance an opponent. His arms circled my waist and he pulled me down with him. He rolled me over, not realising this was exactly where I wanted to be. I grabbed him round his waist with my legs and held him down. He groaned, part pleasure, part pain. I squeezed harder. Harder. His breath came in stifled rasps. I looked down at him and realised I could see green eyes staring out of the mask. Unable to resist the temptation, I ripped it off. Why hadn't I known at once? I released my grip and allowed James to sit up. I pulled his hood off and looked into his eyes.

'Was all this really necessary?' I asked angrily.

'I thought you might refuse to see me again.'

'Why would I do that?'

'Come now, Lili, we didn't part on the best of terms, did we? Now, I have paid a great deal of money for my hour. Stop wasting my time talking.'

'Just one more thing. Did Dexi know who you were?'

'Not when I made the booking. I gave a false name. I did say I'd found you on the Internet, which is of course true. Er . . . Dexi did know me, of course, when I arrived. I persuaded him not to reveal my identity.'

'I'll have words with him.'

'Don't blame him. I knew you wouldn't be really angry.'

I nodded, satisfied, excited, flattered. A whole surge of adjectives hit me. I had to win. Most of all I had to win. He already owed me a punishment, I remembered as I felt my hot, wet pussy throbbing in anticipation. If I beat him again, we might both get well satisfied, eventually. I grinned at him and dived for his legs. He was caught unawares, unprepared for the sudden move. I twisted hard and he rolled over on to his front. I moved to sit astride his lower back and pulled his legs up. I tucked his feet under my arms and leaned slowly back. I had to move carefully or I could damage him. As I mentioned, a broken back or strangulation isn't good for business. His body became limp and I glanced behind me at his head. I felt his hand move against my back, which I rightly took to be his submission sign. He groaned and turned over.

'You're a full-blooded bitch, aren't you? You won't do that to me again.'

I laughed and threw my head back. This guy hated being beaten, I could see. I'd got his measure here, on my own territory. However fit, wealthy or anything else he may be, I was undoubtedly the champion in the wrestling arena.

'You're a bastard, so we're well suited. Bitch and bastard. Ready for more yet?'

I leapt again. This time I decided to treat him to the body scissors he said he liked the last time. I gently lay on top of him, my full length stretched over his. So far, it was purely sexual. I held his arms above his head and moved gently over him. I could feel his prick hardening at once. If he wasn't encased in his lycra suit, I'd have been tempted to expose him. His tool was well worth looking at, I remembered with pleasure. I wriggled against him, still holding his arms firmly. I moved up against his body until my knees were level with his waist and gripped each side of him. He smiled up at me and I felt his own legs beginning to move behind me. Quick as a flash, I parted my own legs and slipped one underneath his body. Immediately, I clasped my ankles together and locked hard. I had him. He smiled again and lay back to relax and enjoy it. I have to admit, I do find this slightly boring. He's lying there apparently in ecstasy, as his pressure fetish is satisfied. I just have to twitch a bit and he

47

comes. What's in it for me? I don't even get the satisfaction of faking my own orgasm. True, I can grind myself against his hip bone a bit, but that takes me only part of the way.

'Let me go,' he gasped, and then remembered to tap my back. I looked down at his crotch to inspect the results of my labours. It was still dry. He leered up at me and grabbed me round the waist. He wrapped his legs round me and began to squeeze. Lucky for me his technique was a bit lacking and I easily managed to wriggle out of it. I saw another chance and gripped his head between my knees, all in one fast movement. It had the added benefit of also allowing me to escape from his hold. I looked down at his face. His expression gave me a moment's anxiety. His eyes looked angry. He was beaten yet again and he didn't like it. I released him, rolling forward as I did so. I gave an almighty heave to my aching body and managed to get my arms down to do a forward roll. I ended standing up at his feet, with him looking slightly astonished at my speed.

'I have been doing this for quite some time.' I laughed. 'Now. You have seven minutes left. Can you manage to beat me, do you think?'

He leapt to his feet and took on an even more determined look. We began circling once more. I heard a click and noticed the door being closed: Dexi was doing his duty very discretely, as usual. If ever there's a silence, he looks in, just to check that all is well. I looked at James, straight in the eyes. If he was going to make the next move, I was absolutely ready for him. His arms swung slightly forward. He was going to try to grab my neck. I ducked and went between his legs, lifting him on my shoulders. Though he was both bigger and heavier than me, he

48

most certainly wasn't ready for this move. His body was caught off balance. He easily toppled forwards, right over my shoulders. I tucked my legs in and rolled away, circling round him so that I could complete the move. I pressed my whole body weight down on to his folded body. As I held him there, I realised that he was in virtually the same position as I had been, when my wrists and ankles were chained together over his bed. I also remembered the spanking I'd received. They often say that people do to their partners what they would also enjoy being done to them. I grinned wickedly. His neat buttocks, though covered in their lycra, were beautifully presented to me. I shifted my weight slightly so that I kept the pressure on him and released my hands. I beat a tattoo of sharp slaps to his arse, using both hands alternately. It was such a good feeling. I'd never have believed anything could turn me on so much. I was practically coming myself without even being touched anywhere. More, more, I thought. I was getting closer every second. My hands were stinging as I beat out my rhythm. I felt his feet kicking against my back but I couldn't stop. My crotch was rubbing against his tight lycra-clad back in time to my hands. It was glorious to feel the power and the excitement of such domination. I felt him moving under me but I was invincible. When I crashed forwards, no one could have been more shaken than me. He'd managed to catch me slightly off balance, too wrapped up in my own pleasure to realise what he was doing.

'You'll pay dearly for that,' he gasped excitedly. 'You crazy bitch. I was hammering at your back to stop. You took no notice.'

I rolled over and stared up at him. I knew my face was red from my exertions.

'Sorry,' I spluttered. 'But don't try to tell me you didn't love every minute of it.'

'Not very professional, was it?' His eyes gleamed.

'I thought I was very professional. Anyone would think I'd been doing it for years.'

'I suggest we forgo the last two minutes of our bout,' he said suddenly. 'I have plans for the evening. I'll see myself out.' He picked up the mask and slipped it on. Only seconds later, he strode through the door. I sat on the mat looking totally bewildered. I'd gone too far this time. I just knew it. I felt an overwhelming sense of loss. I'd thought James Travers had come back into my life. I'd missed him for the past week, I realised. Stupid. I'd only known him for a week so how could I have missed him? He was just another punter. Just a paying client.

'I hope you took his cheque straight to the bank,' I snapped as Dexi came into the room.

'Are you all right? You seemed heavily occupied when I last looked in. New routine, is it?'

'What are you doing this evening?' I asked Dexi.

'I have a date, so I may not be back till morning. We don't need to make an early start, so there's no problem, is there?'

I felt ridiculously annoyed. I hadn't made any plans for the evening anyhow and why I should suddenly feel so deprived, I didn't know. Seeing James again had left me unsettled. The fact that I'd blown the whole thing was nobody else's business.

'Not really. I just feel as though I've missed out on something mega. You did know who that last client was?'

'Well, yes. He begged me not to tell you. He wanted to surprise you. I went along with him; I

50

thought you'd be pleased. Don't let him get to you – he's not worth it. You're doing OK without him.'

'You're right of course, as usual. You go out and enjoy yourself – I'll be fine. Bruised pride, I expect.'

'Not as bruised as his backside will be. I never suspected you had anything like that in your armoury.'

'If you weren't as bent as a corkscrew you might have found out.'

'Now there's an interesting thought. Maybe you should try it sometime. Could easily change my life forever.'

'Go and find your date and enjoy yourself,' I told him. He deserved a bit of fun.

'If only,' Dexi said. 'Why does life always have to be complicated?'

'Complicated? You? You want to tell me about something?' I began.

'No. I'm OK. Really. I'm worried about you though. Are you sure you'll be all right on your own? I mean, if James turns up again, how will you deal with him?'

'He's gone. Said he had plans. Why would he come all this way to see me and then have a date? Men!'

'Bitches, aren't they?' Dexi agreed ruefully. He looked hesitant, as though he wanted to do something but didn't like to.

'Go, Dexi. I'm fine. Go, go, go. I'm a big girl now.' I pushed him out of the door and went up to the suite. I showered, flicked the TV on and surfed through what was on offer. I fixed myself a Scotch and dry from the mini bar and sat to make my big decision: roast duck or prawn curry. Wow!

I'd seen very little of the town and decided to take

a walk before dinner. I pulled on some jogging pants and a T-shirt and went down to reception.

'Oh, Miss Lili? There's a message for you. I was just about to send it up to your suite.' The local girl was very young and thought someone with a name of Miss Lili must be decidedly exotic. She stared at me as if I was about to turn into Xena the Warrior Princess, or something. She passed an envelope to me, still gazing at me as if I was some sort of alien. Maybe it was just the angle. She was about four foot nothing and, at six foot, I certainly towered over her.

'Thanks,' I muttered, wondering whose was the flamboyant scrawl on the envelope. Naturally, I wanted it to be from only one man. I ripped it open. There was no message. Just a time. *Eight-thirty*. Nothing else. What was I supposed to do at eight-thirty? Who had sent it? I asked the girl. She told me a bike-messenger had left it. No description. Nothing.

I went for my walk. I did the entire circuit of the town in around ten minutes. There was an autumnal chill in the air. Everyone seemed to be going somewhere and I was stuck in a town where there seemed nothing much on offer. No wonder my little service was so popular. Saved everyone dying of boredom. I went back to my room and continued to ponder. Was it to be roast duck or prawn curry? There was a knock at the door. A porter stood outside.

'Parcel for you ma'am. Special delivery.'

'Thanks,' I managed to mutter. Who was sending me parcels? 'Oh, hang on a minute.' I fumbled in my purse for some change. I'm useless with money and had only a single two pound coin and nothing else. I handed it to the porter, who raised a finger in a gesture of thanks. Good old Brits – they manage to know their place. I laughed to myself. I turned over the package, looking for any clue about its sender. Nothing. I pulled off the string, never even considering it might be a bomb. It wasn't, luckily. A bombshell maybe. I wasn't quite sure what it was. A series of leather straps, it seemed, attached to a kind of swimsuit, if you could have a leather swimsuit. It was all front and no back. As I held it up, I could see it was definitely supposed to be some sort of garment, rather than purely a set of restraints. I glanced at the clock. I still hadn't decided my menu but, as it was already eight-fifteen, I thought I'd better forget about food. *Eight-thirty* could mean I had a date. If I'd been sent an outfit to wear, it was logical to expect that someone might turn up on time. I was getting wet again. I know that maybe I'm odd, but the very sight and smell of the soft leather was enough. I was getting very excited. It had to be James. He'd said he wasn't short of ideas and this looked liked one of them, to me. I completely forgot that he'd been angry and stormed out. I knew I deserved punishment of some sort and I knew I was going to love every second of whatever he had planned for me. I quickly threw off my joggers and tried to work out how to wear this leather something.

Chapter Four

*A*fter spending the afternoon's wrestling bout with every possible inch of me covered with black lycra, this went to the opposite extreme. The front of the garment – I supposed it was the front – was a long triangle. A halter strap held it up and I clipped the fasteners together. The slightest movement and my tits would be escaping round the edge. The lower edge ended in a narrow strap that went between my legs. A wide belt fastened round my waist, pulled the thong up, tight between my buttocks, cutting right into the cleft. Exciting or what? The belt clipped into my middle very tightly, pulling me into an hour-glass shape that might have sent Marilyn herself reaching for the slimming pills. I shoved my generous tits behind the top, trying to pull it to cover them properly. I didn't expect them to stay there for long. My buttocks were tantalisingly bare, the thong cutting in and emphasising their shape. I just knew that the next time I looked at them, they wouldn't look like two white orbs. The phone rang.

'Your car has arrived,' said my friend from the reception desk. I thanked her, trying not to let her know I wasn't expecting it. Spot on eight-thirty. What was I to put on over the leather, I wondered? I could have worn my casuals, but somehow I sensed that if it was James behind all this, he would disapprove. I pulled a long mac out of my wardrobe and added a pair of high-heeled ankle boots. I felt like a strange mixture of dominatrix and tart. Was I ready to punish or be punished? Either sounded quite delicious. I grabbed a bright red lipstick, just in case I might be the one in charge.

With a totally bland expression, Davis rose to his feet and held the hotel door open for me. I sailed out as if I'd been using chauffeur-driven limos all my life. He opened the rear door and eased me on to the leather seats.

'There is champagne on ice for you ma'am. Help yourself.' He drove off smoothly.

'Where are we going?' I asked.

'The master has rented a house in the country. A short drive out of town.'

'Rented it? Is he planning to stay for long?'

'I'm afraid he does not confide his plans to me. I have no idea how long he plans to stay. Enjoy your champagne.' He slid the glass window between us. I picked up the bottle. It was one of the miniatures they serve on first-class flights. No problem. I'd manage on that very well. After several corners and a lot of twisting lanes, we drew up outside a large country residence, which could have been anything from a private nursing home to a minor royal residence. He certainly did things in style, our Mr Travers, I thought. My leather straps were sufficiently tight for me to be aware of them if I so much as moved an inch. Thank heavens I'd gone without dinner. I sniggered at the thought of curried prawns trapped inside this particular outfit. Not good. Pulling my mac around me, I tottered out of the car on my too-high heels and walked up the steps. I wondered if my friend Davis was aware of what I was wearing beneath the prim mac. Judging from the way his eyes followed me, I'd lay bets that he was. Maybe he'd been the anonymous messenger who'd delivered the gear in the first place.

As I reached the door, it was opened before I even needed to ring. I assumed it was the butler who stood in the entrance.

'May I take your coat?' he asked, trying to unhook it from my shoulders.

'No thanks,' I protested. 'There's something in the pockets I may need later. Thanks.'

'Very well,' he said with disapproval pouring out of his snooty backside. 'Follow me. The master is waiting for you in his room.'

No stairs this time. I followed his snootiness through a baize-covered door, into a dark passage. I shivered. What the hell was I doing here, trussed up in some decidedly kinky leather gear, little more than a few straps, not knowing where I was, whom I was seeing and with no one else in the world knowing about it? What the hell had happened to my built-in safety warnings? What about my usual insurance? What had happened to my stupid brain? Dexi would go ballistic if he knew. I may be strong, a wrestler who could beat most men, but I was letting myself in for something I'd always vowed I couldn't let happen. Not again.

Snooty opened the door after knocking gently. Inside, James was standing. He was wearing tight black leather trousers and a white shirt. He looked every inch a biker having an off day. I did notice his belt matched the assortment of straps I was wearing, almost exactly.

'You shouldn't be wearing a coat, my dear,' he said smoothly. 'Come. Let me give it to . . . him.' He removed my mac, much to my discomfort, and handed it to Snooty. Give him credit: he scarcely blinked at the vision I must have presented. Must be used to it, I thought angrily. How many others did James bring back here for his pleasure? Hundreds, no doubt.

'I assume this is what you expected?' I said to him, after putting up with half an hour of his scrutiny. Well, it seemed like half an hour. The effect of the champagne on an empty stomach was making me less inhibited. I stood straight, my tits immediately jutting out like they'd been starched. With the heels I was actually taller than him.

'You look very tempting,' he said finally. 'Have you eaten?'

'No,' I replied, thinking that food was the last thing on my mind. Tight black leather doesn't cover the sort of bulge he was currently wearing.

'Good. Then you'll have to earn your supper. It could take some time.'

'I assumed you hadn't sent this lot if you were planning to take me somewhere posh to dine.'

'Certainly not. I think you know that you have to be punished very severely for what you did to me today. No one has ever treated me like that before.' For a brief moment, I felt a violent shudder of anticipation run through me. When I saw the look on his face, I also felt a shudder of trepidation. Was I getting into something I couldn't handle? This guy was an enigma. I didn't know what to believe. How to take him.

'But you loved every minute,' I said boldly. 'Don't

try to pretend you didn't.' His face remained impassive. 'Admit it. You loved being dominated. And I'm bloody good, you can also admit that while you're at it.'

'Shut up, slut,' he barked suddenly. 'You need to be taught some manners. Stand by that wall over there.' To my own amazement, I went along with his game. I stood by the wall. He glanced at me before he went out of the room, into what I assumed was a bathroom. I looked at the room I was in. It was a fairly ordinary-looking sitting room. A few antiques furnished it and there were a couple of large flower arrangements. I could smell the roses. I began to wander round but stood back at the wall as I heard him returning.

'You moved,' he snapped at me. 'Now I shall have to restrain you.' He half dragged me into the other room. It was dark, lit only by a dim table lamp. His eyes glittered in the darkness, making him look distinctly sinister. I felt scared, I have to admit. Not for the first time, I wondered what could have possessed me to allow myself to get into this situation. He dragged me to the bed with its modern version of an old-fashioned iron bedhead and foot. He seized one wrist and, bending me over, tied a leather thong round it, attaching it to one side. He took the other and secured it at the other end, stretching my arms out to each side. My chin rested uncomfortably on the mattress. He spread my legs apart and secured both ankles to the legs of the bed with more strips of leather.

'What are you doing?' I whispered.

'Punishing you. I'm going to show you exactly what you did to me this afternoon.' My middle rested heavily on the crossbar and my bare bum was stuck up in the air, exposed and helpless. The thong was cutting into me. The belt round my middle was tighter than ever. My tits hung down low, escaping from either side of the inadequate leather top. His hand caressed my buttocks. I forgot all about my fears and concentrated on the sheer pleasure I was waiting to experience. I would never have believed just how excited I was. Fear conjures its own thrills. I felt his hand, flat and hard. It pounded my backside, at first stinging and doubtless reddening it. He stopped and turned on another light, shining it straight at me.

'I'm so sorry, Lili. You can't see it, can you?' He busied himself with several moveable mirrors, shifting them until I could see every embarrassing inch of myself. The black leather thong had almost disappeared into my cleft and the red marks of his hand were already beginning to show. He hadn't finished by any means. He'd hardly started. He beat out a rhythm that was a repeat of my own poundings of the afternoon. Every inch of me felt as if it were on fire. I wanted to scream out, but I concentrated on blocking the sensations. I was completely held on the edge of orgasm for minute after minute, never quite coming and afraid the sensations would stop if he knew how close I was. I watched his face. The humour was back. His eyes were laughing as he slapped.

'You are quite insatiable,' he said at last. 'I'd never have believed you'd stay for so long without complaining.'

'No choice,' I gasped. I was so nearly there. The leather between my legs had become slick. It moved tantalisingly as he hit me. Did I want more or should I let him finish me some other way?

'I shall let you off the rest,' he said, regaining his serious expression. He released the thongs and belt and helped me to stand upright. I felt slightly dizzy and staggered against him. He looked at me in surprise. 'You all right?' I nodded. He put his finger between my legs and pushed round the leather thong to feel the damp stickiness. 'You seem well lubricated,' he remarked almost clinically.

'What do you expect?' He gave a shrug. I noticed his trousers still contained a huge bulge. 'I think I could certainly accommodate some of that,' I said hungrily, reaching my hand out to brush it lightly. He pushed me back.

'Don't do that,' he said with a snarl. His eyes looked as if he meant it. Again, that tremor of fear shot through me. 'What do you think you have done to earn that privilege? Nothing. You're a greedy whore. Get down on the floor where you belong. On your knees.'

I did as he asked, not daring to disobey. He knelt behind me. I could smell him: hot and exciting. He pushed against me and I could feel the soft, smooth leather stretched tight over his prick. I dared not speak but I wanted that throbbing cock inside me more than I ever wanted anything. I shuddered with anticipation.

'Keep still; I haven't given you permission to move.'

I kept as still as I could. My bum still pulsed from its pounding, my knees ached, and he was still there. What was he doing? I lifted my head a tad, hoping to see in the mirror. Something pushed me down again. It couldn't have been his hand as it was too far away. I felt him stand again and heard a swish. I braced myself. What was happening now? As a sharp pain seared my backside, I knew he held some sort of whip. Now, I've never been into that sort of domination. I gasped and fell forward.

'Get back on your knees,' he hissed.

'God, man, that hurt,' I said in protest.

'Can't take your punishment? You should have thought of that before you tried to thrash me. Now, get back to your proper position and don't dare speak another word until I tell you that you have my permission.'

Grudgingly, I did as I was told. After the first shock, the next blow was far less painful. I imagined the once white buttocks with angry red stripes laid across them. I could imagine what the sight was doing to him. The swishing stopped. He stood silent for a moment and then spoke.

'You may stand up.' It wasn't as easy as he suggested. However fit a body may be, a long stay in one position can make the next movements painful. I staggered to my feet, practically losing my balance in the high heels which, miraculously, I was still wearing. I stood looking at him, my head held high. I wasn't going to admit that his treatment of me had roused any sort of feelings at all. I wasn't entirely sure of his game.

'Spread your legs apart,' he commanded. I obeyed. He lifted his whip, a slender black rod with a small loop of leather at the end. He circled my tits with it and for one dreadful moment I thought he might strike the vulnerable tips. 'Don't you dare move a muscle,' he ordered. I immediately wanted to adjust my position but managed to stay still. He leaned forward and took one engorged nipple into his mouth. The shock stabbed into my stomach, sending a steady rush of fluids to my sex channel. He moved to the other side, repeating his performance and enhancing it with a firm bite as he left it again. My breath was beginning to rasp as I breathed deeply to try to control the turmoil that raged through my body. How could he rouse me to this point so many times and not take pity on me? How did he control himself, I wondered. The swelling of his own prick against the tight leather must have been quite painful for him as well. I licked my lips, still desperately anticipating whatever he was going to offer me. He took his whip and dragged it under my legs. He pulled it backwards and forwards, gently enough not to hurt and yet firmly enough for me to feel every tiny ridge along its length. My orgasm was building again, not that it had ever gone away.

'Remember, you mustn't move even a centimetre,' he ordered. 'If you do, I shall leave you tied up all night, with nothing and no one to give you comfort.' The prospect was not a good one, not in my current state. I've never been a person who could come quietly. I like to scream, pant, yell, whatever. To stand completely still and silent was a totally new experience. I braced myself, as his rubbing began to take its toll. I could feel sweat pouring off me and a shuddering rush as my whole body turned to fire. How my legs managed to support me, I can't remember. I opened my eyes and tried to slow down my breathing. He was looking at me with laughter in his eyes, belying the stern expression on his face.

'Good. Self-control. I like that.' He took both my tits in his hands and gently rubbed at them, making the nipples stand out erect. Despite the fact that I felt marginally satiated for a few moments, they were more than ready to leap to attention and obey his touch. He stared at them thoughtfully, nodded and smiled. What was he thinking? He leaned over and suddenly kissed me, full on the lips. I was surprised to say the least. It was almost a gentle gesture, not that of a man who is fully in control of a punishment session. Perhaps we both had this strange mixture of needs within us. Perhaps this was what excited us both so much.

'Come and sit down. You must be feeling hungry.' I remained silent and immobile. He laughed. 'It's OK. Your silence is over. For now.' He opened a bottle of the inevitable champagne and filled two glasses. 'Come and sit here.' He indicated two tall shiny chrome and plastic stools near to a bar. I couldn't help thinking how out of place they looked. Tacky, in this otherwise luxurious house. I slid over to one of them and winced as I eased my sore buttocks on to the hard seat. He smiled a slightly twisted sort of smile and handed me the frosty glass. I could see myself in half a dozen different mirrors. I looked like a cheap tart, my full breasts hanging out of various strips of leather and reddened buttocks, divided by a strip of black thong, pressed on to a cheap seat. It gave me an unexpected thrill. All I needed was the bright red lipstick to complete the tarty picture.

'I'll ring for supper,' he announced. 'We'll have it in here and then we shall be ready for phase two of the evening's entertainment.'

'Phase two?' I asked. 'I thought we'd finished.'

'Certainly not. I'm sure you need a little more satisfying. I certainly do.'

I was tempted to suggest we skipped dinner and got straight to the action, but that might have looked greedy. When Snooty came, bearing various dishes on a huge silver tray, I barely even blushed. If he thought I was cheap tart, too bad. I'd never see the guy again in my life, so who cared if he even bothered to have thoughts? If I was cast as the tart, I'd certainly play up to the role. I do like to give good value.

'Help yourself to whatever you fancy,' said James, this strange man who had more mood changes than a severe case of PMT.

'Is that an invitation?' I asked, staring hard at the bulge I so desperately needed inside me. Hell, I could eat food any time. The sort of goods he was carrying in front of him were much rarer. He looked at me and his expression changed to the hard man who was my acknowledged master.

'Don't get smart with me,' he snapped. 'I'd intended rewarding you, but talk like that will only get you more punishment. Involuntarily, I licked my lips in anticipation. He'd restrained me, spanked me, humiliated me – the only thing missing was a damned good fuck. Unfortunately, he knew well that was the only thing I desperately wanted. My biggest weakness. He stared at me and shook his head. He got off his chair and took my wrist. He dragged me along towards a metal frame, the kind usually used to hang clothes. It was similar to my own portable rail I used to transport my wrestling outfits. I'd never look at it again in quite the same way. This was not what I had in mind at all, but I didn't dare protest. 'Stand there and don't move,' he ordered. I obeyed. It was perfect for securing someone in a star-spread shape. I knew that someone was about to be me. Obediently, I moved to the frame as he indicated. He pointed at the base and I placed my aching feet against each side of the bars. He tied the leather thongs round my ankles. I made a mental note to remind myself to avoid high heels, if ever there was a next time. My wrists were again tied to the frame, higher up this time. He unfastened the halter straps of my costume so that it fell to my waist. He unbuckled my belt and tugged the strap out of my cleft and the whole thing dropped away, leaving me stark naked, wearing nothing more than the red, angry stripes on my arse.

'I did say it was supper time,' he said briefly as he walked back to the loaded trays. He sat down at the bar and poured himself a glass of champagne. He filled a plate with the wide range of delicacies and proceeded to eat.

'I'm sorry,' I said humbly.

'Shut up. Speak only when you're spoken to. I don't like to be disturbed when I'm eating.'

'I only . . .' I broke off. He got up from his seat and came over to me. He picked up the whip he'd used on me earlier. He struck my buttocks with one sharp, stinging blow. I winced and bit back my cry of pain. Silently, he went back to his supper. My stomach began to cry out for food. I hadn't eaten since a small snack at lunch and I was starving. The bastard must have realised and came over to me. I could smell the delicious piece of chicken he was chewing and looked at the laden plate, my mouth watering. I said nothing and tried hard to think of something else. Anything. Trouble was, I could smell the food and the powerful smell of his musky male body. Both were equally stimulating. He put down his plate a few inches away from me and, keeping his eyes fixed on mine, began to peel off his leather trousers. He wore nothing underneath and his cock stuck out in front of him like a rampant sword. There were two things I wanted, his cock and some food. At that point, I'd have been grateful for either. My whole body was burning and I felt the stimulated sex juices begin to trickle down my thighs. He unleashed my wrists and I waited for my ankles to be released. He gripped my wrists.

'Bend forward,' he commanded. Uncomfortably, I did so. He stepped towards me and my mouth was on exactly the right level to take his prick. He gently pushed it into my mouth and moved backwards and forwards so that I was helplessly sucking him, unable to use any of my own talents for his pleasure but relying completely on him. I was excited and helpless, yet again. I couldn't even protest. My mouth was too full. He was fucking my mouth. He took a deep breath and pulled himself away. He had been right on the edge of coming but had pulled away. I was very relieved. I'd dreaded having to swallow his spunk, afraid I might gag. Maybe now I'd get my reward. Calmly, he went back to his food. I began to straighten up. If I hadn't been quite so fit, I doubt I'd have managed it, held as I was by the ankles.

'Please,' I began. I stopped as he glared at me.

He walked over again and touched my breasts. He cupped them in his hands and leaned down to give a bite to each hard nipple in turn. The pleasure-pain seared my over-stimulated body. His hard expression faded and, wordlessly, he bent to release my legs.

'Get in there and shower yourself.' He pointed at a door in the corner. I hadn't even seen it before. I kicked my shoes off gratefully and went into a sumptuous bathroom. I filled the bath and threw the switch at the side. The bubbles began to rise and I eased my poor, wonderfully abused body into the healing waters. He had ordered me to take a shower but the spa was just too tempting. Maybe there would be more punishment for my disobedience but, at that moment, I didn't care. I closed my eyes to make myself relax. Every inch of my skin was alive, sensuous, tingling with sex. I heard the door open but kept my eyes closed. I felt him step into the tub beside me and he leaned over, soaping my body with gentle, slow, sensuous movements. It seemed impossible this could be the same man who wanted to be my master and keep me subservient. I opened my eyes to look at him.

'Hi,' he said softly. It seemed he'd moved into yet another role. I'd almost have dared say that he looked like a lover. But I knew better. He obviously had a number of personalities: there was the one that enjoyed being dominated during our wrestling bouts; he was, undoubtedly, an experienced SM master and now I was seeing him as some sort of lover. He must also have the various business facades that enabled him to be so rich and successful. I once more wondered about my own safety. To hell with it. I enjoyed his different roles as much as I enjoyed my own. We were a volatile, lethal combination. As long as we could separate our roles and coincide with correct moods, this was going to be one hell of a relationship. If the roles conflicted, the excitement could really get going . . . big time!

While the bubbles were blowing around us, I lay back and let his hands do what they would. He probed every available piece of me, fingers pushing into hungry orifices. He kneeled and pushed my legs apart, pushing two fingers deep inside me. He added more fingers to his exploration and I began to experience the fluid motions, the beginnings of my orgasm. I leaned back, resting my head on the side of the huge tub. He rubbed more and more insistently until my body was a single river of fire, concentrating on the one point he was rubbing. He stopped suddenly. Lifting me out of the bath, he pushed me down on the thick pile of the carpet. He lay on top of me in the almost unfamiliar missionary position and began to push himself in and out. I couldn't stop myself responding, whatever he might have wanted. I lifted my legs round his waist, holding him firmly in place and pushing against everything I needed to in order to find relief. We moved in harmony until I felt myself soaring with him. I felt him come deep inside me as I reached my own peak. It was probably the most satisfying sexual experience of my life, so far. God, I had to watch myself. I'd already allowed the word lover to creep in. I'd be falling in love if I wasn't extremely careful. Women like me don't do love. Never. It hurts too much. Dexi was probably the only man I could allow myself to love, and that was something totally different. The brother I never had.

I have the strangest mind. Why, after glorious, fulfilling sex, should I suddenly think of Dexi? Maybe he's deeply embedded in my innermost conscience or something.

'Stay with me, Lili,' James said suddenly.

'I can't,' I whispered hoarsely. It was far more than I dared risk.

Chapter Five

*A*s we moved to the next dates in our tour, Dexi and I were both very quiet. Neither of us seemed to be able to chat in our usual friendly and free manner. After a couple of hours, I broke the silence.

'D'you want to tell me about it?'

'Nope,' he replied, clamping his mouth shut in that determined way he has. His Rock Hudson-type face stared impassively out of the window as the miles rolled on. Stoke-on-Trent next. We obviously hadn't got the routes for our bookings quite well enough organised. An hour's journey between towns would have been so much better.

'I need food,' I announced as we came to a service area. 'Something disgustingly fattening and loaded with unhealthy calories.' I still carried the memory of the delicious-looking food I'd somehow managed to avoid the previous night. I'd finally arrived back at the hotel with barely time to pack. As Dexi had obviously done the same, neither of us had mentioned it.

A week in Stoke followed, with all the usual routines, until the last day arrived. I'd been silently hoping that James would make a booking, as he had the previous week. Only three clients had booked my services on the final day. We looked forward to an early finish. Dexi had even offered to take me out to dinner. He must have been desperate. Perhaps he was going to break his silence and tell me what was bothering him. I finished off my final client, a weedy little man with a high opinion of his own abilities. Hoping never to see him again, I quickly disposed of his ego, his prowess and his cheque. He wasn't too pleased that he hadn't held out for more than a few minutes. He asked for a signed photo of me, which I gave. I wondered if he'd keep it in his wallet. I also wondered how he would carry my memory. I doubted I would go down in his personal history as the woman who beat him in five minutes flat. As I showed him out, Dexi was waiting.

'How much were you looking forward to that dinner?' he asked.

'Why?'

'Someone just e-mailed a request for an evening session. In a club somewhere near.'

'I don't think so. I'm not into audience participation.' I hated doing public bouts. They're something I gave up long ago. Nothing like as lucrative as my current programme and always highly competitive. 'No. Definitely not. I've done all that stuff.'

'He's offering double rates. Claims he's the owner of the club. Purely private affair. Just one on one. You and him. He sounded OK. I don't mind missing dinner. Two hours. It's a lot of money to turn down. He even offered a bonus if you win.'

'I'd need you with me. Just to make sure all is well.'

'I'm cool.'

'So much for an early night.' I couldn't afford to turn down what might amount to almost two grand. Think of the plates and cutlery Penny Jackson's restaurant could buy with that.

'So, do I call him and accept?' Dexi asked. 'He gave a phone number.'

'I guess so. What's his name?'

'Straver. Mark, I think it was.' I shrugged. Names meant nothing to me.

We cleared up the room we'd taken for the bouts and decided that a club wouldn't need us to take any of our own equipment. At least we'd be ready for an early start the next day. I selected a purple suit from the rack and silver boots. It was a one-piece with a high front neck and dipping back. Mr Straver hadn't suggested anything in particular, so I grabbed whatever was near at hand and shoved it in my bag. Dexi came in with a tray of snacks.

'Thought you might need something to keep you going. You'll eat after the fight, I suppose?'

'Sure, but this looks good. I don't want to run out of energy at the crucial point. It'll probably be near midnight before we're finally through. Do you reckon they still have food at that time of night up here?'

The club was in a seedy part of one of the five (or six) towns. Urban regeneration hadn't quite made it to this particular area yet. I wasn't sure exactly where I was as everywhere seemed to point at the City Centre, whichever city it was. The dingy street was deserted and I mentally pulled Dexi closer to me. I didn't fancy being left here on my own. There was a strange tang in the air. Smoky. Chemicals. I wasn't sure. The door of the club was in desperate need of paint. Not promising at all. I hoped the owner, whoever he was, realised exactly how much tonight's little battle was going to cost him. If he had that much dough to spare, he could surely have afforded a can of paint for the door.

The door was unlocked and we pushed our way in. The stairs led up from the tiny hallway. We went up. Wooden stairs covered with dark-brown, battered linoleum. It was utterly depressing. At the top was a rather cleaner door, with a bell. I pushed it and waited. A huge burly guy opened it. My heart skipped a beat. I certainly did not fancy two hours with this brute. No way was I going to fight with Dexi outside the door. He was going to stay right in front of us, witnessing the whole wretched bout.

'Come in, love,' he said in a rasping voice, ruined by too many cigarettes and booze. His whole body reeked of it. I wondered how I could get out of this. I went inside, Dexi close at my heels. He was looking equally dismayed at the prospect ahead of us.

I blinked at the array of lights in what was clearly the main room. The floor was well sprung and covered with a huge, custom-made wrestling mat, virtually identical to our own. A few tables and chairs ringed the arena and there was a bar in one corner. The room was deserted, apart from the three of us.

'You can change in there, love,' the ox of a man said, pointing a grubby arm at the corner behind the bar. I carried my sports bag through, wondering if I should refuse now or later. I might wait and see how he shaped up when he was dressed in more appropriate gear. I was uneasy, worried and cursing myself for being greedy.

The dressing room was more like an up-market ladies' room – mirrors everywhere and a couple of cubicles. I stripped my outdoor gear off and was halfway into pulling on the purple suit. Hanging on the wall was a white suit. It was shiny vinyl, long sleeves and high neck and with high, cutaway legs. It would be most uncomfortable to fight in but something told me it was there for my use. I also knew the seedy guy who'd let us in wasn't my partner after all. Straver. I thought about the name. Travers. What was the name he'd used last time? Vestrar. Anagrams. Bastard. He was following me round the country. But he owned this club? Unlikely. Improbable. But not impossible. The outside belied the inside. Maybe he did own the place and kept the other guy as a doorman. He couldn't leave the place unused for the rest of the time, could he? Perhaps he sponsored fights or rented out the premises for some other use. So what, I shrugged. I pulled on the shiny vinyl creation, grimacing slightly at the feel of the unyielding fabric. I laced up the front, tightly. It fitted to perfection, just as I'd known it would. I looked around for boots of some sort. I thrilled at the thought of the possible punishment if I did anything even slightly different from his expectation. A box was lying on the shelf and I opened it, pulling out the matching white vinyl thigh boots. The soles were very soft and light, of course, so that no damage would be caused to either of us. I laced up the boots, pulling them tightly so they showed off the shape of my legs. That was what it was all about, wasn't it?

I brushed my hair into a high ponytail and fastened it with an extra-tall clip so that it stood several inches above my head. I took a deep breath, tried to calm my pounding heart and pushed the door open. Dexi and the big man were drinking at the bar. Holding my head high, I walked over to join them.

'Wow,' slobbered ugly features. His hand drifted

towards his crotch and I managed to stifle the bile that rose into my throat. Was I mistaken after all? There was no sign of James W. Travers. 'Want a drink, darlin'?'

'Still mineral water, thanks.' I sipped from the glass, looking in desperation for a clue from Dexi. He knocked back his drink – brandy, from the smell that drifted my way. To my horror, he announced that he was off.

'Wait a minute,' I protested.

'You'll be fine. Don't need me or anyone else around. Eric will look after you.' He spoke calmly with only the faintest hint of a smile at the corner of his mouth. 'Have fun, darling. I'll see you in the morning.' What the hell was he playing at? I'd had only a brief fantasy that it was James awaiting my fighting skills. I hadn't even told him about the possible anagrams of his name. Before I could say anything else, he left the room and clattered down the uncarpeted stairs.

'Boss is on his way. Won't keep you waiting long,' the man, Eric, told me. I breathed a sigh of relief and immediately began to enjoy the prospect of the evening ahead. My skin-tight vinyl creaked slightly with my every movement. Should have used the bright red lipstick after all, I thought. I was going to dominate tonight. Well, for the first part at least. After that, who could tell?

After a few more minutes, the bottom door opened and I heard light steps running up the stairs. Eric went over to open the Yale lock and let him in. My opponent was dressed in a dark business suit, white shirt and tie and carrying a briefcase. He looked about as ready as the man in the moon for a bout of heterosexual erotic wrestling. Mind you, the idea of taking him in his present garb was more than a little tempting.

'It's OK, Eric. Thanks. You can take the rest of the evening off.' Eric looked disappointed.

'I wasn't expecting to leave you, sir,' he said gruffly. 'I ... er, you might need something. You might want a few pictures taking ...' His voice tailed off.

'Go, I said. I have everything I need,' he said, looking straight at me. I felt that wonderful swoosh the stomach makes when it anticipates something good. Eric got up and went to the door.

'Door locked or left open?' he asked.

'Locked,' James replied briefly. As Eric slowly left, looking over me salaciously before he went, I looked back at James.

'I'm pleased to see you, Mr Straver. Surprised, but pleased. I take it you are ready to go? I like the idea of a business suit.'

'Let me look at your outfit,' he commanded. I stood and even gave him a twirl. 'Good.'

He went into another changing room in the opposite corner and I went over to the mat and began to do some warm-up exercises. I stretched and flexed various muscles. I knew my opponent by now and I knew what he was capable of. I must never underestimate him. James W. Travers was as full of surprises as a cartload of monkeys. He came back into the room wearing the skimpiest white trunks I had ever seen. Nothing else. I stared at his broad chest and narrow waist. He hadn't a spare ounce of flesh on him and every muscle looked finely honed and trim. He was beautiful, I realised with a pang. Everything a woman could want. Sexy, good looking and unlimited wealth, evidently. If circumstances had been a little different ... Why had I refused his offer of living with him? I must be crazy. If he asked again, I'd probably say yes, yes, yes.

He walked on to the mat and stood waiting. I felt strangely shy. The thought of his sexy body bending over mine as he spanked me got me totally horny once again. I remembered the feel of restraints round wrists and ankles, leaving me powerless to defend myself against anything he offered. Then I remembered. He'd also humiliated me in front of that snooty butler and his chauffeur. Made me show off fetish gear and behave like some lewd trollop. I'd now got myself angry, in the mood to fight. I gave a whoop, worthy of Xena the Warrior Princess herself, and cartwheeled towards him. He was taken totally by surprise and collapsed on to the floor as I leapt on him, my feet wrapping themselves round his neck and holding him down. He lay helpless and I jumped up again, beckoning for him to get up and join me. I was wearing a wicked grin, taunting him, challenging him. I held out my arms, innocently waiting for him to step forward. My wrist went straight under his chin as I turned him and held him in a headlock. With a heave, I lifted my legs round his middle and he staggered round the mat, impeded by my whole body weight. I bounced to make it even more difficult for him. He began to collapse down on to the mat and I pushed against him with my hands, released my legs and did a back flip, landing beside him in a standing position. He laughed.

'You certainly mean business tonight.'

'You'd better believe it,' I almost shouted. I felt good, high, like no amount of dope could make me. I'd used it a few times but decided the after effects weren't worth it. Now I confined myself to alcohol in moderation and fitness to excess. I crouched in front of my prey, feeling like a tigress, ripe for action. The white vinyl suit and high boots looked almost sleazy. If that's what he wanted, he could have it, cartloads of it. I pounced again. I layed him flat on the mat and sat on his chest. I carefully placed my vinyl-clad boobs over his face – a well-known smothering sort of technique. You really have to know what you're doing and let them go only so far. The very second I felt him beginning to relax, I moved away from him. He grinned up at me and made his own countermove. He'd been feinting. His legs came up behind me, knocking me forward right over his head. I whooped again and rolled over forwards, ending in a sitting position.

'You'll never better me in the ring,' I called out challengingly.

'I don't need to. I have my own ways of bettering you. And don't get too cocky, madame. I have moves in my repertoire you don't even know about.'

'You look like the cocky one to me,' I shouted. 'You're all cock from where I'm sitting.' I sat watching him, panting. I'd already fought for several hours today but the adrenalin was flowing now. Admittedly, not one of them had taken up much of my energy. Most of them were relatively inexperienced and largely wanted the vicarious thrill of being beaten by a beautiful woman. Short of sex with a prostitute, where else could they grapple with a powerful sexy woman? No pro would do what I do and they get the same sort of relief, let's face it.

James rose to his feet and held out a hand to pull me up beside him. I couldn't quite decide whether he was about to make some new move and so allowed him to lift me, pulling down heavily on his arm as I did so. That way, he was kept off balance and couldn't possibly pull me into a new hold. I stepped back and hitched at the neck of my suit. It was rubbing a bit and I needed to release the pressure. Fast as lightning, James leapt at me and grabbed at the high collar. He tore at it, splitting the fabric away from its fastenings. I always knew vinyl wasn't a good idea and told him so. He raised both hands and, with a powerful wrench, ripped the whole thing from top to bottom.

'Get out of it,' he ordered.

'Don't give me orders,' I said, pushing him to the ground. I placed one booted foot in the middle of his stomach and pressed him down, hard. He gasped and I saw realisation dawn in his eyes. 'Apologise for ruining my clothing.' His jaw tightened and he tried to get up. I pressed him back with one foot, transferring the weight as if to place the other foot on top of him. I didn't like the idea at all, as it might make me lose my balance. With a man like this, you didn't offer him even the slightest chance. He flopped back and held his hands up in surrender. 'Apologise,' I commanded.

'I'm very sorry,' he whispered.

'Louder.'

'Sorry,' he said almost audibly. I didn't stop until he practically shouted it. I allowed him to get up.

'Take the rest of my beautiful suit off.' He stood in front of me and slowly peeled off the sleeves and took the remains of the top down. I stood naked before him, except for the high boots. It felt good, having him kneeling before me like this. I pushed my legs apart and lifted his chin. I moved forward so that my pussy was right in front of his mouth. 'Eat me,' I ordered. His eyes met mine. I didn't waver and stood, my breasts jutting out proudly above him. He leaned forward obediently and pushed his tongue into me. I opened wider and stood towering over him. He continued to lap and I continued to provide plenty for him to lap. Several times over. His tongue kept brushing my clit. I felt the first rousing of orgasm but, each time, I stopped myself. I wanted it to last until I was ready to have him inside me. He gripped my ankles to support himself. It sent a conflict of emotions. I loved being in control but adored the feeling of being out of control. Suddenly, I wanted to be restrained, to feel the tight bands of something restricting my every movement. But I needed to keep this control until I'd had all of what I wanted from him. Hopefully, my own punishment and his own thoughts and need to dominate would be fulfilled.

'Enough,' I cried out. 'That's enough time spent gratifying you. You haven't thanked me for the privilege.' His look was one of almost hatred.

'Thank you for allowing me to pleasure you,' he said meekly.

'Good.' I spoke softly and moved towards him again. This time I waited until he was reaching forward for me. The timing had to be split-second and I lowered my back so that he fell forward. As he was actually moving, I stood up and quickly swung him round over my shoulders. I hurled him to the ground in a full body slam and dropped on top of him. He was quite winded and quite helpless. I pressed my body over his upper torso and held him down. It would have been counted as a fall to me, if we'd been playing that sort of game. As it was, I held him down until I could feel his breathing returning to normal. I straddled his face, leaving damp, bare pussy once more near to his mouth.

'Thought you could catch me out, did you?' I

shook my head sadly at him. I was kneeling on his wrists. He was powerless. 'You know what to do,' I said. He obliged until I could feel my eyes glazing over again and my head swimming with the joy of my heightened sex. His tongue was warm and moist, making its way over and round the parts of me that mattered most at this moment. His tongue reached my engorged clit as he drove me into a frenzy of need. His teeth caught it and nipped it almost to ecstasy. I felt weak and fluid through my entire body. There was only one thing I wanted now. His glorious prick filling me where it could accomplish everything else I needed. I hadn't quite worked out how I could achieve that yet. Once he had me down and powerless, he'd surely keep me wanting him, just as he always did. This time, I was not prepared to endure hours of agonised waiting. I wanted him now. I lifted myself slightly, putting myself out of his reach. His face was wet with my juices. I turned, not letting him move at all. I peeled off his trunks, what there was of them, and released his hugely erect cock. I leaned down to lick him and squeezed his balls as I did so. He gasped. I squeezed even harder until I felt his body convulsing. His tongue penetrated me once more, swirling round my sex and, locked together in the best of sixty-nine, we enjoyed each other. I felt him beginning to throb and immediately, leapt off him. I swung my legs round and straddled him, riding up and down on his glorious manhood. I felt him slide into me, deeper, deeper until I couldn't believe how much of him was buried. He panted, thrashed and made every display of ultimate pleasure he could. I kept my own fingers busy, working on my clit. The rush of his semen hit me like a power jet. Too late, I realised I'd broken yet another of my strict rules.

We were unprotected. I had no fears of pregnancy but I was terrified of disease. I had no idea of this man's sexual habits, apart from what we'd done together before. He'd always used a condom. It totally ruined my aftermath. I came down far too quickly and allowed it to show.

'It's OK,' he said, almost kindly, reading my thoughts. 'I'm quite safe. I don't have unprotected sex with anyone. Until now. Maybe you'll have to take your punishment next time.' He sounded like the voice of sweet reason. It was almost scary. I flopped my naked body back on the mat and we lay side by side.

'I think my time's up,' he said, after lying beside me for several silent minutes. He rose to lie on one elbow and looked down at me. 'I believe I owe you some money.'

Somehow I felt knocked back. It seemed that he was paying me not so much for the wrestling but for the rest of our little bout. It felt cheap. On the other hand, he had booked me for a bout and even offered a bonus. It was only fair on Dexi to take his money.

'OK,' I said. 'For the wrestling. I reckon it lasted about one and a half hours. You can pay for that but the rest of the encounter was just for me. Because I wanted it. Your punishment, if you like.'

He wrote out a cheque, taken from his briefcase that lay on the bar. His cock had dropped now and his nice, tight arse was looking more than a little tempting.

'Don't even think of it,' he said without turning. I guessed he was getting to know my little foibles rather well. I took his money and tucked it inside one of my boots without even glancing at it. I would hand it over to Dexi the next morning.

'You want to eat?' he asked ungraciously. I almost wondered about saying yes, remembering the last evening we'd spent together.

'If you do,' I replied. To my surprise, he gestured me towards the changing room and I went to dress. I wasn't exactly dressed for anywhere posh and, when I saw him back in his formal suit, I felt rather scruffy.

'Hope you like Indian. Not many other places open in this part of town.'

'Fine,' I said. 'No problem.'

Like any normal couple, we went into the street, slamming the grubby, paintless door behind us. The limo cruised up silently and Davis opened the door for us.

'Good evening, sir. Madame,' he said. He must have been sitting there for the entire evening. Strange existence. James gave him some address and we settled back into the comfortable cushions. I wondered what else the evening held in store. I wasn't even sure I wanted another long bondage, domination or sex session. For once in my life I would have liked to settle down in a comfortable bed and curl up and sleep beside another warm, undemanding body. Hell, I was getting almost broody.

I needn't have worried. He dropped me back at my hotel in the early hours with a casual good night. He didn't ask to see me again and never once had he suggested becoming my one and only wrestling partner. Typical, I thought. Just when I make up my mind that I'll stay with someone when they ask, he doesn't bloody well ask.

Tomorrow would be yet another town, another place.

Chapter Six

*T*hree more weeks and three more cities and we were nearing the end of the tour. The final client in each town had been James. He always used a pseudonym and always managed to keep me guessing as to whether I really would see him as the grand finale to the week. We fought. We took turns with domination rituals. Always, he produced new costumes, new forms of restraint and had enough imagination to keep even the most hardened devotee excited. Though I had almost made up my mind to give up this itinerant life, he never again asked me to move in with him. I'd lost my chance. Ironically, I now knew it was what I wanted most of all.

Dexi had continued to work away at whatever problem had been worrying him and remained unusually silent. He was almost morose at times and I was getting sick of seeing only a miserable face instead of his usual handsome, smiling features. We were at the end of a long day on the Bristol leg of the tour. Dexi had set up the massage table and was working on my back. As always, I was completely relaxed, enjoying the guy's sensual hands smoothing over my naked body. I felt myself drifting into arousal as he circled my anus. His fingers parted the hole and gently, he pushed in one finger and then another, stretching me to the point of near pain. It was unusual for him to be doing this. Only once before had he attempted it.

'I suppose you're going to tell me you could fancy even me, this way,' I gurgled.

'Sorry, love. You don't mind do you? I know what it always does to me though. I thought you might appreciate a change.' I felt slightly peculiar about it. I never actually thought of Dexi's preferences and somehow it made me more aware of him as a man, albeit a gay man. He stopped when someone knocked at the door.

'Who the hell is that?' I asked, pushing him away from me. He flung a large towel over me and went to open it.

'Joel. What the hell are you doing here?'

'I'm sorry Dex but we have to talk. I don't want to lose you. Everything's gone pear-shaped the last few weeks. Dexi, I . . .'

'I am working, Joel. Just now isn't really the time.'

I raised my head and called out, 'Don't mind me. I can just carry on lying here.' Truth to tell, I was more than a little curious. I knew something had been wrong with Dexi lately.

'So this must be the famous Lili,' Joel said, coming across the room and eyeing me for the first time. He was gorgeous. What a waste of a prime physical male, well at least that's how it seemed to me. They made a very handsome couple. 'If you're sure she really isn't shy, do carry on with whatever you were doing,' he told Dexi.

'I'm not sure that's a good idea.' Dexi was stammering slightly. I could understand why he didn't want to continue with the particular form of massage he'd been doing, nor the place he'd been doing it. My anus was still feeling strangely sensitive, stimulated and waiting as it was for, I assumed, that final penetration. My insides were still churning round, waiting for him to complete his intimate massage. I actually felt even more turned on at the thought of Dexi's own favourite lover watching us. Yet again, I wondered if there really is something wrong with my psyche. Joel licked his lips. I could see his own erection beginning to bulge. Dexi gave a shrug and removed the towel. I rolled over to lie on my back, legs splayed apart and nipples standing up to attention. Dexi moved his hands across them and slid slowly down the length of my body along the outside of my legs. He moved back up the inside, his eyes fixed unwaveringly on Joel as he did so. When he reached my pubic area, slowly, very slowly, he pushed his thumbs deep inside me. I closed my eyes, waiting for the orgasm to build. My nub was screaming for attention. Blindly, I pushed my own fingers down to it, rubbing, matching the rhythm that Dexi was weaving. He pushed one finger into my back passage, so that I felt filled in a way that was completely new to me. I could even feel his finger and thumb moving together, pressing the fine membrane that divides the two passages. It was the most amazing sensation and I yelled out before I even remembered where I was and who was watching. As the crisis passed, I lay back panting, fully relaxed and virtually unable to move. When I finally opened my eyes again, the two men were standing silently, their eyes locked together. Dexi's expression was almost triumphant, as if he were silently telling Joel he could have an effect on women as well. Joel's expression was less readable, but then, I didn't know Joel.

'You bastard,' he hissed through clenched teeth. 'So that's your game is it? AC/DC. Bit of everything eh? Well, as far as I'm concerned, forget it. I'm not interested.' Dexi looked impassive.

'This is work, Joel,' he said in a hard voice, quite different from his usual slightly sexy drawl. 'I do what I do and get paid for it. Lili and I have a complete understanding and she enjoys what I do. Her vibrator would do the same job but she happens to enjoy relaxing and letting it happen. If you are jealous then I can do nothing about it. Come to terms with it and we may have a future.'

'Dexi, I love you. Can't you understand what it does to me? Seeing you making love to a ... a woman?'

'Grow up Joel. This is nothing remotely like making love. Of course I like Lili, but what pleasures her does nothing for me. I love you. I couldn't do for you what I do for Lili. With clinical coolness. Emotions are involved with you.' He put an arm round Joel's shoulder and drew him close, kissing him with a depth of passion that made me feel my own insides clench up again. I'd never before seen two men kissing with such intensity. I lay still, hardly daring to breathe in case I brought an end to this drama I could see unfolding. I saw Joel unbuttoning his flies and I glimpsed white satin boxers. Dexi was wearing boxers himself and I could see his own excitement growing.

'Why don't you continue your ministrations to your, er, employer?' Joel suggested huskily. Obediently, Dexi turned me over again and began smoothing his hands down my spine. From the corner of my eye, I saw Joel pulling down Dexi's pants and he leaned over to him, dancing a fully erect penis over Dexi's rounded buttocks. I felt myself getting unbearably hot. An anticipatory orgasmic flush, no doubt. I began to breathe heavily. As Dexi leaned over me, he pressed his naked body closely against my back. His thumbs still circled my anus and made small darting movements into the hole as he widened it, slowly, slowly. He gasped and stiffened as he was penetrated from behind. Joel's arms pushed between Dexi and me and I felt him pulling Dexi hard against himself and they moved in close rhythm. I felt Dexi's thumb inside my anus and thrashed with them, move for move, as I physically shared the vicarious thrill of two men having sex right over the top of me.

I had never known anything remotely like this before. How long it went on, I had no idea. It seemed like hours before Dexi collapsed on top of me and Joel on him. I thought I'd never breathe again for a moment, as the air was pressed out of my body. God, it was exciting. They both moved and I tried to turn over and sit up. It was hard work, as I panted and pulled in great mouthfuls of air. The two men were holding each other close, their naked bodies shining with sweat. They both had well-developed, muscular bodies and looked every inch like figures posing for a stud porn mag. They parted, still holding hands as if they couldn't bear to be totally separated.

'Another first for me,' I announced brashly, sounding utterly ridiculous. I didn't know how else to lighten the tension.

'I'm sorry,' Dexi began.

'No need. Say no more. I'm cool. Well, no, actually I'm very hot. Maybe I should take a shower.' I was babbling on; I knew it.

'It's all right, Lili. I understand now,' Joel drawled in that sexy voice. No wonder Dexi was so smitten with him. He was one helluva man, whatever language you used.

'We'll have dinner,' Dexi told him. 'And talk.'

'Don't mind me,' I told them. 'I'm planning an early night and a take-away.' For once I meant it. It wasn't yet the final day and there had been no sign of James or a booking for my services. An early night would do me good, give me time to think. Where was I going? What was I doing?

Disregarding any fears for my safety, I wandered round the city. Bristol was usually busy. I walked along a shopping street, looking in at brightly coloured displays of Christmas goodies. It surely couldn't be nearly Christmas already? I had a momentary pang. There was nothing to make the time of year special. I had no close friends or family to do the whole tree and crackers bit or share ridiculous presents and wear tinsel crowns. I felt depressed. What had I done with my life? I remembered the very healthy bank account and wondered whether now would be the right time to stop. I definitely had some sort of feelings for James but it was pointless. He hadn't even suggested anything more permanent for weeks now. Obviously, he'd gone off the idea.

A man came up to me.

'You want business?' he asked. 'How much?'

I resisted the urge to sling him over my shoulder and drop down in a full body press, but it was tempting.

'Do I really look as if I might?' I said in my best cut-glass accent. I drew myself up to my full height and I guess I looked so menacing he turned and walked away rather quickly. It certainly was time I took stock of my life.

When we left Bristol we had only a couple of days left in Manchester before we took a break for the damned Christmas holiday. Few men wanted to spend time away from their families at this time of year and besides, I assumed money was generally tight for most people. James had been remarkably silent for over a week and Dexi had made plans with Joel for their own personal Christmas, which I'd bet didn't include any other friends. I was all set to be completely on my own for an entire two weeks. I dreaded the prospect. I sat browsing the Internet on the last evening. Holidays, holidays was all I could find.

'That's it,' I said out loud. 'I'll take myself some-where exotic for a couple of weeks.' That way, the whole awful business of Christmas could pass me by. I did various clicks, grabbed my credit card and booked a couple of weeks in the Seychelles. It cost an arm and a leg but I could always make it up later with someone else's arm or leg. I sat back and grinned. I could laze around, swim, surf or even fish. I didn't care. I'd pack the minimum clothing and luxuriate in a complete change. Sod James and everyone else, I told myself. In a couple of days, England would be far behind me. So would Christmas.

Naturally, it had to be at that very moment that the electronic voice on the laptop told me there was new mail waiting. I clicked and downloaded the message: 'any plans for tomorrow? J.W.T.

I typed my reply. 'Gone away. Back next year. L.'

'Where are you?' came back. I knew I couldn't resist the guy and typed in my current address. Seconds later, the phone rang in my hotel room.

'When do you leave?' he asked, not even bothering to introduce himself. But then, why should he? I'd known it would be him. He could easily find something as simple as my hotel phone number. I still felt gratified that he'd made the effort.

'Tomorrow evening. I have to go shopping tomorrow, so you're a bit too late.' My heart was pounding, the way it always did when I heard or saw him. Just as well I was removing myself from temptation for a while.

'I'd come over tonight but I'm too far away. I could meet you tomorrow – help you select an appropriate wardrobe for wherever you're going.' He was fishing.

'I can manage, thanks,' I told him. We chatted for a little longer and he made no further suggestions about seeing me.

'I'll see you when you get back maybe,' he said finally before putting the phone down. He hadn't even wished me Happy Christmas, I thought angrily. Selfish bastard. Though, to be honest, if I'd really wanted him to know where I was going, I could easily have told him.

Dexi was surprised but obviously pleased that I'd sorted myself out for the next couple of weeks. Though his loyalty would have been thoroughly stretched, I know he wouldn't have let me fester away on my own for the so-called festive season. I set out for the stores the next morning and bought a few goodies for the trip. It seemed at odds to be looking at bikinis while everyone else was heavily into baubles and wrapping paper. I soon gave up and went back to the hotel. I was flying from Manchester to Heathrow and on to the Seychelles from there. I took myself to the airport, hours too early, and sat reading a dirty novel and getting myself unnecessarily turned on. I even began to wonder if I could find somewhere for a quick wank but managed to control myself.

The flight down to London was a good deal easier than driving would have been, but the time I'd wasted at the airport didn't make it any quicker in the long-run. I crossed to the right terminal and settled down to wait for my flight to be called. The bright lights and stream of people kept me occupied. I wandered round the small city that seems to have grown round every terminal and bought a couple of items of duty free. I felt strangely detached and, though not exactly lonely, rather solitary among so many families and couples who were travelling together. At last the flight was called to the departure gate. Even the usually formal stewards were wearing the occasional piece of tinsel in their hats. Christmas spirit, it seemed, was everywhere except within me.

I followed the crowd to the boarding area, telling myself it was positively the right thing to do. As I was handing over my boarding card, someone jostled my back, sending me forward into the desk. I turned, ready to mouth off and, instead, my jaw dropped open. I was staring at James.

'This lady is upgrading,' he told the steward. 'Take her new boarding card please.' He pushed two first-class tickets into her hands and took my elbow, propelling us forward. 'Sorry,' he muttered. 'I forgot they have a separate first-class lounge. I thought I'd missed you.'

'Would you like to explain?' I asked, once we were seated and my heart had calmed down.

'I decided an English Christmas was not for me either. I have enough contacts to find out where you were going. I thought I'd join you. I take it you don't object?' I looked into his beautiful green eyes and just about managed to restrain myself from leaping on him there and then. On the other hand, my prime reason for leaving England was to give myself time to think. I was hardly going to spend any time alone with James on board. Objections? Boy there were plenty. Or, if I were really honest, there were none at all. Fortunately, it seemed that there was nothing I could do about it. I'd better find some way of enjoying this gorgeous, impossible, self-centred, dominant crazy bastard. Sort myself out? It could always wait for a better time.

'No objections,' I replied with a silly grin on my face.

'I think this holiday has quite some potential, don't you?'

'Champagne, madame? Sir?' asked the stewardess.

'Here's to something different,' I said, raising my glass. 'Damn. I haven't got a Christmas present for you,' I added.

'Then you'll have to find a way of making it up to me, won't you? How many times have you joined the mile high club, by the way?'

'Me? Never. I don't fly very often and, well, I've never had the opportunity.'

'We'll have to make up for it then, won't we?'

Anyone who has flown regularly will know that even the first-class toilets on a plane are very small, even for one. When he pushed me inside and followed me, I just about stood upright with the actual lavatory bowl sticking into my backside. Somehow, he managed to sit me astride his rampant cock and I jigged up and down, totally out of control. I was laughing in a way we never laughed during such a serious event as fucking. There was no tension, no bondage – nothing but pure sex. The time and place had maybe made it more of a fun thing as well as a first for me.

The only worrying part was that it was quite out of character for James to behave this way with me. Whatever role I am playing, I usually remain at least partly in control of the outcome. I am always in control of my ultimate destiny, even when he's thrashing me, or tying me in whatever sorts of knots he fancies. If it ever got out of control and I stopped enjoying it all, that's when I'd get out of it. I suppose I was trying to justify to myself my reasons for allowing him to humiliate me. There's something in humiliation that fulfils my deepest fantasies. Something to do with being owned and possessed. But there was no humiliation now – just glorious lustful sex. Maybe we both looked slightly sheepish as we came out of the toilet, rumpled clothing and slightly pink in the face. The queue of one waiting outside obviously knew exactly what we'd been up to.

It was a long flight before we finally circled above the airport on Mahé, the main island of the Seychelles. I gazed out of the window, as the tiny dot in the ocean got bigger. I could see only the granite hulk of a mountain as we made the descent. No sign of an airport or even a runway.

'Hell, where are we going?' I burst out. 'I can't see the airfield at all.'

'It lands along the side of the beach,' he comforted.

I was expecting it to be hot, but not quite so airless. White sand and palms everywhere were just what I'd been waiting for. Just like everyone else, James and I made our way through the tiny buildings that passed for the main international airport. Looking at the two of us, and plenty did, we looked every bit like a normal couple, off on our hols. What would they have said if they knew our real relationship? Dominator and dominatrix. Submissives both of us, at times. I looked at James's suitcase as it was portered out to the waiting taxi. What exactly was in there? If it were to be opened anywhere for inspection, how would he explain any of the more bizarre instruments of torture he may be carrying? I was quite innocent, with my small collection of bikinis and normal holiday paraphernalia. But then, I'd expected nothing more than a normal holiday, relaxing and planning the rest of my life. I gave a slight shiver of anticipation. Having James as my companion was much more exciting. I wondered how the Seychellois would feel about nude wrestling. Although it wasn't my usual thing, here, in this sort of heat, leather, plastic, lycra or anything else were quite out of the question.

I didn't bother to ask about hotels. I assumed that James had altered my booking as well as my flight. However irritated I may have felt about his muscling in on my holiday, I knew it was useless to protest, even if I'd wanted to. Doubtless, he'd arranged a suite in the best hotel and probably booked the fitness suite for the entire fortnight. My muscles positively ached at the thought of daily wrestling. I'd wanted time away from it. I looked at him: calm, self-assured and fully in control. If nothing else, I couldn't resist the thought of fighting him, just so that I could remind myself of his helplessness when I took charge.

Our room was huge, as was the bed. It was probably the largest bed I had ever seen. Positively kingdom-sized, rather than merely king or queen. There was just the one room with an en suite bathroom as its only other luxury. There was a rather primitive air-conditioning unit which ground and rattled against its unequal task. Was this going to be sufficiently luxurious for James William Travers? I somehow doubted it. In fact, I had huge doubts about this whole business. We'd never been together for more than a few hours at a time. What would we talk about? How would we occupy ourselves for two whole weeks? We couldn't be performing sexy things all the time. Our stamina would surely collapse if we tried to overdo things. How does one explain friction burns in intimate places to a foreign hotel doctor?

To my surprise, James behaved as a perfect escort that first afternoon and evening. We strolled along the clichéd silver-white beach and gazed at the azure sea fringed with the obligatory palms. We ate a civilised dinner, enjoying amazingly fresh sea food and sipping cold white wine. Not a word about our usual activities passed his lips. I was curious. I was turned on. I suddenly felt an overwhelming urge to have sex with him. I lifted my bare leg under the table cloth and pushed into his crotch. I wiggled my toes, feeling him harden. His face remained impassive. I pinched his balls hard with my toes. Credit to him – his eyes barely flickered. Who was I kidding when I tried to suggest to myself that I wanted to be alone? I licked my lips and continued to massage him with my feet. He ordered a rich, creamy pudding for us both. I'd have liked him to be licking it off me. Have it spread all over my body ... wow! Instead, unbearably slowly, he was licking it off his spoon, his eyes watching mine the whole time. I could feel the gathering fluids welling deep inside me and even my nipples began to tingle in anticipation.

'We'll have two coffees and brandy,' he told the

gorgeous waitress who seemed to float past our table. He eyed her up and down and smiled in a gentle, sexy way that was more suggestive than a gilt-edged invitation. I felt unbelievably jealous. Why didn't I inspire a look like that? I was just a toy to him. Someone to fulfil his needs. What the hell. I had needs too and he knew he could completely fulfil mine, however strange they might seem to anyone else.

'You look as if you need to do something about yourself,' he said at last.

'Such as?'

'You'd better bring yourself off. Go on. Do it.'

'Here?' I asked, somewhat foolishly.

'Naturally. Go on. I shall enjoy watching while I drink my coffee.'

I glanced round the busy dining room. Couples were staring into each other's eyes. No one would take any notice.

'Do it,' he hissed. He had the look in his eyes that I recognised. I knew I had to obey him. Slowly, I slid my hand under the cloth and pushed it into my pussy. I felt hot and sticky and my clit was already engorged. The very gentlest of movement was enough to set it throbbing and I half closed my eyes as the beating pulses took over my mind. The wonderfully familiar feeling of melting began to spread through my body. I felt almost drowsy and lethargic but the drive for relief was pushing me on. I groaned silently. I needed to rub harder and harder. I opened my eyes, crashing back to earth as I realised where I was.

'Go on. You can't tell me you've come yet,' James said in a voice that was slightly too loud. The couple at the next table looked askance. I felt myself growing hot and blushing. 'Do it,' he commanded. I scraped gently with my finger nail right over my clit. More, more, but the feelings were dissipating with the circumstances. I knew it wasn't going to happen now, however long I masturbated. Dare I fake it? He might well keep me sitting there otherwise. He glared at me and looked angry. I thought I'd probably be punished later and that did turn me on again. I rubbed myself with renewed vigour and very soon felt the glow of familiar orgasmic sensations. Gently, quietly, I got there. I leaned back against my chair. The afterglow filled my head and I didn't care much about anything or anyone.

'Let's make a move,' James said after a moment or two. He rose from his seat and led the way from the dining room. I expected him to go straight to our room but he walked off down the beach. Almost dreamlike, I followed him. It may have been the wine and brandy but I felt detached and light-headed. We walked along the beach, the moonlight reflecting from the white sands. The greenish phosphorescence glowed at the edges of the breakers, foaming on the beach. When we reached the end of the soft sands, he turned to me. He leaned over and ripped the long wrap-around skirt away. I stood waiting to see what he was going to do next. My own ministrations had gone only part of the way to satisfy the deep ache inside me. Only his glorious prick pumping into me was going to do that. But if I appeared too keen, he'd only make me wait the longer. On the other hand, there's probably very little I wouldn't have done at that moment. My only difficulty was knowing which role he wanted me to play. Either would bring me what I was really waiting for. Eventually.

Chapter Seven

I stood in the tropical darkness, illuminated only by the reflection of a crescent moon on the water. There were strange perfumes in the air and the muted sounds of unfamiliar creatures. I wore only a strip of fabric round my boobs and nothing else. My skirt lay in a crumpled heap on the sand. James, on the other hand, was fully dressed. I stared at him, trying to judge the expression in his eyes. It was much too dark to see.

'A stand-off, I believe,' I muttered. He remained silent. I took a chance and went forward, grabbing his arms by the wrists. I twisted round and forced his arms behind his back. He began to fight back. He kicked his shoes off and he twisted in his turn so that my hold was broken. We faced each other, darting for a hold like two angry wild creatures fighting for domination. I grabbed at his shirt with both hands, pulling him close enough for me to push my legs between his and unbalance him. I felt the delicate silk of his shirt ripping. I gave a momentary grimace, realising that I had destroyed a very expensive garment. It was enough for him to retaliate and he stepped back, regained his balance and managed to push me to the ground. The soft white sand was still warm and we rolled over and over until we were both in the shallow water, sand caked all over us, scratching our skin as we fought for superiority. We broke apart and I ran deeper into the water, trying to remove the sticky sand. He did not move. In a ripped shirt and soaking wet trousers, probably even more expensive than the shirt, he looked a sorry sight in the dim light.

'Come here,' he called softly. 'This isn't what I intended at all.'

Damnation, I thought. I'd got the wrong message. This whole thing was a ghastly mistake. This holiday wasn't at all what I'd been planning for myself. If he'd butted in on my trip, he'd have to take the consequences. I paddled back to him and stood before him. Either my eyes were getting dark adapted or the moonlight had increased. I could see his expression was almost one of bewilderment.

'What is it?' I asked.

'I don't know. I don't think I was intending to begin wrestling. It wasn't what I meant to do. I think I . . .' He broke off. Swiftly, I interjected.

'OK, so I misread the signals. Don't go strange on me. We both know what we mean to each other. Bondage. Domination. Bloody good fucks. Nothing more. No complications. Right?'

'I guess so. Must be the alcohol. The heat. Jet-lag. I don't know. Let's go back to the hotel.'

'I'm ready for bed. And I mean bed – to sleep.' I picked up my skirt and wrapped it round myself. At least I looked reasonably decent. He looked a total wreck. 'Maybe sharing a room was also a bad idea. I might see if they have any spares.' I felt totally confused. Hell, wasn't it what I had wanted, to spend some time alone? Here I was with the sexiest guy on legs, suggesting separate rooms. Something was seriously wrong with me. Too early in the trip for sunstroke. Jet-lag, I finally decided. Definitely jet-lag.

I went into our room and picked up the phone to dial reception. He came in seconds behind me.

'No need for that. I'll leave you alone if that's what you want. This bed's quite large enough for us to have our own space and still leave plenty to spare.' He dumped his soaking clothes into the bottom of the bath-tub and showered himself down. His body was magnificent. I looked at the gleaming flesh and cursed myself. His cock was enormous, even when it wasn't erect. Delicious. I felt myself getting aroused once again but I could do nothing about it. Once he was asleep, I'd have to make use of my vibrator. Lucky I'd packed it. But, as I'd expected a solo holiday, I thought I'd need it. There were unlikely to be other means of satisfying the urges I knew would doubtless be haunting me. He towelled himself down, still remaining silent. I watched as he got into the bed. Was I really going to spend several nights with this man and never fuck once? I doubted it. However much I wanted him, I wasn't about to admit it. If he could do without then so could I.

I showered, dried myself and climbed into the other side of the bed. I switched off my bedside light and lay in the darkness. I heard his steady breathing. I could smell his body, musky, sexy. I knew at that moment that I was desperately wanting him, at any cost. I'd have to make subtle moves in this vast bed if I was to make him think we'd touched by accident. Was it really only a few minutes since I'd vowed I could do without him? Consistency has never been my strong point.

Jet-lag must have really been genuine. I slept as peacefully as a baby on Mogadon. I awoke to see bright sunlight streaming in through the windows. My bed-fellow had gone. I could hear the shower running in the en suite. I stretched, luxuriously, enjoying the space, the warmth and the joy of having nothing important to do. Was it really December? Was damp and dreary old Britain busily trying to conjure up canned Christmas spirit?

'Hi!' he said, coming into the room wearing a small towel round his waist. My body did a jump start at the sight. 'You slept well.' He sounded like a husband. Someone used to finding the same woman in his bed every day. I bit my lip nervously. Serious problems ahead?

'Morning,' I replied. 'How about you?' He nodded.

'I've ordered breakfast.'

'I don't eat breakfast,' I lied.

'OK. I can probably eat two. I'm starving. I thought we'd do a tour of the island this morning. If that's OK with you.' I shrugged. This was definitely turning into a cosy holiday for two – a cosily married couple maybe.

'I haven't thought about it. Perhaps I'll just take a walk round here somewhere.'

'Not many places you can walk. It is a tropical paradise, you realise. Probably hoards of tropical creatures to go with the tropical weather.'

'Maybe,' I said, stalling for time. I had no intention of giving in to his every suggestion.

'I've booked a car for the day. You can please yourself if you come or not.' He pulled on a shirt and shorts and slipped into some sandals. There was ring at the door and he opened it to admit a waiter and his trolley. The waiter was informally clad in shorts and white hotel T-shirt. It seemed that even uniform was minimalist here.

'You want coffee?' James asked.

'Thanks,' I said, pushing back the sheet and standing up. He ran his eyes over my naked body and smiled.

'No need to dress for breakfast. It's all quite informal.' I wrapped a pareo round me and sat near the trolley.

'Might as well eat something, as you've bothered to order,' I said, grabbing a plate of fruit and my coffee. I followed it with the delicious fresh rolls and smeared some exotic spread over them. I wandered to the window and out on to the balcony. The sea was sparkling and the palms gently swaying. I sniffed the clean air and felt good. He moved behind me and stood silently looking out. He went in to get more coffee and filled my cup. I felt ill at ease, not knowing what I was expecting or what was expected.

When I saw the fun little buggy that turned up as his hire car, it was simply too tempting to miss. Why punish myself? I was here to have fun and relax.

'I need a couple of things from the boutique,' I told him. I wandered down, unable to hurry in any way. I picked up a large hat, a couple more sarong-type garments and a large straw bag. I took them back to the room and stuffed in everything I might need for a day of sight-seeing. I could do the tourist bit as well as the next. I slung my bag over my shoulder and went back to the reception area. James was sitting in the vehicle, waiting like a dutiful escort. It was spooky.

We drove into the mountains, up and down the sort of gradient that would make even the strongest stomach churn. We pulled up near the top and sat gazing at the amazing views. Other islands were dotted around the expanse of blue sea, looking mysterious and exotic, even at a distance.

'We have to talk,' James said seriously. 'I'm not having the stress of us being together and not really speaking. If you want to be on your own then say so. I can move to another hotel, find myself other companionship.'

'James, we've never had this sort of relationship. Not a relationship at all, if I'm honest. I'm confused. I don't know what you want of me.'

'I needed a holiday. I hated the idea of you being away and the pair of us unable to share whatever it is we do have. Especially at Christmas. Everyone goes completely potty at Christmas, grinding your face in it, if you happen to be alone. I simply couldn't face all the pseudo-kind invitations from well-meaning folks. They all seem to think I should join in with the jollies. I hate it. But, if you really do want to be alone then I'll find some other diversion. I'm still hoping you'll consider my suggestion. I want you to be my personal wrestling partner. Companion. Whatever. We can discuss details later but I'll provide you with whatever you need – gym, facilities in the town. For now, can we please get back to normal? I've had enough of pussy-footing round in case it isn't the right thing.'

I laughed. I reminded him he wasn't too keen on *normal* the previous evening.

'Even tycoons get jet-lag,' he replied.

It was going to be all right. All right? It was bloody fantastic. If there was anywhere we didn't manage to access at some time, I'd be surprised. We used the fitness suite for our more athletic enterprises. My own *punishments* were mostly carried out in our room. He invented several ways to hold me prisoner. One of the most interesting was when he tied me down using thin strips of palm. They were fragile and would have broken if I'd dared to pull on them. I was forced to remain virtually motionless, a great test of endurance for me. Imagine being restrained, wanting and waiting for punishment and not knowing what he might do if I broke the inadequate bonds. It gave a whole new dimension to my treatment. There were plenty of times when we just fucked. Plain, honest, sensual screwing. Whatever we did, we did it to the best of our ability.

I had resisted the urge to examine the contents of his suitcase. I was intrigued but didn't want to spoil any surprises. I was introduced gradually to a small collection of leather straps, fine chains and several items he could use to spank my backside. He loved it when he could see me reddening. Hand marks sometimes. Thin stripes when he used his whip. Even a hairbrush (my own). He was careful, knowing I'd be wearing a bikini most days. He enjoyed having me totally obedient at times. Controlling my every movement and seemingly dominating my every thought gave him pleasure. I loved it too. Let's face it, how could I have allowed it otherwise? For a whole week, he was my master and I was his slave. His total slave, bowing to his every wish.

One evening, we learned there was to be a special buffet, put on by the hotel for visitors and residents alike. It was to be a formal affair with several important members of the local society. James was eager to attend, hoping to pick up a few contacts for future business, no doubt. Inevitably, I wondered what to wear. What counted as formal in this place?

I foolishly thought I'd pick up something suitable at the boutique. James had other plans. After a lazy day, lolling by the pool, sunbathing and swimming, we went back to our room. To my surprise, he seized my wrists and shackled me to the bedpost. I protested but he left me there for a couple of hours. Every now and again, he would come into the room and tease me with the odd slap, a tonguing in the most sensitive places or even an occasional massage driving me to the point of frenzy. Talk about total control! As the time for the evening's entertainment approached, I tried asking politely if I was to be allowed to accompany him or not. If the answer was to be 'yes', could I please go and buy something appropriate to wear? He told me that he would be dressing me for the evening. My heart throbbed with anticipation. What on earth could he be planning. It wouldn't have surprised me to discover he had some fantasy bondage gear tucked away and was about to parade me, firmly shackled to him. Whatever, I thought. I wriggled in pleasurable anticipation. Nobody knew me here. I had no reputation to keep up. Little did I know that I would soon have a reputation I'd rather not have to keep up.

At eight o'clock he came to the room, showered and changed into a white dinner jacket.

'Very James Bond,' I dared say.

He came over to me, lifted my legs into the air to expose my arse and slapped me hard.

'Speak when you're spoken to,' he snapped. Evidently my hours of privation had done nothing to relieve him of his dominant needs. 'Apologise,' he ordered. I opened my mouth to tell him where to go but thought better of it.

'Sorry,' I mumbled.

'Say it clearly. Sorry, master.'

'Sorry, master,' I said marginally more clearly.

'You will address me as master for the entire evening. Do you understand?'

For a moment, I looked at him with loathing. If he thought I was going to lick his boots or his backside for a whole evening of socialising, he had another think coming.

'I said, do you understand? Your choice. I can leave you here while I go and enjoy myself. I'd have thought you would be looking forward to some decent food.'

I looked away. My stomach had been rumbling for hours but I wasn't giving him the satisfaction of knowing. He slapped me again and picked up his whip, ready to use it once more.

'Yes, master, I understand,' I said quickly. No use suffering for the sake of it, I told myself.

'Very well. You will find your outfit in the bathroom. Wear exactly what I have put out for you. Nothing more; nothing less.' He unlocked my wrists and slapped me to get up. I was stiff and had to stretch to be able to move after so long in one position. 'You have ten minutes. Don't keep me waiting.'

I went into the bathroom and took a very swift shower. I pulled open the plastic bag to see what delights he had left for me.

A white, frilled, see-through blouse was the first thing. It was awful. Cheap. Tarty. Obvious. There was no bra. A black satin skirt came out next. I should have expected something like this. It was little more than a pussy pelmet, covering nothing that mattered. Further foraging in the bag revealed fishnet stockings and a narrow black suspender belt. Now, why wasn't I surprised? Cheap, shiny red stilettos completed the hateful outfit. Angrily, I thought of dumping the lot in the trash but I knew I'd probably regret it if I did. How could I attend some formal event looking like the worst kind of tramp? How could I not? I pulled on the dreadful ensemble. I dumped the bag in the rubbish and heard a clunk. I felt in the corner of the bag and pulled out a pair of huge hoop earrings, brass of course. I hated them but, obedient as any slave, I took off my own gold studs and slipped them through the pierced holes. They looked revolting. What was a man of his obvious wealth doing with the cheapest-looking tart he could hire?

I held my head up high and walked into the bedroom, as confidently as the ridiculous shoes allowed. My bum swung from side to side, allowing my exposed arse to be displayed to anyone who cared to look. My bare nipples were pressed hard against the transparent blouse, which was also a couple of sizes too small. I knew he'd done that deliberately too. Everything he bought for me was always a perfect fit.

'Allo, darlin',' I mouthed, as I plonked myself beside him.

'Stand up,' he ordered. 'I haven't seen the full view yet.' I stood again. 'Your seams need straightening at the back.' He forced me to bend over. My bare pussy was open to his view, just as he intended. 'Haven't you got any bright red lipstick?' he asked. 'Just to complete the effect?'

'I have, but you said no additions.'

I added the most tasteless, bright colour I could find and used lip gloss to emphasise the horror. I looked and felt an utter slag as I presented myself to him for a final inspection. He eyed me and gave a sneer as I wiggled my way across the room. Heels this high made normal walking impossible. My tits were thrust hard against the flimsy blouse, my nipples showing dark through the transparent fabric. My butt stuck out behind, pushing the skirt high over the stocking line.

'Your hair's all wrong,' he informed me. He grabbed my brush and swept my hair on top of my head. 'Do it in that ponytail thing you do. Fasten it high, so it flops to one side, over your face when you move.' I obeyed, almost splitting the tight blouse in the effort to reach. 'Look at yourself,' he ordered. I did so and pulled a face. 'What do you look like?' he asked.

'A cheap tart. A slag.' He glared at me. 'Master,' I added.

'Precisely. A tart. A slag. Someone available to any man who'll pay enough. Let's go.'

I didn't know why he wanted me to look so cheap. I guessed it was just another domination kick. I teetered after him, struggling to keep up with his long strides. Despite it all, I was so hot for him I'd have fucked him right there and then, if he'd let me. Maybe the costume gave me the mind of a tart who could be hot for any man.

More than once during the evening, he made me bend over for him. Each time, there was some stud-type nearby, also getting an eyeful of pussy. I began to play up to my role, flirting and drinking with anyone he allowed near. I respectfully called him master and winked at the first chance at whoever was out of his vision. I leaned over him, stroking his prick on several occasions, gazing tenderly at him. I licked my lips suggestively, usually when he was discussing something seriously. Most of the women in the room were avoiding even looking at me directly.

They clung to their partners as if afraid I might leap on them at any moment.

'Come here,' he said when I finally got near the buffet. I was starving and would have killed for a handful of the prawns I'd spotted. He pulled on one nipple, dragging me closer to him. I almost yelled in pain as he gave it a vicious twist.

'She doesn't eat after nine at night, do you, Doris?' he announced to the group he'd been talking to.

'Doris?' I exclaimed.

'Now then,' he warned. 'What have I told you?'

'Yes, master,' I replied. 'Sorry, master.' The men in the group sniggered. I looked contrite and stood slightly to one side.

'She fights very well,' James told one of the men. 'Would you like to watch her?' The stranger looked slightly embarrassed.

'You'll demonstrate, Doris, won't you?'

'Yes, master,' I said through gritted teeth. I suddenly wanted this evening to end. I'd had enough of the game. I felt weak from lack of food. My ankles ached after standing on the ridiculously high heels for so long. His hand was working its way between my thighs as he was talking. Suddenly, he caught my clit between his finger and thumb nails. He scraped at it until I was almost screaming. Somehow, he was still talking quite casually to his new friends. I no longer cared what they thought of me. I just wanted his cock deep inside me, thrusting, pummelling into me, bringing me satisfaction and taking away the ache that I had been nursing all day.

'I'll book the fitness suite for tomorrow afternoon then. Three-thirty? You won't be disappointed, I'm sure. You certainly don't mind topless, do you, Doris?' he was saying. What the hell had I been missing? What else had he promised? He scraped my clit hard and gave me a sharp jolt.

'Topless is fine, master,' I hissed. I never wrestled topless. It wasn't my scene. Men who demanded topless weren't in it for the right reasons.

'I think we'll retire now,' James said eventually. 'I feel rather weary.' I couldn't swear to it, but I thought he winked at a sleazy-looking guy whose tongue was practically hanging out. I hoped he wasn't my opponent the next day. I might be compelled to hurt him, just a little.

When we finally got back to our room, I sank on to the bed in gratitude. I kicked off the shoes, wondering if I'd actually wrecked my feet permanently.

'Exactly what are you doing?' James asked.

'Sorry. I was relieving my feet.'

'Master,' he snapped. 'How dare you? Put those shoes on immediately. A slut like you behaves as her master orders. Understand?'

'Yes, master,' I said meekly. The game wasn't over yet, apparently.

'Show me some more pussy,' he ordered. I bent forward, my bare pussy just a few inches from his face. I wondered if he could actually see my whole sex glistening. I was so wet for him. My clit was probably bruised from his abuse of it. I was excited like crazy. There had been something oddly masochistic about showing my bare pussy to every man in the room who cared to look. For James, there was the added bonus that it was his own personal pussy. Look but don't touch. Now, I hoped he would make use of his own personal piece of pussy. He poked an exploratory finger in. The position I was in made it effortless for him. He stuck in two fingers, and then another. I was beginning to feel my orgasm

110

building and he was aware of it too. He pulled his long fingers out and I was temporarily bereft. I waited anxiously. Was he about to push his cock in there, at last? Whatever else is pushed in, there's nothing like a living organ for complete satisfaction.

'Kneel,' he commanded. I obeyed. He began to rub at my anus. He parted my bum cheeks and gently rubbed at the narrow opening. He moistened his fingers with my own juices. He pushed his cock against the tight hole and slowly began to push harder and harder. I pressed back against him, barely keeping my balance. I was still fully dressed, with the black satin strip that passed as a skirt almost round my armpits. The blouse had finally split open, leaving my tits hanging down, relieved to be free at last. The stockings afforded no barriers and merely added to the titillation of my circumstances. He circled and pressed until the tip of his cock had forced itself into the dark narrow passage. He pushed more, more, until I felt as if I was going to split open. I was beginning to come in a way that, truly, I had never experienced before. Apart from Dexi's fingers, my back passage had never been entered before. His arms went round me to pull me even closer to him. His fingers probed into me from the front. As he was finally deep inside my rear passage, gently at first, he pumped until I was screaming out. The pain was utterly exquisite as his fingers worked at my sensitive clit and his prick filled me from behind. I felt him climax and he shouted with me. This time, whatever he might order from me, I collapsed on to the ground, feeling him slide out as I fell. I couldn't move. I was totally exhausted and, I had to admit it, totally satisfied for once. I felt him peeling my clothes away. He took me into the bathroom and dumped me in the deep bath. I felt as helpless as a child. He washed and dried me. He carried me to the bed and lay me down, covering me with a sheet.

'You've been a good obedient slave,' he told me. 'That's why I rewarded you so well.' I was so tired, I barely responded. I fell into a deep sleep, no longer caring that just a little while ago I'd been feeling light-headed with the lack of food.

When I awoke the next morning, I was held tightly in James's arms. He was still fast asleep and looked almost innocent. Was this the same man who had spent an entire evening humiliating me and then providing me with the most exciting sex I'd ever known? He'd fulfilled so many of my fantasies. I smiled gently. I planned to order some food. Once I'd eaten the most enormous breakfast of my life, I knew that today was going to be mine. Despite the aches in places I'd never even realised had feelings, I was ready for a spot of retaliation. If memory served me, I'd been volunteered to do some topless wrestling. As long as my opponent was willing to fight bottomless, I'd have no objections. As for James himself, I'd thought of one or two ideas for a spot of torture of my own. I may not have much in the way of fetish gear with me but my imagination was certainly running riot. He stirred and looked at me.

'Morning. How are you today?'

'Just about to order breakfast. Why don't you stay in bed and I'll serve it to you, like a good slave should.'

'Sounds interesting,' he said. 'Do put something on before you open the door. I don't want to witness your embarrassment.' I nearly choked. Last night he'd done everything he could to show my most intimate parts to anyone who cared to look. Maybe today I was something different. Maybe he realised

I was no longer his personal tart. I hoped he was unprepared for what I had planned. The look of surprise on his face would be something I anticipated with great pleasure.

Chapter Eight

I slipped into one of his own shirts to serve him breakfast. He ate the food eagerly and lay back to enjoy my ministrations. I was sweetness itself, as I fed him succulent fruits and fresh warm rolls. I remained subservient throughout the whole proceedings, until he was drowsy again and lay back to enjoy his pampering. I had put aside a few of his small collection of straps and added some things of my own; I was about to adapt. I hid them in a towel as I stepped out on to the balcony.

'It's glorious out here,' I called.

'Always is in the Seychelles.'

I sat and waited. He would soon come out to join me. If I had been kept tied down for half a day, I wanted retaliation, revenge. Now it was my turn to restrict him. When he appeared, I sidled up to him, lovingly submissive. I was his adoring slave for just a few moments longer. He leaned over the edge of the balcony, a towel draped round his waist. Perfect. I took his hand gently and drew it over my bare breast, pressing his fingers across my taut nipples.

'Greedy,' he murmured. I slipped one of the hand-cuffs on to his wrist and twisted him quickly round to snap the second one in place, taking in the cross-bar of the balcony as I did so.

'What the hell . . .?' he said angrily.

'My turn today, lover,' I told him almost coyly. I eased him to sitting position, his back to the rails and feet stretched out in front. I put a cushion under his knees. I'm thoughtful like that. I splayed out his legs and fastened each ankle to a convenient upright, using his own leather thongs. He smiled at me.

'Just what do you intend to do with me?' he asked.

'Haven't quite decided the whole plan,' I said airily. I stared down at his cock as it was beginning to spring into life once more. I knelt in front of him, leaning over the cushion. I stuck my tongue out and licked the tip, watching fascinated as it thickened and darkened. I licked some more, watching until a tiny spot of semen moistened the tip. I reached for the piece of elastic I'd been saving and slipped it over, right down to the base of his cock. I pulled it tight and fastened it with a bow. He gasped as he realised his predicament. I wasn't finished. I opened the towel and took out another of his own thin leather straps. This one I wrapped tightly round his engorged balls and fastened it, round the base and across the middle, dividing them somewhat pain-fully, I imagined. I didn't really care. His protective towel had fallen away and he was lying helpless, trussed to the balcony with his genitals exposed to the world. He moaned slightly, as the blood pumped uselessly. He thought he might relieve himself if he could only come but I knew that it would be practi-cally impossible.

'How could you . . .?' he began. But I was in charge now.

'I'm going for a swim,' I announced. 'I'll pull the blind over you so you don't get sunstroke.' I dropped my sunhat over his head and finally added a yellow bow to the tip of his cock. Maybe I'd suffer later but his face was the picture I'd been waiting to see. As I was leaving, I remembered my camera. I took several shots of him. I did wonder if his expression really did indicate some sort of apoplexy, but I didn't care.

'Bitch,' he exclaimed. 'Bitch. I'll make you pay for this.'

'You had your fun last night. I'd call it quits.' I walked away from him, feeling guilty as hell. If he really did feel like retaliating, I knew it could all backfire. With my hair loose and more normal clothing, no one seemed to recognise me this morning. If they did, they weren't showing it. I swam lazily round the pool and dried off on one of the sunbeds. Though I'd only been away for an hour or so, I felt the need to return to my prisoner. Just thinking of him lying there was enough to get me going. Insatiable? Me? I stretched and rose from my warm place. I casually strolled back to our room and called his name. Silence. I frowned and went to the balcony. It was empty. How could he have escaped so quickly? Surely, he wouldn't have asked for help? Yet I couldn't think how he'd managed to get out of the handcuffs. The room was empty. I shrugged and sipped some iced water from the mini bar. I sat on the balcony, looking around the hotel complex. Everyone was lazing in the sun or wandering along the beach. I wondered if any of them did the sort of things we did. Not many people will even admit to their own secret fantasies, let alone perform them for real. I'd almost dozed off when I heard a knock, before the door opened. It was one of the chambermaids.

'Excuse me, ma'am. May I remove the sheets now?' I waved a casual hand. 'Your man asks you to join him,' she added.

I turned to look at her. She was grinning in a way that suggested she knew something.

'Really? Where is he?' Not like James to send someone to fetch her.

'He in gym, ma'am.' She gave a giggle.

I got up and obediently went towards the gym. I remembered the bout he'd promised to some stranger the previous evening. And I was to be topless, too, I remembered. I was not in the mood one little bit. I felt drowsy and relaxed and not at all ready for wrestling. I had done no exercise, even though our various activities had kept me in trim. Somehow, it didn't quite equate to his request for me to be his partner, exclusively. I pushed the door of the fitness suite and went inside. He was sitting astride one of the benches, relaxed and wearing boxers. I could see his hard-on still pressing against his pants.

'Am I allowed to ask how you escaped?' I said in a cold voice.

'No. But I am still wearing your more intimate restraints.' I dropped my eyes to his crotch. I wondered if the bow was still in place as well.

'You must be very uncomfortable.' He smiled and licked his lips.

'Amazingly uncomfortable. It's agony. I may have to beg you for release.'

'Sounds promising,' I said, suddenly relishing the idea of a domination session. 'So, what gave you the right to try to escape?'

'I didn't like your choice of venue. This is much more my sort of place, don't you agree?'

I was wearing my pareo over a bikini. It somehow didn't seem like the right gear for a dominatrix. He seemed to read my thoughts. His eyes moved towards yet another of his plastic bags. It contained a bikini, made of soft tan leather. The straps were inevitably studded and there were several other straps, presumably for restraint. I wondered where it had come from. I glanced round the room. Several pieces of the standard equipment may have been suitable but I was feeling more creative. I bound his wrists together and attached him to a convenient bar along the side of the room. Obediently, he parted his legs, when I kicked at him with my foot.

'You will stay still, like that. Don't dare move.' He nodded, a wicked glint in those green eyes. I took off my clothes and fitted the leather outfit into place. I picked up the lower part of the old bikini and stuffed it in his mouth, securing it in place with another of the straps. I saw shock in his eyes and he moved his leg slightly. 'Still, I ordered. Don't move.' His head began to nod and so I picked up the last of the leather straps and began to whip him on his legs. His eyes closed briefly as he savoured the sensation of my blows. I gave the boxers a tug. Hampered by his spread legs, they didn't fall off so I indicated that he should allow them to drop. He complied. His prick was still engorged, dark and restricted by the elastic that was still in place. The bow had been removed but the tight binding round his balls was still there. I nodded my pleasure.

'Good. It must be painful,' I said with an evil smile. I dragged the strap across him, lifting it slightly to strike him. I saw his eyes flicker for a second and then he winced as I struck him, very gently at first. My second blow was slightly harder and I saw the pain fill his eyes. I was wandering into new territory here. This was something I hadn't experienced and I wondered just how far it was safe to go. Pain was one thing. Damage was something else. This may have started as my revenge for the treatment I'd suffered the previous day but I didn't want to ruin him for life. I could be the main loser if I did that.

'If I allow you to speak again, you have to beg for your release. Agreed?' He nodded. I took away the gag and pulled my pants from his mouth. 'Shall I let you go now?'

'Please take off the bands.'

'Beg,' I snapped.

'I beg you,' he said, his voice sounding quite different from his usual confident self. 'Please.'

I lifted the strap again, as if to strike him. He closed his eyes and grimaced. I felt slightly afraid that I could damage him. Besides, how would I cope without my regular doses of his beautiful cock? He opened his eyes, waiting for the blow. Instead, I flicked at his erection, making it strain even further against its restriction. I leaned down and flicked my tongue over him, cupping his tight balls in my hands. He groaned and gasped as I gave him just the tiniest of squeezes. I felt power surging through my body. I leaned against his body, the tight leather bra top grazing against his own hard nipples. I straddled his cock, rubbing my leather-clad mound over his tip. He looked as if he was almost ready to pass out. I stuck my finger into the elastic and gave it a slight tug. He shouted out as the pain seared through his body. I untied the elastic and pulled it away. Instantly, his semen pumped out, relieving the huge pressure that had built up. His balls seemed to remain hard, secured as they were. I looked at his eyes, trying to read the message. They were icy hard, like two pieces of jade. I could tell nothing of what he might be thinking. Very slowly, I released him. He sighed and for a moment I waited.

'Are you sorry for punishing me yesterday?' I asked.

'Yes.'

'Yes what?'

'Mistress?' he asked with a question behind the word. I nodded.

'A proper apology,' I insisted.

'I am truly sorry, mistress.'

'And you will never suggest that I wrestle with anyone other than you in a state of undress.' His eyes hardened again. He obviously did not relish this kind of blackmail.

'I'm not sure you have the right to make such demands.' I picked up my strap again and thrashed his legs. I lifted it towards his balls and drew it across them. His eyes gazed at me steadily. I knew he would positively bleed before he gave in to this demand. I let it drop.

'Maybe we should take time to talk properly.' I untied his wrists and he rubbed his arms. I took one of them and began to massage it gently, allowing his circulation to return. 'You know, I don't like being told who I am to wrestle, and certainly not topless. I don't do topless. Well, maybe if I choose to but I won't be ordered to do it. Were you really serious last night? Who was that creep you were trying to make me partner?'

'A business deal. I can never resist the challenge of gaining new clients, even when on holiday. He's a South American. Brazilian. He can provide a number of very lucrative deals in future. It was a good chance to satisfy one of his fantasies. He'll pay you well, I don't doubt that.'

'That's not the point. Dexi would never book anything that he considered dubious. How do you know what this guy is capable of? Does he wrestle? I could get injured without my back-up.'

'I'll back you up. If he looks like turning rough, I'll be there for you. I promise.'

For some foolish reason, I was willing to believe him. I knew deep inside that I was doing the wrong thing. I had a bad feeling about it. Being punished by someone you believed you could trust was one thing. I didn't even know why I was so apprehensive. Heavens, I was fighting strangers all the time. I never knew my opponents before they turned up at whatever venue I was using at the time. I never realised before how much I relied on Dexi to use his instincts to sift out problems. I wished I could ask his advice but I knew what he'd say: *Don't do it if you are uncomfortable with it.*

'OK. Just this once,' I said doubtfully. 'And only to save face. Your face.'

'Good girl. I may even reward you later.' He dropped a kiss on my forehead. It felt weird, almost too familiar. It seemed to be a part of our relationship that wasn't supposed to exist.

At three-thirty we went along to the gym again. James pulled out an exercise mat and spread it over the floor. It was far too small for my usual routines. I just hoped that I would be able to beat this slob as fast as possible.

'You will stay and referee?' I said, more as a statement than a question.

'If he doesn't object. His name is Ramon,' James

told me. It had to be. When was there ever a South American villain-type who wasn't called Ramon?

'Object or not, I don't fight without someone stationed nearby.'

'You fight me.'

'That's different. I know you.'

'Do you really?' he asked, a strange look on his face. He was right to question it. I didn't know him at all really. The door opened and slob features came in. He was wearing shorts and his well-developed pecs were bulging in terrifying mounds. He was overweight and a couple of inches shorter than me. At least something was in my favour, slightly.

'Ramon, meet Lili,' James introduced me.

'Hi,' he drawled lazily. 'I thought you were called Doris.' He had only a trace of accent.

'Only for last night,' I said with a leer at James.

'I thought you looked a bit white-trash for such a high-flyer as James,' he said. 'So, Lili, have you been wrestling for long?'

'Long enough. Shall we get started?'

'He promised topless. You are covered. I like to see tits. I like to feel tits when I have a woman.'

'You're not exactly having me,' I said desperately, in case his understanding of English was flawed. I looked anxiously at James. 'What exactly have you promised this ... this ... man?'

'You have to win to get paid. If he wins, he gets you. Only temporarily.'

I glared at him. How dare he make promises like that on my behalf? I loathed him suddenly. How could I even consider giving up my career and staying with him? Bastard.

'Let's go. Take off that top and fight me,' Ramon demanded excitedly. I was wearing the leather bikini James had given me. I unhooked the bra and allowed the sleaze to run lascivious eyes over my naked breasts. I shuddered at the thought of his touch on them and took a deep breath. Whatever happened, I had to fight harder than ever before, to beat this jerk. No way was I going to be his plaything, even for a few minutes. We faced each other and circled on the inadequate mat. He stabbed a hand at me, narrowly missing my left boob. It seemed that my tits were his only target. That was good. It showed a weakness. I noticed James sitting down quietly in a corner. Ramon held up a hand, evidently noticing the same thing.

'Hey, James. Disappear. This is private, OK?'

'Lili wants me to be around,' he said quietly.

'Get lost. Understand?' I panicked slightly as James gave a shrug and left the room.

Bastard, I thought. How dare he land me in this mess?

'OK, lovely. Let's go.' He smirked.

I felt I was almost fighting for my life, and took no chances. He could crush me with sheer body weight, if I allowed him to get the advantage. I was fit and reasonably nimble and knew I had to keep the advantage at every moment. I quickly legged him down on to the floor and before he knew what I was doing, I grabbed one of his plump legs and pulled it up with me, high against his body. I had him pinned down and helpless. He gasped as the air rushed out of his body. He stuck a tongue out and licked the tip of one nipple that dangled a bit too near his ugly mouth. I almost gagged. I bent his leg hard and stamped on it as I stood up again. He writhed for a moment and then gave a chuckle.

'Tough cookie,' he clichéd at me. 'Got plenty of fight in you, have you?' He pushed himself up and we circled again. He reached for my neck but I ducked, throwing my arms round his legs as I dropped to the ground. He crashed down as I rolled out of harm's way. Quick as a flash, I sprang to my feet, almost kicked him over on to his belly and grabbed his arms. With an enormous effort, I pulled him back into a half-nelson and then the other arm to make it a full-nelson. He screamed with pain as I put the pressure on to his arms.

'OK. OK. I submit,' he shouted out. I let him go. One up to me. I knew he was angry. Macho men like him are never beaten by a woman.

The process began again. I circled and jabbed to catch him. I could tell that he was not going to fall for any of my tricks again and was wary, on guard. He grabbed my neck, ready to toss me to the ground. I knew how to get out of this move very easily. I leaned slightly forward and he followed, trying to keep his grip. In a trice, I had him unbalanced and with a huge heave, managed to throw him over one of my shoulders. It was more of a topple really, caused by his own weight being displaced. I grabbed his arms as I gave him a cross-press, shoving his shoulders down on the mat. I spun round so that my knees landed on his chest and held him down. I leaned forward. I swallowed the bile that rose as he tried to seize my nipple in his great red mouth. I did the smother hold, leaning over him so hard that he was gasping for breath.

'I think that counts as two falls to me,' I said hopefully.

'I'm entitled to my money's worth. We did not stipulate a particular number of winning moves. I expect another half an hour at least. Of course, if you are too weary, I can think of other things to do.' He leered up at me from his supine position. I wasn't having any of it.

124

'I'll take half the fee and we can give up now.' I rose from my position and went to put my bra top back on and wrap a robe round me. He rose to his feet and walked over to me. His hands came round from behind, catching my breasts firmly in his spade-like hands. He kneaded them hard and tried to turn me to face him. I felt anger roaring through my body. No man did this to me unless I invited him. Letting go of one boob, he caught hold of my hair and dragged my face close to his. I could smell his sweat – sour, acrid. I saw his mouth descending close to my own and, unable to move, could see no escape. I closed my eyes, waiting for the worst.

'That is not part of the deal,' said James's voice from the doorway. I nearly fainted with relief. I shoved him away from me. His grasp of my tit was still holding firm and he pulled at me savagely. I almost screamed with pain. Strange, I thought irrationally, I endure endless pain at times and find it hugely stimulating. Now, with far less discomfort, I am in agony. Pleasure-pain must depend entirely on desires. James can do it for me. Ramon disgusts me. Now where's the logic in anything?

'I don't think much of your bitch,' Ramon was saying. 'I can find you a dozen better than her. You like me to find you a couple of girls for the rest of your stay? Lovely girls. Obedient girls. You can do whatever you like with them. Not like this bitch. She really tried to fight me. Really tried to win. I don't like that in a woman.'

'Excuse me,' I protested. But James shook his head. I was silent.

'She's trained to fight. She is a professional, not someone playing at the fighting game. If I'd known that's what you wanted, I could have saved you the time. There's no fee, of course.' The Brazilian appeared mollified. He nodded.

'You want me to get you a woman?' he asked almost conversationally. James shook his head.

'I can get my own, thanks. We're going back home tomorrow anyhow.'

Sleaze picked up his towel and wandered lazily over to the door.

'Pity about her temperament. Might be worth knocking her into shape. She's got such great tits.' He left us.

'I am not a commodity to be bought and sold,' I began angrily. 'Talk about a chauvinist.'

'It's the macho male. Has to display his prizes.'

'Like you were doing last night? And what's that about us leaving tomorrow? I have at least another couple of days.'

'I was saving you from him, Lili. I thought you might prefer to accompany me back now, rather than hang on till the bitter end. I have to get back tomorrow. Business.'

'I'm not sure.'

'Suit yourself.' He shrugged.

I went to take a shower and heard him closing the door behind him. I put on a towelling robe and wandered back to my room. A large dress box lay on the bed. I wondered what particular brand of fetish gear would be waiting inside. I wasn't in the mood for anything else today. After Sleaze, I was ready to be quiet. Maybe do a spot of sunbathing. If I really was leaving tomorrow, I might have left it too late to acquire a decent tan. I ignored the box and removed the leather gear. I was a holidaymaker and not someone's fantasy for the rest of the day. Of James, there was no sign. I rubbed sun lotion over my body and lay naked on the balcony. I must have slept as it was almost dark when I opened my eyes. I stretched and sat up. The room was in darkness. Maybe James had taken up Ramon's suggestion of finding him a woman or two. I was almost too lazy to care. I showered and opened the wardrobe to find something to wear. I looked at the box again and, almost unwillingly, opened it. A creation of dark chocolate-coloured fabric lay inside, protected by several layers of tissue paper. I lifted it up and held it against me. It was so light, the fabric must have been silk or something similar. It was gorgeous. Elegant. Stylish. Though it was revealing, there was nothing about it that suggested it was designed for anything other than a formal occasion. I slipped it on. Naturally, it was a perfect fit. I stared at myself in the mirror. I looked as good as any model wearing 'that dress' at an opening night. A pair of strappy gold sandals, high-heeled, naturally, completed the outfit. I rolled my hair into a sophisticated French pleat and clipped it firmly in place. I was certainly all dressed up and wondered if I had anywhere to go. I looked in the box to see if there was a card or message of any kind. There was nothing.

I went to the bar. Surely, James must be there somewhere. Several men stood around drinking. I turned down a couple of offers of drinks and sipped my own glass of wine. I noticed some of the men from last night but they didn't seem to recognise me. Why would they? Doris the tart was long dead. I'd decided that I would be dining alone, when James entered the bar, accompanied by Ramon and four young girls. They giggled and hung on the arms of the two men, as if scared to let them go. I felt myself blushing: embarrassment? anger? jealousy? This was almost more humiliating than last night's spectacle when I was forced to play the role of Doris. Was I supposed to sit and watch their performance now? I finished my drink. This beautiful dress must have been given to me for some reason or other. I could only guess. I stood tall and walked slowly out of the bar. I didn't want dinner after all. I did not give another glance at the noisy group in the corner. If that's what James wanted, he was welcome to it.

By the time I was back in our room I was almost shaking with anger. He'd known I wouldn't be able to resist showing off the dress and that I would behave exactly the way I had. He'd planned the whole thing. What a devious bastard he was. He lured me with promises, suggestions. He abused me and then treated me like this. I guess I'd asked for it in a way. Left myself wide open to it. I pulled the dress off and flung it to the ground. I lay on the bed and allowed my anger to run riot. After that, I felt a damned sight worse. I was jealous. Pure, rotten jealous. Was he having some exotic sexual romp at this very moment? Two at once eh? Every male's idea of the perfect fantasy. The girls had looked all of seventeen, I told myself angrily. Lovely, dark-skinned kids.

I began to pack my things. James could please himself. For me, Christmas was well and truly over. I'd managed to avoid the festivities and now I could manage to avoid the aftermath. England, even in the middle of winter, seemed very appealing.

Chapter Nine

I awoke at around two o'clock. James was still missing. I thought of a few more names to call him and tossed around for another hour or so. I was incredibly hot. The air-conditioning had died. I longed for cool water. I contemplated going for a swim in the sea. I wasn't sure whether there were any nasties lurking out there and settled for the pool. I flung a robe over my naked body and went across the lawn to one of the huge hotel swimming pools. A rope hung across the entrance, disclaiming anyone's rights to sue in case of accident out of hours. I stepped over the rope and dropped my robe to the ground. I dived in and swam lazily to the other side. It was heaven. The water was cool, refreshing. I floated on my back, looking up at the stars. Palm trees rustled in the darkness and faint jungle sounds filled the balmy air. What would be my lasting memory of this place? Perhaps I could make this moment the one to take away with me.

I heard a slight splash and looked around. There was nothing. No one. I swam some more, slowly. A pair of arms surrounded me and I almost screamed. A hand went over my mouth. I fought it, struggling to tread water, as I was out of my depth.

'Shh,' whispered a voice in my ear. 'Don't be frightened.' I tried to turn to see who it was but the arms held me tightly. We moved along in the water until our feet touched the bottom. The hand was removed from my mouth and was replaced by warm lips. I stopped fighting and allowed the tongue to penetrate my mouth. It was nice. I needed something gentle like this to soften my anger. Strong hands began to caress my body – breasts, gently massaged to arouse me, followed by probing fingers that explored every inch of me, even the hidden inches. One arm was supporting my shoulders, while the other continued its exploration. My legs were parted and held by his leg, half floating, half standing. I closed my eyes. I didn't need to know who this stranger was. It was enough to feel his naked body making love to mine. Gently, he lifted me out of the water and laid me on a sunbed. He lay on top of me, his body warming mine in the gentle breeze. I felt his prick rising and pressing hard against me. He pushed my legs apart and drove it deep, deep inside. It was pure sex. Straighter than an arrow. Nothing kinky, nothing demanding. He knew exactly the right places to touch me. Slowly we rode to a climax. On any other occasion, I'd have probably said it was boring and conventional. This particular night, it was wonderful – mysterious, satisfying and tender. He lay still when we'd finished and quickly slipped out of me. I didn't even care whether he'd used a condom. I couldn't see anything of him at all in the darkness. There was no moon and we were just beyond the glow of the hotel's lights. He pulled me up and led me back to the pool. We walked in slowly, the water now feeling quite cold. It was like silk running over our bodies. Nude bathing is so much more sensuous. I swam alongside him and he suddenly dived under and swam away. I didn't try to follow him or even watch to see him leave the pool. My mysterious lover was gone. I didn't care. Somehow, the strange little encounter had restored my calm, not to mention my confidence. How on earth could James expect me to move in with him if he treated me the way he had?

When I finally returned to the room, I discovered James lying on the bed, apparently fast asleep. I lay some distance away on the huge bed. No way was I going to allow myself to get closer to him. My unknown lover had restored me completely and, for once, I had not a single thought of sex in my mind. Long may it last, I thought, as I turned over to sleep.

The sun streamed into the room when I awoke. A fly or other insect was crawling over my back and I tried to swat it away. I rolled over, straight into James's arms. He grinned at me and began to fondle my breasts. I was beginning to feel that they were the only part of me that mattered. They'd been very much overworked lately. He kissed me gently, quite unlike his usual self. I was about to kiss him back when I remembered.

'What the hell were you playing at last night?' I demanded angrily.

'Don't start getting jealous, Lili,' he said coldly. 'You knew it was business. Ramon was angry at the way you treated him. I was trying to salvage the situation. The dress looked good by the way.'

'I don't understand you,' I said, still angry. 'Why

organise a beautiful dress and then flaunt your bimbos in front of me?'

'Ramon's idea. He felt you needed a lesson in manners. For a *bitch*, you didn't meet his standards of how a *bitch* should behave.'

'And they did, I suppose. Enjoyed both of them together, did you?'

'Don't ask questions, Lili. I haven't asked you anything about how you spent your evening. I haven't asked you to explain your own absence from our bed – you were missing when I returned – just as I don't ask about your life back at home.' I listened to him in silence. Had I behaved so very differently myself? Did I ever? Dexi may be gay and therefore not a direct challenge to any man I spent time with, but he finger-fucked me quite regularly. Besides, there was the stranger in the pool last night. It had been nice. I closed my eyes dreamily and my hand wandered down to the usual place. James brought me back with a jolt.

'I see you've already begun packing. I take it this means we are returning together?'

'I guess so,' I muttered. Damn the man. He always managed to get his own way. All the same, it was time I got back to work. A couple of days to work out and we could get moving again.

We didn't talk much on our flight back. It seemed to have been assumed that I should return to James's house with him. When the redoubtable Davis turned up at Heathrow, I got in beside James without giving it a thought. The window separating us from the driver was closed. James leaned forward to one of the cupboards and brought out a bottle of champagne, which he poured into two glasses. He handed one to me.

'We have decisions to make,' James announced

formally. 'This is what I propose. I shall set you up in a gym in town. Dexi can stay on as your agent. You can continue your business but I have priority. If I send special clients to you, you will fight them. You will not have sex with anyone other than me. I don't like using condoms and as long as we are both exclusive I see no problems. You will, of course, ensure that you do not become pregnant. I can guarantee that you won't get bored for the foreseeable future.' It sounded like one of his business deals to me.

'You've thought it all out, haven't you?' I replied.

'Naturally. You will of course live with me in my house. Davis will drive you whenever you need it.'

'I have to discuss it with Dexi. I can't decide for him, as you must realise. And only straight fights with anyone else. None of the Ramon stuff.'

'OK. You have until Thursday. Two days from now. Perhaps we can relax for the rest of the journey, catch up on some sleep.'

We sat in silence all the way. I expect we both dozed for much of the time. I still felt totally confused. Did he really want me or not? He'd been happy enough to sleep with his two girls the previous night. What was there to say he wouldn't again, whenever the fancy took him in future?

We arrived at his home. It was freezing outside. I'd forgotten it was still early January. I huddled my jacket round me, wishing it was twice as long and twice as thick. I ran inside and shivered some more. I remembered the imposing hall and that was about all, apart from the bedrooms. There was a huge log fire in the lounge, one of the rooms I hadn't seen on my previous visit. I moved over to the fire, luxuriating in the warmth.

'We'll have something to eat and I'll show you

round. You've only seen a very small part of the house. I have plenty more to show you, to tempt you with. You won't be disappointed, I'm sure.'

His voice was full of sexy innuendo. I felt myself beginning to boil inside. God, what a hopeless case I was. A couple of suggestive remarks and I'm lost. Whatever sort of bastard this man was, I knew I couldn't resist him. Providing Dexi agreed, it was all a foregone conclusion.

We ate an almost civilised meal, prepared by Davis's wife, whom I hadn't yet met. We began the tour. A study, formal dining room, three different sorts of sitting room with television, musical instruments or just for sitting in, I guessed. The kitchen at the back, I ignored. Kitchens are not my scene. We moved upstairs. I gathered the staff quarters were also somewhere at the back, well out of earshot, or so I hoped. Upstairs, there were the various rooms I'd already seen. James's bedroom was mirrored in several others, until we reached the locked door of his mysterious special room. Somehow, I knew this would not be a disappointment to me.

With a grin, James took out a key and pushed open the door. It was a large room, mainly empty of furniture. It reminded me of our old drama studio at school. There were lights, a sound system and several curtain tracks, presumably to divide the room for whatever reason. Round the edges there were various cupboards. Two other doors led off the room but I was not allowed to see what was behind them. A large wrestling mat was rolled up at one side of the room. Altogether, the room gave little away as to its real purpose. Over the months to come, I should no doubt learn more.

'So, what's in the cupboards?' I asked, more for

something to say. Nothing else in the room really gave much to comment on.

'You'll have to wait and see. Can't give away all my secrets at once, can I?' I shrugged.

'I don't see anything very special. It's just an empty room.'

'But that is the whole point. I can make it into whatever I want it to be, with a few lighting effects, sounds and even projection on the walls.' He opened a cupboard and slid out some sort of computer. He pressed a few keys and the lighting changed to spinning colours. He produced the sound of a busy street, then jungle sounds and, finally, haunting notes played on panpipes. It was bizarre. Another cupboard held clothing, all neatly hung in rows and looking like rainbows of colour. I could only guess at the contents of the other cupboards, but I could look forward to finding out. What a strange man he was. Who else would keep a whole huge room like this, just to act out his fantasies? I suppose I had never really known anyone else quite this rich and eccentric.

I was given the room next to James as my own base. There was of course an intermediate door so that we could wander freely between the two.

'You will of course share my bed, but there may be times, such as when I have to travel, when you'd prefer not to be disturbed.'

'I see,' I replied. It seemed strange to me to be actually moving in with someone. I wasn't sure I could handle the restrictions. 'This is always assuming I do agree to your proposals. I shall see Dexi tomorrow and we can discuss the future.' His smile flickered for a moment. I knew he had quite forgotten Dexi and my intention of waiting to give him an answer.

'Yes, of course. Maybe you never will get to know all the secrets of my playroom.' I smiled sweetly and turned to my unpacking. 'Lili?'

'Yes?'

'Why not come and play awhile?' He took my arm and pulled me towards the door of his playroom. I followed, still curious to know more. He opened the door of the clothes cupboard and flicked the hangers along. He glanced back at me and made his selection. 'Go into the bathroom there and change.' He gestured towards one of the doors and I took the garment and obediently went to the room he indicated. The room was mostly black marble, with mirrors and bright lights everywhere. The bathtub was more like a small swimming pool, set into the ground. I looked at the outfit I was to wear. It was made of something very fine and flimsy, black with a silver thread and completely transparent. As far as I could see, it was designed to reveal my breasts completely but otherwise covered every inch of me. I slipped off my travelling clothes and pulled on the body suit. It fitted tightly with a very fine long zip at the back. It was impossible to fasten it on my own. I went into the room again and asked James to oblige. He pulled the zip, encasing me completely. I loved the sensation. My boobs hung exposed through the holes at the front and looked very vulnerable. He put his fingers under them and lifted them gently. I was already excited, just by my clothing. As I caught sight of myself in the mirror, I saw that I might as well be totally naked. The thin fabric revealed every inch of me, the lights catching the shiny fabric as I moved. I felt good.

The wrestling mat was unrolled and James went into another room to change. I wandered round the strange room, looking at the various bunched up curtains and wondering what on earth he planned to do in there. More to the point, how did a man involved in something as macho as the construction industry become involved in all of this? As he came back, I turned to him and approached him, ready to make any response to his moves. He carried a small box and ordered me to lie on my back on the mat. I obeyed, wondering what on earth he was up to. He opened the box and took out two small metal circles, designed in star shapes. He lifted each breast in turn and clipped them to my nipples. As he pressed them into place, I felt them tighten and a click secured them in place. It was painful but extremely sensual. I felt myself churning deep inside, unbelievably turned on by something so small as the nipple clips. He smiled down at me and pulled gently on the loops at the peak. I gasped at the pressure and felt the connection between my thighs. Why is it that everything seems to have some internal switch to send that particular message? However the clips had been made, they were not going to pull away easily. He was pleased with the effect, it seemed. He beckoned me to stand. Somehow, he seemed to think that my adornment could survive a wrestling bout. But he was not yet finished with me. He turned me round and fondled me from behind. As he worked on my breast, I could feel his cock hardening next to my bum and he wriggled to press it into the cleft. My nipples hardened in anticipation and, once more, I gasped as the clips gripped even more tightly. I actually began to wonder if they would ever come off.

James laughed and began to move round me, challenging me to make a move. We had several attempts at squeezing each other. My shielded nipples might become a weapon to use against him, I thought. But the pressure had its effect on me. Each time we pushed together, I was so turned on that I could feel orgasmic rushes wetting my whole sex. My breasts seemed to have become the main pleasure centre of my whole body and stood out erect and inviting. James seemed highly amused and kept up the pressure. At last we both went down to the ground and rolled over and over. I sat up and managed to grip one of his legs. I clamped my ankles together and held his leg firmly, while I grabbed his other leg and pushed hard with both hands. I held him in a wide leg spread for several seconds, pushing harder to make the spread wider, bit by bit as his muscles relaxed and stretched. I could see his cock tightly held by his trunks, the fabric stretched tight over his erection. He almost cried out as I made his legs part even more. If he'd been upright, he'd have been performing the splits. I could see from his expression that he was loving it and so I held him there. I hoped he would submit soon. My own legs were aching from holding the position.

'Submit,' he called out at last. He couldn't reach my back to tap it in our usual signal. I grinned at him as I slowly released the pressure. 'God,' he murmured,' that was bloody fantastic. You are very strong. Incredibly strong. I was using everything I could to resist. Dangerous lady,' he added.

'And all that after a holiday. Maybe I don't need too much of a workout to get back into shape.'

'None at all. But then, your holiday was pretty active I seem to remember.' He leaned up to me and touched my nipples. The immediate response made me gasp slightly. 'I think these things have potential, don't you?'

'How on earth do they work?' I asked, panting slightly as my body responded to the stimulation.

'Some ancient Turkish device. They have a catch to release them, but that is my secret. I had them specially made for you. Sadly, they hadn't arrived before the holiday. I have several ideas for using them in any number of ways. The little loops – think what potential they might have.'

'I am.' I smiled, thrilling at the particular potential he may be thinking of.

'You can keep them in place for now. I may decide to let you out of them at some stage in the future. Now, I believe you have the first throw in our bout.'

We played some more, nothing too serious. At every opportunity, he managed to inflame my tortured nipples. Each time they swelled, the wretched metal seemed to grip harder. Just when I thought I was getting used to them, he would make some movement to keep my senses fully alerted. After his second submission we were both too weary to fight any more. We lay side by side on the mat and he stroked my pussy through the fine gauzy material. I felt weak with desire and waited for him to release the zip down my back. I rolled on to my front and hoped he'd take the hint. He lay on top of me so I could feel every inch of his body pressing down on mine. I felt him pull out his prick and waited for him to unfasten me so that I could take it into me. He rose to his knees and pulled me on to my back again. Evidently, I was not going to be released. Did I say I felt sexy in this garment? I suddenly began to hate the restriction. I wanted him inside me but there was no way in.

'Tonight is nipples only,' he said evilly. He kneeled, straddling my head and leaned forward. He took my breasts between his hands and stuck his

139

magnificent cock between them. He pumped and pumped. I felt almost giddy with the sensation. I was beginning to feel my own pleasure centres reacting to his stimulation. Though nothing was touching my lower erogenous zones, excitement was driving me to my own peculiar sensations. Unbelievably, I was building an orgasm for myself. He slid in and out between my engorged breasts until finally his semen spread out all over my stomach. Amazingly, his whole action was enough. I gasped and finally screamed as I came myself. He lifted his head and laughed, releasing his hold on my tits. He moved over me again and slid his naked torso over his own spunk, rubbing it into the thin fabric of my imprisoning suit. I was floating helplessly on my own cloud. He tweaked my metal caps again, sending a new rush of hot need between my legs. I was more than ready for him. Bastard. He'd had all he wanted and, once more, I was left with nothing more than a new, raging hot need. He then stood over me, staring down at my frustrated body.

'Stand,' he ordered. I did as he asked. 'Turn.' I did so. He pulled the zip down, peeling the garment away from my body. It was sticky with his spunk and my own juices. Still he did not touch me. He pointed to the door of the bathroom. I moved towards it.

'I just hope you've the courtesy to provide at least a vibrator,' I muttered as I went into the bathroom. Someone appeared to have filled the bath for me. Scented bubbles rose in the steamy water. I wondered who had been in the bathroom and whether there was some other way of getting in there. I could see no doors anywhere, just mirrors. I didn't like the idea of James's staff knowing exactly what we were doing all the time. I stepped into the huge bath and lay back luxuriously. I examined the metal clips over my nipples. There did not seem to be any way of releasing them. Curious. I pressed all round them, a process which seemed to make them clasp even more tightly to my nipples. I pulled gently on the small loops but this had no effect either. I was stuck with them, presumably until James chose to remove them.

I closed my eyes, wondering how and when my desperate need for a fuck would be satisfied. He was quite OK, he'd had his release, but I was still a churning mass of intense need. I masturbated but it gave me little or no relief. I glanced around, hoping to see something I could use. I still had my vibrator in my suitcase. It would have to do, even if it was no substitute for a rampant living cock. I stepped out of the bath and dried myself on a warm soft towel. I felt sensuous, warm and inviting. My silver-tipped nipples stood out eagerly.

I went into the main room. The mat had been put away, as had my clothes. I walked into the corridor, naked. Davis was watching and he nodded and smiled. I've never been reticent about displaying my body but it felt somehow wrong to be flaunting it to him. I went into what was supposed to be my room. My case had been unpacked and the meagre contents hung in the vast wardrobe. I must sort out the rest of my clothes and install them here, I realised.

'There's a dress for you to wear for dinner,' James said as he came into the room. He handed me a short, scarlet shift dress with the softness of silk. I slipped it on and looked down at the sharp points that protruded. I almost giggled but knew it would be wrong. In his present mood, I had no idea what James might decide to do.

We ate dinner in the large, formal dining room. I

felt ill at ease. It seemed so strange to be eating a delicious meal while wearing such strange adornments beneath a silk frock and just after a heavy session in his playroom. He poured wine and chatted as if we were some old married couple. I had the distinct feeling that this arrangement was going to be difficult, if it even worked at all.

I looked forward to speaking to Dexi. I realised I'd missed him. I wondered if he and Joel had sorted their differences and what he would say about my proposed new lifestyle.

'What are you thinking about?' James asked suddenly.

'Dexi.'

'Charming. I suppose I'd be jealous if it were anyone else,' he said somewhat pompously.

'You can't expect to control my thoughts,' I told him. 'At least not all the time.'

'And when can I?'

'You know perfectly well. You practise often enough.'

'I like being in full control of you. You are the very best slave I've ever had. I mean it Lili.'

'I like to control as well, don't forget. I think I could be a great dominatrix. Because I enjoy it from both sides, I think I know exactly what you like.'

'This isn't the usual relationship, I have to admit. Seriously, I've never been into submission before. I've always enjoyed wrestling but few female partners have your talents. I'd never have believed, let alone admitted to anyone, that I enjoy what you do to me. Perhaps I have discovered a new dimension to my character. I've always enjoyed fetish clothes and had many fantasies of my own. You seem to be willing and able to match my imagination, perfectly.

I think we are sufficiently alike to make a success of it. Do your best to persuade Dexi. Please.'

I stared at him, surprised by his frankness. He was obviously sincere. Ours was a rare combination. Both of us wanting the same things. I knew it would work well, just as long as we could judge the other's mood. We needed to learn to read each other's signals, so that we assumed the right roles at the right times.

Life was about to become a darned sight more exciting. If only the bastard would fuck me right now, I couldn't want for a better life. All I got that entire night was constant stimulation of my nipples, which did nothing to dull the intense ache that was growing in my dark passage.

Chapter Ten

James hardly spoke to me the next morning. He left early for a busy day at the office and I wanted to see Dexi. We had a lot to talk through.

'How was Christmas?' he asked when we met in the appointed bar in town.

'I hardly noticed it was Christmas. How about you?'

'It was OK. We did all the Christmas stuff. I've got a whole lot of news for you, though. Mega plans.'

'I have some ideas too,' I said cautiously. 'How are things with Joel?'

'Problematical. He's so jealous of everything I do without him. I seriously need a break to decide how we are going to move on. That's where the plans for you and me come in.' Dexi wouldn't look me straight in the eye. Warning bells rang. 'But, tell me about your holiday. What did you get up to?'

I thought about some of the things we'd done. Could Dexi possibly understand?

'Actually,' I began, 'James came along too. We spent the whole two weeks together.'

'Good Lord. He must be keen.'

'He is. Look, this is what I have to talk about. He wants me to move in with him. He's agreed that we carry on the business, though we'd stay here, in the Manchester area. He's offered a proper facility for us to use. A permanent site. What do you think?'

'I'm not sure. Do you think it's practical?'

'We're never short of customers anywhere.'

'But will they travel here? And what about the ones who may pester you if you're in one place?'

'Dexi, with you in charge of my bookings there won't be a problem. You always manage to sort everything out for me. I love the idea of not moving around so much. If things work out with Joel, you can even have your own personal life back.'

He stared down at his finger nails. He was brooding, I could tell.

'Let me think about it. I don't suppose you'll be interested in my ideas anyway, assuming you've already made your own decisions.' I felt bad. I knew he was right; I had already made my decision.

'Go on. Tell me.'

For the next five minutes, he put out the most exciting plans I could have dreamed of. He'd spent a lot of time on the Internet and had come up with a whole tour programme for the States, north to south and into Mexico. I could see how excited he was at the prospect. How would James take the idea of at least a two-month tour? I couldn't predict the man at all. What I did know was that I wanted James to be a part of my life for the foreseeable future, at the very least. The thought of him actually made me tingle. I felt the sensation rush through my body, causing a tightening and a stab of pleasure-pain through my still-clamped nipples. Dexi would laugh when he saw the latest attachment to my body. He was probably not averse to the odd punishment session himself, as long as some man he liked was in charge. We'd had very limited discussions on the subject, over the years. He'd once mentioned the pleasure-pain when his balls were tied up, rather the way I'd fastened James's just the other day in the Seychelles. Maybe Dexi would be a source of other ideas to try on my new sexual partner. I knew that, whatever we all decided, I wanted to stay here for a while. Talk of tours would have to wait.

'I guess we start looking for suitable premises and I'll get the bookings rolling in,' Dexi said with a grin on his handsome face. 'Maybe we'll still do a tour in the future sometime.'

'Maybe we will. But I'm glad you'll agree to stay here for a while. I know it's what I want to do. But I'd never just dump you, Dexi. I'm very fond of you, you know that.'

'And I of you,' he replied softly. I noticed two girls at a nearby table suddenly lose interest. They'd obviously been fancying him like crazy but gave up when they saw him look at me the way he was doing at that moment. I grinned and stuck my tongue out at them. Little did they know about us.

I found life very strange for the next few weeks. Living with a man who went to work, had meetings and had business dinners was a totally new experience. We had nothing like a marriage-type of relationship. I don't believe too many married couples wrestle and perform the sorts of sex we did. James must have spent hours finding the outfits he brought home. Some he had specially made. We learned what worked for our wrestling bouts and what didn't. In some gear, I was unable to move freely enough to fight and so we ended in a slave

146

girl session, even when this was unplanned. I adored his strange costume designs and, whatever role I was playing at the time, I found immense satisfaction. I was almost becoming complacent, until Dexi brought me down to earth with a list of fights for me.

We had leased space in a building in town. We had turned the top floor of an office complex into a perfect area for bouts and put in changing rooms, showers and a small area for the office. The whole area was sound-proofed, so we didn't expect to interrupt too many business meetings on the floors below. My selection of costumes was hung in cupboards and, at last, Lili was ready to resume her career. Several old clients returned and enjoyed my attentions. I soon fell back into the ways of the business and the routines. Somehow, though, I'd lost my interest in the whole thing. Maybe I was being spoilt at home, with James.

'You mustn't be complacent,' Dexi said severely one morning. 'You have to keep your bank account rolling. James may tire of you and then where will you be?'

I knew he was talking sense and tried to be more professional about everything. James had not yet called on my services for his clients and I'd almost forgotten that part of the deal. I was therefore shocked when he announced one evening that he had a number of clients for me, the following evening.

'I don't do public performances,' I tried to remind him.

'You do when I order you to,' he snapped. I frowned.

'OK. Nothing extreme though. No bare tits or see-through clothes. These are for you and only you.'

'You'll wear what I tell you to wear.' His face was impassive and I could tell by the tone in his voice that I was about to be his slave for the rest of the evening. I went upstairs and into the playroom. I sat on a bench and waited for him. He liked it when I was submissive from the start . . . sometimes. When he came in, he was carrying a box. He put it on the floor and lifted the lid. I tried to see what he'd brought but he snapped at me to behave. I knelt down before him and hung my head in my best possible submissive gesture. I saw him take something from the box and step nearer to me.

'Get up,' he ordered. I obeyed. He wound a wide leather basque round me and began to lace it tightly. I was reminded of the old stays, worn by girls with eighteen-inch waists. He knew how I liked to be tightly encased but I did wonder how those girls had managed to breathe. It pushed my boobs up high and left them resting over the top. Was it going to be another tit night? I had hoped it might be lower down that received his attention today. My arms and legs were wrapped in cross straps, like old-fashioned garters but pulled much too tight for comfort. He somehow looped the leg straps between my legs, this time across the tops of my thighs, pulling my pussy wide open. I was spread in a star shape and attached to his favourite frame. He disappeared into one of the bathrooms and came back bare chested but wearing his tight leather trousers. I looked apprehensive for him, waiting to see how he was about to spank me. I licked my red lips in anticipation. He stopped and reached down into the box again. He took out a rubber gag and put it in my mouth, fastening it round the back of my head with another strap and buckle. I wasn't sure about this. How could I ever tell him to stop when I'd had enough? He slipped a mask over my head so that I was not only dumb but blinded as well.

I felt his hands run over me. His fingers slid under my bonds and he caressed the bare bits of my flesh with something cold and hard. It felt like metal but it was pliable. He pressed something against my buttocks and I felt him lift an arm, as if he was about to strike. I braced myself but there was no contact. I let my breath out again. Several times he repeated the exercise, obviously enjoying my suspense. He pulled the hood off my eyes and I saw him pacing round me like a lion tamer. He slapped a piece of leather against his hands and raised it to tan my backside. As he raised it again, I tried hard to scream. He laughed, assuming it was part of my game. I screamed, silently. The gag prevented me from making much of a sound. I didn't much like being silenced. He must have read my mind. He took off the gag.

'I can't hear you begging for mercy,' he said wickedly.

'Do I need to?' I asked.

'Yeah,' he drawled. 'Turns me on.'

'You know your trouble? You're too ready to dominate.'

'Look who's talking. You really are asking for it, aren't you?'

I didn't get the chance to reply before he swiped me again, right across my buttocks. It hurt. I yelled.

'Please . . . please stop.'

'Beg me. I am your master, after all.'

'I beg you, master. Please spare me.' I waited, half of me hoping he'd stop and get on with the main course. The other half was busily getting myself to that wonderful point where you can hardly breathe, hardly bear to wait any longer.

149

'Greedy, aren't you? Tell me why you think you deserve my beautiful prick inside you, relieving your greedy appetite?'

'You've got the best prick in all the world?' I suggested insincerely. He shook his head.

'Not good enough.' He raised the strap again and I braced myself. He stood waiting, watching. He cupped my extravagantly high breasts as they rested on my leather basque. He pushed his face into them, obviously enjoying himself. 'Maybe I need something else from my personal body slave.' He pushed a finger into my hot wet slit. I closed my eyes again, trying not to show him just how much I was wanting him. He unfastened his tight trousers. His cock sprang out, hard, engorged, ready for action. He pushed it in front of me. I was trussed too tightly to move much but I felt the tip searing against my pleasure centre. I felt as though I could draw it into me, right where I stood. He moved back and suddenly snatched at my bonds. I moved away from my imprisoning frame and rubbed my wrists. I grinned at him and made a suggestion.

'Why don't you come to bed and we'll have glorious sex. Fuck me, James.'

To my amazement, he did. I kept on the leather gear. He tugged at various parts of it, keeping me seriously turned on all the time. We had a seriously passionate fuck. James got turned on when my nipple shields began to dig into his nipples. When we'd finished, he reached over for a bottle of wine and poured a glass. Like some old married couple, we shared the same glass.

'How did you begin this wrestling career of yours?' he asked. I stared. He'd never asked me anything much about myself. I hesitated.

'Why do you want to know?'

'Curious. Just curious.'

'It isn't so remarkable.'

'Go on.'

I really wasn't sure he should know too much about my past. This wasn't what we were about. For a moment, I thought of giving him a fantasy explanation. My mind raced at thoughts of impresarios discovering me, wanting to make me a star. It was so much simpler than that in reality.

'I liked the idea better than anything else I could have done.'

'Meaning?'

'I wanted to earn money, and fast. A lot of money. I didn't see me earning enough if I did shelf stacking at the local supermarket. I'd always been very fit. I was tall and strong. I worked out at a gym and did a bit of judo. One of the guys suggested I could make money wrestling. I tried it and, sure enough, it was very well paid. I toured with a somewhat dubious small group. I never really liked wrestling other women much and hated public performances. I had the idea of mixed bouts. Heterosexual bouts paid very well. Most of the men fancied themselves and were usually shocked when I won. My then manager insisted that I'd earn twice as much if I threw in sex. I didn't want that. I choose if I'm having sex with anyone.'

'How old were you?' James asked.

'Seventeen. I pretended eighteen to make it legal. I fought as Rio. It sounded exotic, romantic even. My manager didn't like it when I refused to fight. He was an utter bastard. He sacked me, dumped me in the middle of nowhere and with no money. I was completely on my own. I went to work in the town as a waitress. I was useless and got the sack. Then I

151

met Dexi. We used to run every day, along the beach.

'I hated myself and didn't know where I was going. Dexi helped me to find self-respect. I worked to get a completely new image. I owe him everything. We set about building a high-class, expensive business. Very expensive, as you know. The price weeded out the worst dross. No more public bouts and never without Dexi being there. The Internet allowed us to make it, big time. I've a very useful nest egg waiting for me. I'd never quite realised how much demand there is for the services I provide. And, what's more, I don't ever do sex as part of the deal. Only when and if I want to.'

James sat silently sipping his wine. He made no comment. I wondered if maybe I'd done the wrong thing, telling him so much. Somehow, knowing about a person's past gives a different picture.

'Say something,' I demanded.

'I've nothing to say. I asked; you told me.'

'What about you? Do I get to hear your life story?'

'Nope. I shall remain the mysterious stranger, purveyor of fantasies.'

I laughed. There was an unusual tension between us. I didn't like it, nor understand it. James took a deep breath.

'We're going to have to spend some time apart. I have to go away for a few weeks. Quite soon. You can stay here if you like. We'll decide where we're going after that.'

'I see.' I felt cold suddenly. It wouldn't do to show how important to me he had become. I spoke again. 'Dexi wants us to do a tour of the States. Maybe that would be a good idea.'

'OK. I'll miss you, Lili,' he added, almost as if he'd only just thought of it.

'I could always come with you, if you like,' I suggested.

'I don't want you tagging along with me. I have too much riding on this.'

'I see,' I said. I felt slightly hurt. I was only a part of his life. 'And are you placing restrictions on me?'

'I'm not sure. Leave it for now. I need time to think.' He looked much more thoughtful than I was used to. It was most disconcerting. What was going on in that devious mind of his?

For several days, we seemed to be totally estranged. No games. No sex. No fighting. Fortunately, Dexi kept me working hard and taking my mind off James. We even spent the odd evening together, eating Chinese take-away from cartons, just like the old times. I wasn't in any hurry to get home. Dexi knew there was something amiss.

'What are you going to do?' Dexi asked one evening.

'I think we should go ahead and plan our tour. Maybe after that, we both need to think about our futures. Maybe it's approaching the time for Penny Jackson to reappear and consider a very different future,' I told him.

'Joel and I are discussing setting up some sort of joint project,' Dexi announced rather too casually.

'Good Lord,' I exclaimed. 'When?'

'He's looking into it. If we go away, that should give him time to get things moving.'

'So, this looks like being our final big fling,' I said softly. I wasn't actually upset, I realised. Maybe it was really time for me to grow up. I still wasn't sure about settling down in any way but a few weeks away might settle my thoughts.

A couple of days later, James gave me the dates of his trip.

'I have a week completely clear before I leave. Let's do everything we have ever dreamed of before I go,' he suggested. 'I'll live out my wildest fantasies and you can live yours. What do you say?'

I licked my lips in anticipation. My own fantasies largely involved being dominated. I guessed James would be more than ready to accommodate me. I loved the idea. We sat for hours, revealing to each other our greatest turn-on ideas. Over a couple of bottles of wine, our ideas were getting wilder and wilder, more and more extravagant and diverse. I could see James mentally storing up my suggestions. We laughed a lot, both of us growing very excited over our plans. Once tomorrow was over, we would experience a week of utter debauchery. The orgy to end all orgies. He promised to spare no expense as we devised ways to live out our ultimate fantasies. If we achieved only half of the mad schemes we had suggested, it would be a totally crazy time. It would be an experience neither of us could ever forget.

I had a couple of wrestling bouts booked in town for the following day. Once they were through, I planned to leave Dexi to spend the coming week sorting out our tour. I wanted no interruptions of any kind for the next seven days. If this was to be the end of James and me, so be it. But I knew it would be the grand finale to end all grand finales.

Chapter Eleven

'Get up, whore,' was the greeting on our first morning. Obediently, I got out of bed and looked with interest, to see what I was supposed to wear. A peekaboo bra, black and very tarty, was the first garment. A pair of lacy, black, crotchless pants followed. Fine black stockings and suspender belt completed my get-up.

'Don't I get anything else to wear?' I asked.

He was wearing a suit and tie – somewhat over-dressed compared to me and not exactly what I'd been expecting.

'Later. We're making a couple of business calls. You will behave yourself and be quiet for the dura-tion.' His voice was cold and hard. Masterful.

I stood in the dreadful outfit, waiting for my next orders. He gave me a lash across the buttocks, leaving a red stripe above the pants, visible enough to turn him on for a while. He indicated high black stilettos. I saw myself in the mirror and sighed. I had admitted to a fantasy of being a whore and sex slave in front of a large audience. Maybe I hadn't meant to look quite such a slut as I did now. As to an audience, I couldn't begin to guess what he had in mind.

'Make-up?' I enquired.

'In the bathroom.'

I went in. False eyelashes, bright lipstick and pancake make-up were on the shelf. I did the job and knew I looked like the cheapest tart anyone could pick up. Doris lives again, I thought, remembering the Seychelles. I was expected to walk down the street like this, presumably.

'God, you look foul,' James said. 'Put this on.' He gave me a leopard-skin print, almost see-through plastic mac, which left very little to the imagination. I cinched the waist tightly. He shoved me down the stairs and into the waiting limo. Davis, to his credit, didn't flicker an eyelash. We drove to a building site near the centre of town. He shoved me out of the car and I stood there while a row of builders cheered me on, calling out obscenities and whistling loudly. I stuck my hips out and wiggled a bit. Hidden behind the coarse make-up, I could play the role admirably. I strutted along to the building and waited outside while James did whatever it was he was doing. I glanced round the site. There was virtually no work being done since we'd arrived.

'What the hell are you doing?' he bellowed when he came out. 'You're my tart. Stop flaunting yourself. Everyone can see what you are.' He lifted the back of my short mac, pushed me over a rail and proceeded to slap my arse until it was red hot. The builders were getting very excited. I began to wish I'd never mentioned this particular scenario. All the same, I was so hot and sexy, I would probably have enjoyed a gang bang.

'You might look just a little contrite,' James

snapped. 'Now, get over to that lift.' I looked at where he was pointing. A crude lift went up to the top of the site. He rammed a plastic helmet on my head and shoved me inside the cage. He pushed the lever and we rode high above the site to a crane cab. Needless to say, the initials JWT were plastered over every available space. We reached the cab and he pushed me inside. It was cramped and there were levers everywhere. He snatched away my plastic mac, ripping it as he did so. He leaned out of the window and dropped it.

I took stock of the situation. I was high above the ground, in the glass cab of a crane, wearing trollop gear, hideous make-up and with several dozen workmen staring up to watch the boss, presumably, having sex with a tart. Wonderful. There was nothing for it. I had to perform. Careful not to move any of the levers, I leaned down to unhook his pants and reached in to pull out his prick.

'Go down on me,' he ordered. I nearly protested, needing something drastic doing to my own hot pussy. I tried to reach him with my mouth but it was too confined a space. He hitched my backside high against the window and spread my legs. I knew that everything I had was perfectly visible to our audience below. My wet pussy gleamed, neatly framed by the black lace edges of the pants.

'Bastard,' I whispered. He somehow reached over me and swiped my bum yet again, surprisingly hard.

'Suck me off, tart,' he ordered. I did as I was told. 'Harder, harder,' he shouted. I bounced up and down, my tits still sporting their metal tips, visible through the peekaboo gaps in the ridiculous bra. My cunt was pressed against the window, sliding up and down as I moved. I could still hear the noisy men down below. As James finally came, I lifted my head. My eyes pleaded with him to finger my sex slit at the very least. He read my message and indicated the knob on top of one of the levers. Somehow, I managed to hook myself over the knob and eased myself against its hardness. I rubbed at my clit, feeling the smooth metal beginning to bring me the much needed relief.

'Stop that,' James commanded, just as I was beginning to feel the warm smooth flow at the start of my orgasm. 'You're too greedy. Stop it. Now,' he roared. I glared at him with pure hatred and did as I was told. I fingered the edges of my open pants and he slapped my wrists hard. 'Stop it, or you'll suffer,' he threatened. Somehow, I knew that I had to obey him. He meant every word.

'Get back into the lift.' I stood shivering in the open cage. I could see my plastic mac – little enough protection but at least it had kept the wind out. It was lying on the ground near the bottom of the lift. I lifted my head as we reached ground level. The men were strangely silent as we got out. I could tell that several of them had been having a good old wank while they watched our display. A couple of them stepped forward with the mac, both fighting to help me into it.

James glared as the man, drooling as he did so, hooked it over my arms. I'd been standing practically naked in the winter air, goose bumps covering every inch of me. To stop myself shivering too hard, I planned my revenge on the bastard who was now leading me out of the building site and into the street. Erect silver nipples pushed at the torn mac as I clutched it round me in the icy wind. The rest of the skimpy outfit did nothing to protect me from either the cold or the public gaze. I held my head high, trying to pretend this wasn't happening, and fiercely kept my fingers away from the place where my desperate need was screaming out. After what seemed like hours, the limo drew up and I sank back gratefully into the deep seats.

'I hope you enjoyed all that,' James said. His smile was one of intense satisfaction.

'If being this turned-on is supposed to be enjoyable, I'm not sure.' I pushed a finger on to my aching clit and began to move it.

'Stop it,' my tormentor snapped. 'I'll allow relief when I'm good and ready. Slaves do not have time to pleasure themselves.'

'I'll remember that,' I threatened. He reached over to me, flung me across his knee and proceeded to paddle my backside once more.

'Don't you ever dare threaten me again,' he snapped. I believed he meant it. Davis drew up in front of the house and came to open the door for us. Somehow, my dignity had to be recovered. Tottering on four-inch heels allows little dignity: my tits jutted forward and my bum stuck out at the back. Red stripes and hand marks covered my buttocks and I had blotchy make-up to complete the picture. How could anyone find me attractive? I moaned to myself. Attractive or not, my sex was boiling over. I needed to be alone for a few minutes at least, just to get rid of the ache.

I was sent into the shower and began to rub shower gel over myself, anxious to find some relief. Immediately, my master came into the shower and grasped my wrists. He clicked them into handcuffs and hooked them over the shower. He turned the pressure on high and I was forced to endure the punishing blast. He leaned over my nipples and, using a small key-like device, unfastened the metal clasps. My nipples immediately rose to accept the icy water falling over them. He leaned forward and licked them, his tongue warm relief from the cold. My juices immediately started flowing again as the connecting link joined the nerve cells through my body. He turned off the shower and released my hands.

'If you touch yourself, you will be restrained again. Understand?' I nodded. 'Now dry yourself. I've ordered lunch.' He towelled himself and went out of the room. I dared not even try to rub myself. Somehow, I sensed that he would be aware of anything I did. I went into the bedroom, naked, still damp and awaiting my next orders.

'You may sit at my feet,' he allowed graciously. He had a tray of food and was already eating. It felt more like dinner time to me. I was starving. I looked up hopefully. He handed me a piece of chicken, which I gnawed hungrily. Other delicacies came my way until the tray was empty, apart from some fruit. He pushed the tray to one side and demanded that I feed him grapes, true slave-girl-style. Corny or what!

'I need a rest. We'll wrestle later. I don't want you giving yourself any satisfaction meantime. I want you hot and ready for me.' I'm sure one eyebrow must have flickered at his words. Immediately, he knew that he couldn't trust me and bound my wrists together. He laid me on his bed and secured me to the bed post. I was helpless.

Exhausted by my morning's activities and unable to move much, I dozed beside him, trying to forget the dull ache between my legs. Later, I watched him sleeping. I was happy to be his total slave. I was turned on like crazy, practically all of the time I was with him. His body was beautiful, lean and hard.

There was a chemistry between us like nothing I'd ever experienced before. I knew I'd been able to trust him completely from the start. I could never decide whether I was more turned on as his slave or when he was mine. A complex situation. Despite the humiliation, this morning's activities had been wildly exciting. Performing sex high above the heads of a group of salacious workmen had thrilled me beyond words. I knew they had all wanted me. Every one of them was lusting after me. Hidden behind my make-up and tart clothes, I represented their own fantasies. The fact that the nearest I had come to satisfaction was with a gear knob meant nothing. The thrill of still being kept waiting was almost more pleasurable, however frustrating. I felt myself oozing with desire. The smallest movement proved it to me. My slick passage was screaming for attention, for pleasure, to be screwed within an inch of its life.

'Don't even think of it,' James's voice said beside me.

'I can't help it.'

'Filthy whore. You have no decency in you. Spread your legs.' I did as he asked, hoping that, at last, the ache was going to be removed. He passed his finger across my deep cleft. He held it up, wet with my own juices. He wiped his hand across me and I groaned. I was still on the verge. My bones were fluid; I felt weak.

'Go on,' I whispered.

'Why should I? I don't want to. You are nothing. A mere slave. Why should I care about you?'

'I'm sorry, master,' I whispered.

'You should be.' He pushed my legs even further apart and lay looking at my most intimate places, places I had never even seen myself. He stretched a lazy finger to my clit and scratched it lightly. I knew it was swelling, responding. I felt the orgasmic flush creeping over me and tried to lie still, in case he saw my satisfaction. I couldn't bear him to stop. I hardly dared breathe. 'You won't fool me,' he laughed cruelly. 'I can see exactly what state you are in. It's dark, throbbing and very enlarged. He pinched the bud between his nails and pleasure-pain shot through me. I was powerless, teetering right on the edge of the orgasm to end all orgasms. I was panting. I closed my eyes, practically praying for him to finish what he'd started.

'Please,' I whispered at last. 'I beg you.'

'Sorry. I have an appointment with Madame Lili. She has a very modest costume to wear today. She wouldn't like to think I was being unfaithful. I dread to think what she might do to me if I allowed some slut to accept my pleasuring.'

So that was the way it was going to be. If I wanted any satisfaction today, I was to earn it. Earn it doing what I probably do best. He reached for the straps binding my wrists and loosed me. He led me into the playroom, where the mat was already placed on the floor. Some of the many sets of curtains were drawn across and I could see strange shapes behind them. He glanced around.

'Some special things for later in the week. No peeping. I have so many plans. I guarantee that you will never have a better week's orgy than this.' He pushed me into the bathroom. I was still being kept under supervision, presumably in case I tried to relieve myself. A gold lacy lycra suit awaited me. It was short, with the legs cut high, almost to my waist. It fitted snugly under the crotch, too snugly even for a finger to get inside. It had a plunging neckline, just low enough to show the start of my cleavage. It was good to fight in but not much use for any purely sexual pursuits. He handed me a pair of soft leather boots, laced high up the calf. James was wearing tight gold lycra shorts, which showed off his well-endowed crotch to perfection. His arse looked neat too. I do like a nice tight arse on a man. The slave was about to become the master . . . or . . . mistress.

James was not yet quite ready to relinquish his role. He stood proud, his head high, ready to give me a good match. Bastard. I could give as good as I got and was more than ready to do it. We grappled for several minutes. I was controlling what had been my prime desire, to get laid. I flung him to the ground but he did a head roll and stood again. We grasped each other's waists and tried to bear hug each other into submission. Impasse. I tried winding legs round his to unbalance him but he wouldn't let it happen. We parted again and walked round with small jabbing movements, nothing more than threats. I glanced round. There was masses of space. I stepped away from him and built myself up to take a flying kick at his shoulder area. I even managed a Xena whoop as I flew through the air. He went down and I landed half on top of him. I rolled to grasp his head between my thighs. I pulled and the muscles responded, clamping his head so tightly that there was only one way out. After several moments he tapped my back. He lay on the ground, exhausted, winded. I stood over him, my legs apart.

'Get up, you dog,' I snarled. 'Now. I said, get up.'

He obeyed me. At once I had achieved dominance. From then on, my fight was simple. Whatever he tried, I countered. If he tried to grab me, I could kick his hands away with no difficulty. I took him down into a body scissors, my powerful thighs crushing the breath out of him. He was totally helpless. When I saw his cock rising, getting ready to shoot, I let him go.

'You don't get your relief that way.' I laughed. He was still lying back and I seized my own chance for payback. I ripped the tie from the top of his trunks and snatched away the fabric. Once more, I trussed up his cock, right at the base. The ends of the tape I wrapped round his balls, straddling the tie across the middle to divide them. He was practically crying out with pleasure-pain. I stood and placed my foot victoriously on his chest.

'How did you escape the last time I had you like this?' I asked, suddenly remembering that morning in the Seychelles.

'The chambermaid,' he said guiltily.

'She must have enjoyed the sight,' I said with a grin. 'How much did she charge you?'

'We made a deal,' he said enigmatically. 'Now, what do you intend to do with me?'

'You're my slave now,' I reminded him. 'I shall decide.'

I rolled him with my foot and he lay on his stomach, his cock stuck painfully under his body weight. I pushed his legs apart and stuck the toe of my boot into his crotch. He groaned again. I finished yanking off the shorts and twisted them together round his ankles. I felt proud of my innovative start to the evening's activities. I looked for a weapon to slap his backside. I picked up a flat-backed brush and began to slap his arse. Once it was nicely red, I stuck my boot beneath him and indicated that I wanted him on his back again. It wasn't easy now that his feet were secured. He held up his arms to me, as if suggesting I lie with him.

'Forget it. Don't you have the first idea of how a slave should behave?'

'Sorry, mistress,' he replied.

Suddenly I had the strongest desire to humiliate him. To really bring him down and endure some of the things he had made me do. It hadn't been discussed in our fantasy confessions.

'Get to your feet.' He struggled up and stood waiting. I took two pairs of handcuffs from the rack, ones with long chains between the bracelets. He kept an extensive selection for every possible use. I unwound the pants that I'd used to secure his legs and clipped one ring to each ankle, fastening his wrists to the other end. He was slightly bent forward but I could still see his engorged cock, secured in its binding.

'I'll order dinner. I trust Mrs Davis is still providing meals?' He nodded. I wondered if Davis had ever seen him with the roles reversed. 'Or perhaps we should go out for dinner.' My mind was racing – it would be good to have him sitting opposite me in a posh restaurant with various parts of his anatomy bound as painfully as I could manage. His eyes looked anxiously at me but, credit to him, he remained silent. I fixed a leather belt around his waist and pulled it tight, as he would have done to me. I tied a thin strap round the end of his cock and pulled it up towards the belt, tying the end off tightly. It obviously hit the mark, as he bit his lip to stop his protest.

'You can hardly take me out like this,' he said, indicating the chains on his ankles and wrists. I nodded and loosened them. I collected a fine white lawn shirt from his room. I pushed his arms through the sleeves and fastened leather straps from his wrists to the belt. He was unable to lift his arms

165

more than a few inches. I pulled on thin linen trousers, giving me a clear vision of his imprisoned cock. I pulled the ends of the straps over the waist so that I could use them to control him if necessary.

'Do you have somewhere in mind?' he asked in a voice considerably less confident than usual.

'Green Dragon,' I said, remembering our first date. He gulped.

'But I always take my business clients there,' he whispered.

'So you do. Now, do I have to put a collar and a lead on you? Or are you going to behave while I get ready?'

'Lili . . . you don't mean it, do you? Not the Green Dragon. Besides, you'd never get a table at this notice.'

'Really. You're being most tiresome.' I gave a slight tug to the straps holding his cock in place. He yelped in pain. I wasn't sure if it was truly pleasure-pain that time. 'You do make a fuss. Any more from you and I shall have to use one of your own gags.' I picked up a mobile and scanned through the list. I knew the Green Dragon would be there. I dialled.

'Oh, hi. This is James Travers's . . . er, secretary. He'd like a table for two for the evening. Yes, I do know it's short notice. No, a private room is not necessary. The main restaurant will be fine. Thank you. See you soon.' I smiled sweetly at him. 'No problems. You're obviously well known there.' He shrugged. There wasn't much else he could do. 'Now, what shall I wear?'

I flicked through the many outfits in the cupboards. There were plenty to choose from. I chose a black rubber dress, short and close-fitting. Starting just below my cleavage, it was laced down the front for its entire length. I tugged the laces together. My breasts were pushed high, barely covered by the rubber top. Tantalising glimpses of flesh were revealed between the lacing. I pulled on long black thigh boots and fastened a studded belt at my waist. For an extra touch that I knew would infuriate him, I added a whip, tucking it into the wide leather belt. I swept my hair into a high ponytail and clipped it with a silver buckle. I wound the loose hair tightly round the rest, giving me a tall spike, very phallic, on top of my head. I'd grace any rubber fetish bar and looked every inch the madame I now felt myself to be.

'Ready?' I asked.

'Lili . . .' he began.

I pulled the whip out of my belt and flicked across his flies. He instantly sank back, biting his lip.

'You were saying?'

'Nothing.'

'Good. I don't really want to take you out wearing a gag. Now, I'll call Davis to bring the car round.'

I wiggled my way along the corridor, dragging James behind me. I was about to enjoy myself. Once more, I had to admire the total lack of expression on Davis's face. The man was showing discretion like I've never seen.

We were shown to our table with only a hint of raised eyebrow. Inscrutable is a phrase often used of the Chinese. I believed it that night. I fingered the whip threateningly if he looked like saying anything and pushed my booted toe into his crotch if he took his eyes off me. I ordered for us both, choosing my own favourites and disregarding his own preferences. I ordered him to eat every scrap on his plate and threatened him if he left anything. He struggled to reach his mouth with the restrictions on his arms and had to lean down. If a waiter was close, I made sure that James called me mistress in a loud voice, ensuring that everyone knew exactly who I was. It was a most pleasurable evening. I could even use the blunt end of the whip to massage my own dire needs. I closed my eyes as I came. Bliss. It was a relief that caused me to call out softly. He glared at me.

'You are a disobedient slave,' he muttered under his breath.

'How dare you?' I snapped and shoved my boot into his bondaged prick. He grimaced and lowered his head.

'Sorry, mistress,' he said abjectly.

'Sign the bill,' I ordered.

'I haven't got a card, mistress.'

'Then they'll have to send you an account.' I'd forgotten all about paying, in my haste to leave the house. I rose and went to the reception. The lovely Chinese lady I'd met on my first visit was at the desk. She looked at my outfit and frowned slightly. I explained that James had forgotten his credit cards and arranged for a bill to be sent to his office.

'And now, perhaps you will phone for our car.'

'Madame, I . . .' The woman looked at me as if she wanted to say something but thought better of it. I wondered if she was about to initiate me into the Chinese way of treating a gentleman.

'You wouldn't understand,' I said softly, smiling at her. She smiled back and shook her head. Her voice took on a new tone.

'Don't you believe it, love. The Chinese are an ancient people.' Her wonderfully demure accent quite disappeared and she sounded as if she truly came from this northern city.

When we arrived home, I felt quite exhausted. But I was not ready for bed without the fuck I'd been looking forward to all day. I undressed James and took off his straps. His cock was still taut and erect and I unfastened the ties. I pushed him on to the bed and straddled his body. The rubber suit was hot and sticky. I pulled the whip from my belt.

'Take out the lacing,' I demanded. I lay back and he climbed over me to oblige. I pointed at my boots and he carefully unzipped them. When I was naked, I lay back, running the whip between my fingers. I pushed it behind his waist, using it to pull him down on top of me. He sank with a sigh but I rolled away. I was going to remain on top for a bit longer. I stroked his erection until it stood hard and proud again. I lowered myself on to it and ordered him to remain still. I moved up and down its length, savouring every second of rub of skin on skin. I felt him beginning to come and I wanted more so, again, I gripped him hard at the base, to stop his ejaculation. He was weak, blurred with his own needs. Again I rode him, pressing forward so that my clit slid against his hard cock, bouncing up and down until I felt the roar of my orgasm beginning. I let him go and he pounded his hips against the bed, gripping my waist and drawing me into him. I felt his cock deep inside me, grinding way beyond my pelvis, or so it seemed. Hot with primal need, I ignored his cries. I pushed my fingers into myself so that every necessary part of me received the attention I craved. I screamed out with relief, before collapsing over him, totally exhausted. After several minutes of silence, he pushed me off.

'End of day one,' he said

Chapter Twelve

We slept late the next day. Hardly surprising. It would be hard for either of us to keep up this pace for a whole week. While he seemed to have given a lot of thought to what we should do, I was somewhat better at improvising. Several fantasies had been covered already. Somehow though, I sensed that we wouldn't be repetitive. It was almost like the Seychelles again. Plenty of time and no real need to hurry.

We drove to the coast and spent a quiet day, wandering deserted beaches. Mrs Davis had packed a delicious picnic lunch. The day sounded quite tame by many standards but it had its moments. It was too cold to lie on the beach so we found a sheltered hollow in the sand dunes. He reached over and lifted my T-shirt, exposing my naked breasts. I hadn't been in the mood for a bra that day. He gently pressed my nipples, already swelling and dark. He caressed my body and I lay back, enjoying the feeling of passivity that overtook me. His hands slid down inside my jeans and began to follow their accustomed path. I stretched out languorously, luxuriating in the promise of easy, satisfying sex. James slid my jeans off and pulled the T-shirt over my head. I lay naked, the sea breeze blowing over me. He removed his own clothes and pressed himself over me.

Neither of us spoke as he used his fingers to blaze the trail for his cock to follow. I was as weak as a kitten, waiting for the pleasure to reach a climax. As he slid deep into me, I shuddered as the recognition of his member filled my soft, dark, wet channel. His finger worked on my clit, stimulating, teasing, driving me frantic with the pleasure of it. We moved in perfect unison, each of us pumping, pumping towards the ultimate goal. I could hear the sea crashing to the shore and felt the waves pounding across the beach to reach me . . . us, as with a jolting shudder, we arrived at the moment of definitive pleasure. I heard someone approaching us, obviously a family walking up through the dunes. I was too lazy and too sated to move. I kept my eyes closed so that I couldn't see them.

'What're they doing, Mam?' asked a childish voice. 'They ain't got no clothes on.'

'Come away. Disgusting. Should be ashamed of themselves,' said an angry female voice.

I giggled.

'Probably do her good to enjoy a bit of uninhibited lust,' I said softly.

James withdrew from me and rolled off me. The breeze was chilly and I shivered. I sat up and dressed again. I flung James's shirt over to him and, lazily, he put it on.

'Let's go,' he suggested. 'I want to call on some old friends on the way back.'

Call we did, mainly to swim in their private pool.

We had it to ourselves and swam naked. We even managed to wrestle in the water. I performed leg spreads on him and stretch exercises that got him more than ready for another bout of sex. He held me over the Jacuzzi bubbles until I was practically coming with the flow across my clit. It was nice but less than satisfying. Though we both almost managed to climax, it was hard to judge the moment. We failed to coincide completely. He massaged me in the most appropriate place, while I clung to his cock, rubbing, pulling, feeling the skin sliding over his hard centre. At last, we were both satisfied, for the time being.

I remembered the Seychelles and the gentle man who had made love to me in the swimming pool. I must have let something show, as he promptly questioned me about it. I said nothing at first but he kept prodding me for the truth. What the hell, I thought, and told him about it. For a moment he looked angry. I pointed out that he had deserted me for no less than two young girls. He glared but said nothing. I could see he was still angry with me.

Later, he told me that he wanted me exclusively. He said again that he was not prepared to risk disease and hated using condoms. I protested about his two companions.

'You little fool. I wouldn't ever have sex with anyone like that. However pure and innocent they might look, don't you think I know their history? Meanwhile, you go and take unbelievable risks yourself.'

'I'm sorry. But I was angry. Hurt. I didn't even know who it was. I thought it was you at first and when I discovered it wasn't, it was too late.'

'Only thought? I should have tried to be certain if I'd been you. Before taking risks.'

'Well, now you know why I didn't want to tell you about it. Please don't let it spoil our time together.'

He said nothing as we drove home. We ate a silent meal and went to bed. It had been a nice day but my big mouth had spoiled it all. Maybe I did need a gag.

The week flew by after that blip. I have never had so much satisfying, intense sex, nor in so many places and ways. It was one long orgy all right. We reached Saturday morning all too soon, and sadly, I realised that we only had until Monday before he was flying out to Rio. He was to meet the South American, Ramon, whom he'd met in the Seychelles. I wasn't really sorry to be left out of that trip, after all. I wondered if he'd manage to resist the streams of women he'd doubtless be offered. I knew that, for once, I did really care. Fortunately, it wouldn't be too long before Dexi and I were leaving for our own tour.

'I have made plans for the rest of our time,' he announced on Saturday morning. 'The ultimate fantasy for both of us. I hope you didn't have anything else in mind.' I wriggled expectantly. 'You promise to be obedient, submissive to everything?'

'Is there a choice?' I asked innocently.

'Only if you wish to abandon the whole thing,' James said calmly. 'Once the game has begun, there is no going back.'

I looked at him curiously. Was there any doubt about my enjoyment? I'd more than proved how far he could go. I'd accepted everything he'd done to me and given as good as I'd got.

'I guess so. Is there something you're not sure about? Something you want to check out?'

'No. You'll never forget this next two days, I promise you. I trust you will find it everything you could dream of.'

I was excited and wondered which of my fantasies he was about to fulfil. I was already beginning to boil, deep in my usual places. I wondered if I dare suggest a quick relief before we started. I realised that wouldn't do at all.

'I can't begin to imagine what you're planning. I'll take a shower,' I said, leaping out of bed.

'No. Later. We're having a champagne breakfast to start.' He pressed the intercom and seconds later Davis arrived with a trolley. He took the covers off the dishes and opened the champagne. He smiled and left the room.

'To sex, fun and the ultimate fantasy,' James toasted. I clinked his glass. He downed the wine quickly and picked up the bottle to refill the glasses.

'I won't remember much of anything at this rate,' I complained.

'Drink,' he ordered.

We ate fresh croissants smothered in honey followed by exotic fruits I couldn't even give name to. He fed me with pieces of fruit, gently, sexily teasing me with his tongue and fingers. He was the perfect lover – gentle, thoughtful. He caressed me and kissed me tenderly, in a way he had never quite managed to achieve before. He stopped short of making love, fucking or screwing. He reached to his side table and picked up a jewellery box. I was frankly puzzled. Was he about to propose to me? That was ludicrous – we didn't have that sort of relationship. He handed the box to me and I began to pull off the lid, looking into his eyes for an answer. Suddenly, he snatched it away.

'Later,' he said. 'You'll see what's in here later.' I stared at him curiously. Was this part of his game? What was he trying to tell me? He gave me more champagne and watched me drink it down rather too quickly. I was beginning to feel light headed, slightly dizzy. He picked up a bell and rang it imperiously. Two strange girls came into the room. They were wearing what I could only describe as harem pants and gold bra tops. I stared, fascinated. They were identical twins, both with long dark hair, braided with gold threads. They were tiny, reaching only up to my breasts. They had almond-shaped eyes, outlined in black, and the pair of them moved exactly together. They came to the bed and took my hands, leading me out of the room. I cast a glance back at James. He was lying with his eyes closed, seemingly ignoring the proceedings.

The game was beginning. Feeling slightly tipsy from the champagne, I almost floated through a door I did not recognise. The blaze of light dazzled me as I realised I was in the marble bathroom which led off the playroom. We had come through the door I had never been able to find. It must have been the way that someone had come in to run my bath at different times. The room was different. Candles were burning everywhere, reflecting in the mirrors and giving the dazzling light. Oil burners filled the air with some exotic, unfamiliar perfume. It was heavy, musklike, dreamlike.

I stood naked, as the girls drew me into the scented water. They accompanied me into the water and began to soap me all over, rubbing gently, smoothing my skin. It was curiously erotic. I've never been one for appreciating other women, never even had any lesbian experiences, ever. In fact, fighting other women had been something I'd never really liked. But these two beautiful girls seemed unaware of what they were doing to me. They rinsed the soap away and took my hands, leading me out of the water. They lay me on one of the marble steps, on a soft white towel, and began to pat me dry all over. Completely synchronising their movements, they dealt with each part of my body. I felt myself floating, as if I was drugged. It was strange, ethereal.

When they were satisfied that I was dry, they took me, soundlessly, through the door into the play-room. It was dark and I recognised nothing. Through a set of curtains I saw a table, like my own massage table and lit from above with a pale pinkish light. They indicated that I should lie on the table. They brought warm oils and began to rub my body, gently, smoothly. I felt myself drifting away again, relaxing as they ministered to me. The champagne had obviously lulled me into a stupor and the per-fumed air and gentle bathing had transported me to some strange land. Their small, probing fingers explored me, visiting even the most intimate places. They knew exactly where to touch. I felt the familiar ripples begin to drift through my body. Mindless and unable to resist anything, I experienced the most delicate orgasm I could remember. The girls giggled slightly. I saw them begin to finger each other in their own search for satisfaction. I couldn't take my eyes away from them as they both panted slightly and seemed to reach their climax. They turned back to me and caressed me once more.

Once I was relaxed again, they took my hands and led me away from the table. I was losing all sense of time and place. I wondered briefly what James was doing while all this was going on. Between more curtains there was a stand with clothes awaiting. The girls stood, one at each side of me, and put their small hands beneath my breasts, rubbing my nipples to make them erect. Once they were satisfied, they each picked up a golden circlet and clipped them in place. I felt the grip of the metal; erotic stabs of pain ran through me. My nipples were once more encased with metal tips, gold, this time. The design was different, though the principle was the same. The centres were exposed, pink buds in the midst of the gilded flowers. I stared down and the girls giggled slightly, before tightening the clamps even further, to ensure a very close fit. I winced slightly as the metal bit into my soft flesh. It was pure pleasure-pain. They clipped slave bangles high up my arms and wide gold bands round my wrists and ankles. My lower body was still naked as I awaited the rest of my costume. A gold band was clipped round my waist, pulling me into the familiar wasp shape that I knew James liked.

I was then taken through the maze of curtains to another table. My handmaidens pressed me back and I was fastened down to the table, making use of the various ornaments that had been placed around my body. A strap was fixed across my forehead, preventing me from making any more movement. What the hell was going on now? The curtains moved and a short man came through. I stared at him. His naked torso was pierced in every possible place. His nipples were speared with gold shafts; his navel bore a large ring; his eyebrows held a small forest of studs and rings; broad sweeps of rings, graduated in size, went round his ears. His baggy pants were made of silk, doubtless all part of his role in my weird fantasy. When I had described my Arabian Nights fantasy to James, I could never have believed he would have created it in so much detail. I was being prepared for the delectation of a master.

The eunuch, if such he was, nodded at the girls and they lifted my legs, slotting them into metal poles at each side of the table. They then moved away the lower section of the table, leaving my bum close to the edge. It looked like a delivery table in a maternity hospital only with the patient trussed in place, totally unable to move or resist. I strained to see what was on the trolley that was wheeled in next. It smelt like hot wax. A strong light was switched on and I was blinded for a moment. The odious little man moved my stirrups so that my sex lay wide open, exposed and vulnerable. He painted hot wax on my pubic hair and proceeded to rip out the fine dark hair that concealed my mound. At the first tear, I screamed. I can take bikini line waxing, just about, but this was too much. My eyes streamed as the pain seared through me. I yelled and immediately, he clapped his hands. My two fiendish handmaidens appeared and I bellowed at them to release me. Foolish thought. Instead, the treacherous little bitches firmly clamped a gag round my mouth and pulled the silk scarf tight to smother my screams. I tried to fight back, impotent and useless. More wax. More tearing. I felt weak, angry and impotent. How dare James cause this to happen? Bastard. I'd show him later. My nipples were tightly held in the metal, the exposed buds pinched in their prison. I felt uncomfortable and pissed off – as far from a fantasy as I could hope to be.

If this was what he wanted, James could take a running jump. I didn't want to play any more. He'd made me promise to accept whatever he had planned but this was pushing it beyond the limit. The euphoria I had been feeling had now evaporated. I felt stone-cold sober. As if realising my thoughts, the Pierced Fatso ordered the gag to be removed. My head strap was released and the girls came to give me something to drink. I protested but they forced it between my lips. I tasted brandy, a good-quality cognac, I noticed stupidly. I felt its warmth spreading through me and the pain lessened. I lay down again, unable to resist, if I was honest. My straps were replaced and once more the evil little man began his torture. I couldn't believe there could be any more hair on my body, anywhere. He told them to lift my arms and he peered beneath. Thank heavens I had already removed that particular hair myself.

He sprayed my poor naked flesh with something that stung like hell. I made my silent scream once more and then relaxed as the stinging subsided. The girls smoothed a soothing balm over my nude pussy and I was left alone. I must ask what the balm was. It certainly worked well. I relaxed and I suppose I was half dozing, listening to the haunting music that was playing. I felt like that slave girl, exotic and unable to resist whatever my master demanded of me. This was my fantasy, just as I'd described it, though the reality was something less than pleasant. Things must begin to improve soon. I was being prepared for my master's pleasure. It was my duty to do everything he wanted. To obey his slightest wish. I thought myself into my role and felt composed and ready for whatever would happen next.

The girls returned to me and removed the restraints. They took off the bands from my body and led me into the bathroom again. I was bathed once more and dried. I felt helpless, totally without any spirit of my own. I watched fascinated as they shaped and painted my nails. Gold talons seemed to extend from my fingers. My toenails were coloured in the same way. My eyes were outlined in kohl, making me look like a 70s advertisement for Turkish Delight. I looked like them and nothing like myself. Next, my hair was pulled tight into a metal band and clipped away from my face. For a moment, I wondered if they were about to remove all the hair from my head. I would have objected most strongly to that infringement. They wound my hair into a tight bun and clamped it in place with a small, gold, jewelled cage. I felt already exotic, a stranger even to myself.

I was taken through silken draperies and adorned with the gold bracelets, anklets and slave bangles. A huge filigree necklace was hung about my neck, spreading a lace-like pattern of gold across my chest and reaching down below my nipples. Flashes of colour were threaded among the gold and I began to see myself as some exotic princess, probably about to star in some dreadful, thoroughly exciting 'B' movie. I was clothed in harem pants, full, transparent gold silk. They were tied with golden cords around my hips. They picked up a huge red stone, perhaps it was a ruby. I looked down as they measured it against my navel. They smeared cement on to the back of the jewel and, somehow, stretched the hole to push it in. It was held in place for a few moments, presumably until the cement dried. Even that unaccustomed sensation felt strange. It was as if every part of my body was given a new dimension. Discomforts were there to make me aware of every inch of my flesh.

When they were satisfied, a gilded circlet was pressed over my forehead. Flimsy veils were attached and pulled around my head. My face was covered, leaving only my eyes showing. Talk about Salome . . . I was already beginning to work out how to wiggle my hips to entrance my new master.

They showed me my reflection. I was unrecognisable. I stood tall, dwarfing the twins. I held up my head proudly. I was indeed a slave-princess.

I heard a gong being sounded. I could hear movement and the music grew louder. My handmaidens slipped golden chains on to my wrist bands and taking one each, led me in to meet my new master. I was no longer a princess. I knew that I was a mere slave, purchased for his pleasure. They pushed me down on to the floor and made me lie flat. I was not allowed to look. I heard someone clap their hands and I was ordered to kneel. I lifted my head and saw my master, magnificent in silk robes, lying on a couch. He nodded to me and I rose, moving forward. He stared at me and finally smiled and nodded. Evidently, I had passed.

As the haunting music began again, the twins began to dance. I found myself swaying to the music and they danced past me, pulling away my veils, one at a time. When I was finally revealed, the master clapped his hands and the music stopped. He beckoned me to approach him. He leaned forward and fingered the core of my nipples. They promptly stood to attention, causing me to wince slightly as the metal once more bit into me. Pleasure-pain. He beckoned me to lie on the couch beside him and he ran his hands over me. I was sick with longing. My pussy was there, waiting, denuded and smooth. Whatever the balm that had been used, the pain had quite gone. I wanted him to see me smooth and clean. My heart was pounding with the expectation. I tried to think of all the old movies I'd once loved, when slave girls had been used by their men.

I was one of the poor girls, with nothing of their own. I was there purely to serve.

The master lay back. I half rose to caress him, uncertain as to whether I was performing as I should. The twins moved silently forward, pulling me back down to the couch. I watched as they removed his flowing robes and massaged his cock until it stood straight and erect. I noticed a gold band circling it at the base, which they tightened as his erection stood proud. They turned to me and moved my legs apart. I realised that the voluminous pants were crotchless and they began to stroke my smooth mound. It felt strange to be so completely hairless. They held my arms out and my legs apart. It seemed that we were to be observed while we loved, fucked ... whatever slaves did. The master rolled over me and inserted his cock deep inside me, while one of the twins reached out and stroked my clit. I felt as if I was taking off, aiming high towards the sky. He pumped into me, without any preamble or delicacy. Bang, bang. The movement was enough to bring me to the necessary point but somehow, after the exotic lead up, it felt a great heap of nothing. I think he came. I didn't really care. I could see his eyes, teasing, laughing at my evident distress and disappointment. He moved out of me. I could see at once that he had not allowed his own orgasm. The clip that had been placed at the base of his cock, much as I had tied him before, prevented him from coming. Evidently, it was a strategy he'd enjoyed.

He lay back against the cushions, indicating that I was supposed to do the same. The two girls disappeared behind the drapes and returned, carrying a large double-ended dildo. They straddled it and began to rock on it, their feet and arms intertwined. They threw back their heads and we could both see them laughing as they came. It was surprisingly erotic and I felt my juices beginning to gather. When they were finished, I saw that the master was smiling and he nodded to them. They came to me and turned me on to my stomach. My legs were once more spread apart and they began to massage my bumhole, at first gently and then more insistently. I felt something being pushed inside. The ring of flesh was taut, stretched. Even now, I felt as if I might tear at any moment and kept very still. When I felt as if I was as full as it was possible to be, the object was removed. I opened my eyes and realised that I could have watched the entire proceeding through carefully placed mirrors. The rubber dildo was being pulled from my bumhole and the master was moving forward to replace it. I was about to be buggered.

His cock was still huge and erect as he pressed against my backside. His arms pulled me close into him and he slipped into my lubricated passage, filling me to the hilt. I waited, scarcely daring to breathe, let alone move. Gently, he pulled me down over him until I was lying on top of him, speared on his prick. The twins came forward and spread my legs. The dildo was pushed gently, deeply into my cunt. While one of them moved it in and out, pressing it hard against my pubic bone, hard against my clit, the other was kneading my tits. I felt the master moving up and down, the girls matching the rhythm perfectly. Never have I ever felt anything quite like it. I was a seething mass of orgasmic fluids. I was no longer a body made of flesh and bone but one incredible pleasure centre, blood pounding almost painfully through an orgasm that never seemed to be stopping. I felt my master come in a huge rush and my own pulsing form was liquid fire. I had no

idea how long I lay there. I had no sense of beginning or end. I lay supine, doing nothing at all to
achieve the amazing effect. If I never had another
orgasm in my life, this was something I could never
forget. Someone must have lifted me off my master
but still my hips were thrashing spontaneously. I
saw my master looking down at me and he clicked
his fingers, indicating that the precious dildo should
be removed.

'Wow!' I breathed. He raised a warning finger to
quiet me. Evidently, it was not allowed to speak to
him.

'Silence, slave. You speak only when told.'

'I'm sorry, master,' I said with bowed head. He
rose to his feet and picked up a whip. He rolled me
over with his foot and began to pound my backside.
Red stripes crossed my back. He grinned and put
the whip down.

'Think yourself lucky that you performed well.
Otherwise, you would have been severely punished
for daring to speak. Bring food, wine and music,' he
shouted suddenly. I felt too weak to move. Truth to
tell, I don't think I'd even begun the climb down
from my dizzying experience.

Music began to play, haunting and foreign. More
exotic, musky fragrances filled the room. A low table
was carried in and several trays of strange-looking
foods. Fruit, meat, honey and nut cakes. I realised I
was ravenous. Maybe some food would restore my
energy, ready for whatever else lay in store. Fantasy? This was no longer some game that was being
played out. I had become the part I was playing. I
would enjoy every second of what remained. I sat
up, ready to partake of the feast. Surely, such a
favoured slave would be allowed to eat with her
master?

A couch was brought for me and we lay opposite each other, feasting on the unfamiliar dishes. Rich, heavy wine was poured into silver cups, refilled as soon as they were empty. When we were replete, everything was cleared away. I waited silently, wondering what was to happen next. James was sustaining his role well and I was now totally wrapped in my own. I was his slave and there to be used for his pleasure alone. Not that I wasn't getting my own pleasure on the way through. I felt deliciously lethargic, sated. The mood wasn't allowed to last for long. Perhaps it was the wine or the outlandish setting. We were both ready for more activity. I did not know the time of day or night. I had no clue about how long we had lived in the strange world.

He took me into what had been created as his bedroom. It was arranged like a tented camp and I imagined desert stars above us. He had the girls remove my pants and the heavy necklace. I was wearing the wrist, arm and ankle bangles and my gilded nipple rings and nothing else. He touched the ruby in my navel and gave it a tweak that sent a shot of pleasure-pain through me. It also sent erotic messages to my sex. He stroked my body and indicated that I was allowed to arouse him once more. This time, we were alone and I felt freer to respond to him. He spread my legs and kissed my naked pussy. He liked the clear flesh and I knew I no longer held any resentment towards him for inflicting that particular pain on me.

He reached to a side table and produced the jewellery box I'd seen earlier. He opened it and took out a gold ring. I stared in fascination. It looked like a wedding ring. I was suddenly flung back in my own time. I wasn't ready to make that sort of commitment. But then, neither was he. I began to sit up, ready to make my protest. He pushed me back and slipped the ring on my third finger. Before I could speak, he took out a second ring and placed it on the other hand. Two more rings were taken out and pushed on to my fingers. I looked down at my hands and smiled at him. If I wondered why I had suddenly been given them, I pushed it out of my mind. He began to give me much better things to think about. I enjoyed his smooth body as we rolled, played and had some of the most gloriously satisfying sex one could believe possible. I knew I should never meet another man, ever, who was able to perform with such magnificence, such frequency. I was in sexual heaven.

It was some hours later that I was to learn exactly why he had given me those rings. They were most certainly not *wedding rings*.

Chapter Thirteen

I lost all track of time as we enjoyed sex, wrestled gently, dozed and had more sex. We drank wine, champagne, brandy at times. We had moved into a state of total euphoria, where the world did not exist outside the silken drapes that surrounded us. I awoke from a deep sleep to hear a gong sounding. I tried to work out what it was, and where I was. Dazed from sleep, wine, whatever, I felt detached and unable to think.

'Lili? I want you to do something for me. Will you?'

'Depends,' I murmured lazily. He sighed and leaned up on one elbow, smiling at me. 'Sure I will,' I said with a grin and opened my legs again. I was well past caring.

'Listen to me,' he said more firmly. 'I'd like you to wear the rings I gave you.' He picked up my fingers and spun the rings. 'I want you to wear them somewhere special.'

'Through the nose, for instance?'

'Close,' he said. 'You're into piercing, aren't you?'

'Not averse to it. What do you have in mind?'

'I've heard,' he said softly, fingering my smooth pussy, 'that rings strategically placed on these lips can enhance the excitement no end.' He tweaked the naked flesh between his thumb and fingers, sending sharp stabs of pleasure through me. He gently dug his nails into the same spot. Despite the excesses of the past days, I was getting more than a passing interest.

'What do I have to do?' I asked. I sat up and looked him in the eye. I'd become very interested indeed. 'Why are you being so coy about it? Not like you at all.'

'I wasn't sure how you'd take it. It's a sensitive area down there, now isn't it?' He was driving me wild yet again, as his fingers caressed and played around the area in question.

'Can I think about it?'

'For a few minutes. Think about the gentle pulls against my prick as it passed the rings. Think how it would feel if every tiny movement I made, was enhanced by your golden rings.'

I lay back, wanting and waiting all over again. He teased me with his stiff cock, gently pinching at my pussy with one hand as he held me open with the other. He plunged again, satisfying, throbbing. His fingers rubbed hard on my clit. I pushed against him, wondering what it would feel like with the enhancements. I'd certainly looked at various sites on the Internet, where genital piercing was suggested. Wow! I knew immediately, I couldn't refuse.

As I came, I screamed out.

'Yes. Yes. Yes. Do it to me.' I collapsed as his orgasm shot through both of us. For a moment we lay still. He lifted himself and stared down at me.

'Was that an agreement I heard?'

'I love the idea,' I said firmly. It was going to be the biggest turn on ever. I wriggled with pleasure at the thought. I looked at the rings on my fingers. 'All four?' I asked him.

'I thought so. Two on each side. It won't be without pain, you realise.'

'Pure pleasure-pain,' I said happily. I guess I was too high on my clouds of fantastic sex to think properly. We lay side by side. Relaxed. Fulfilled for the present. He rose and poured wine for us both. I sat up and gazed at my fingers and the four gold rings. I would have the piercing, just as soon as I could get it done. Perhaps a surprise for when he came home.

James produced a sheet of paper from beneath his pillow. He handed it to me to sign. I looked briefly at the jargon and decided it was all too complicated.

'You need to sign it,' he told me.

'What is it?'

'Consent form. For the piercing.' I shrugged. So what? I'd made up my mind hadn't I? I took the paper and a pen and scrawled my signature, the one I use for autographs. I didn't care.

The twins returned to our bedside and, at a nod from James, led me away. He stared after me. I looked back at him longingly as I was led away from him.

The marble bathroom was once more lit with candles and the oil burners were filling the air with relaxing perfumes. They stripped me of everything, except the four rings. The slave bangles, the red jewel from my navel. Finally, my hair was released from its clips. I was once more bathed and dried by the handmaidens. When they had finished, the same table was brought in, where I had been secured for the painful removal of my pubic hair. I gave a small shudder at the memory but I knew that, in the long run, I hadn't really minded. I made little protest as I was fastened down to the table. My legs were once more hoisted into the stirrups and this time secured with chains wound round to prevent any movement. Extra bands were placed round my body and I couldn't move even a single muscle. I waited in some trepidation. The door opened and I waited to see who was entering. A trolley was being wheeled in. No smell of hot wax this time. I saw my tormentor from earlier, the pierced man. James came in and looked down at me.

'What's going on?' I demanded.

'Trust me. You said you'd like to be pierced. I've arranged it all for you.' James spoke dispassionately.

'What, now?' I gulped. 'I didn't think you meant it right away.'

'I'll see you later, darling,' James said.

Darling? What the hell was he playing at? He'd never called me that, except when we were doing a tramp act and it was said in a jokey way. He disappeared through the door and the twins began to work on me again. They removed the four rings from my fingers. I hoped they weren't about to make off with them. They dropped them into a dish containing some liquid that smelt faintly antiseptic. I watched as much as I could watch, as Fatso came close and peered between my legs. He grasped the lips of my sex and pinched it together. He was carrying out a major inspection of my pussy. He pulled a chain down, from my waist level, and clamped it down through the cracks at the top of my legs, holding my bum even closer to the table and preventing me from even twitching. He sprayed something from a can and I immediately felt as if my pussy lips were frozen solid. I squeaked and made some curses that made the three watchers smirk at my total impotence. Still, I was into it. Something else cold pushed into my senses. I felt a slight pricking sensation across the flesh of my sex lips. Another. Another. I counted four. The bastard pierced me on both sides. The rings were soon going to adorn the lips of my pussy. I felt a mixture of pleasure, excitement and discomfort, not in that order.

'Bastards,' I yelled, as the pain was hitting me, seriously now. 'I didn't mean it. I didn't want it yet.' I made up my mind to sue, the instant I was released. James would be first and Fatso second. The twins would make a nice ending. The fact that I had given my consent was far from my mind. At that moment, my attention was caught by a new activity.

I watched as Fatso reached for the rings, and somehow, opened them. 'I'm going to clip each into place and clamp it with a pair of pliers,' he said. The girls were watching, totally fascinated. He handed me a mirror. 'See?' He pointed to them, fingering the clip.

The twins looked into my eyes to see my reaction. I nodded, and all four rings were clamped. Whatever else, I felt wildly excited. Exotic. I was beginning to feel the turn-on value of rings placed in that particular place. It was unbelievably stimulating. Erotic. I knew people often had various adornments in such places. I'd never even considered it before. Maybe I should have. Imagine the look of surprise when a man saw the double row of rings adorning my pussy. It could enhance sex for me, in a new way. Fatso sprayed the stuff on me again and I winced at the cold. Some sort of anaesthetic, I assumed. There was still no real pain, yet. The girls washed away the traces of blood. I expected there would be some pain, a lot of pain, later. After all, even my pierced ears had given me a bit of a problem at first.

'You bastard,' I began to yell. 'You really enjoyed that, didn't you?' Consent given or not, I wasn't yet ready to admit what a turn-on it was.

'Shut up. Listen. I'm leaving you some lotion to use. Bathe the rings at least three times a day. You've got piercing already, so you know the drill. They'll heal quite quickly, though I don't recommend you go back to your orgy for a week or two. I shall call tomorrow to check you and see all is well. Throw this lot away,' he ordered the girls, indicating his various piercing tools. Disposable tools – at least that was some comfort. He turned and left the room, taking the rest of his little tool kit with him. Grudgingly, I had to admit that he was very good. Neat job. Almost pain free, so far.

The girls removed the trolley and came back with James. Almost proudly, they showed him my latest acquisitions. He looked down and fingered them, gently.

'Wedded bliss four times over.' He leaned down to kiss my lips. He caressed my body, his fingers sliding beneath the various metal restraints that held me down.

'Free her,' he commanded the girls. 'Then dress her and bring her to my room.'

I noticed he was wearing normal clothes. It seemed that this was the end of the Arabian section of our orgy, as he'd called it. I supposed it had to be in view of my latest restrictions.

The twins gently washed and wiped my pussy and let me out of my restraints. I rubbed my sore limbs and stood. As I did so, the blood rushed back through my body and I felt the stab of sharp pain as I became fully aware of the rings.

'Bloody hell,' I gasped. 'Can't you do something?'

They grinned at me, giggled and reached for a dress that was hanging there. I couldn't even sit down. I felt more uncomfortable than I ever had before. The rings felt the size of hula-hoops as I tried to walk.

I gritted my teeth. The twins slipped a pair of tiny briefs between my legs and tied them at the sides. Presumably a token gesture towards protecting me. They slipped the soft, black dress over my head and pushed my feet into gold sandals. They clamped back the various bangles round my arms and ankles, as if to keep me aware of my status as a decorated ornament. Then the twins led me to James's own bedroom, away from the fantasy land of the playroom.

James was sitting at his desk when I went in. He glanced round and stared at me as he looked over my relatively normal clothing.

'I thought we'd have a quiet dinner for our last night together,' he said softly.

'I've lost all track of time. What time is it? What day is it, come to that?'

'It's late, Sunday night. Our week is over. I'm flying out to Rio tomorrow.' He rose and poured some champagne. 'To a memorable week,' he toasted.

'Memorable all right.'

'I'm sure you will come to enjoy my gift to you, eventually.' His eyes held a glint that I did not understand. So what if he'd adorned me with any number of gold rings? They weren't much good to me – though, to be fair, they were making me well horny. 'They're all gold, you realise. Worth a packet.' He indicated the rings on my wrists, arms and ankles. They were all pretty substantial and if they really were gold, I was wearing some quite serious money. I was slightly mollified. At least I could sell them when I next needed some cash.

After a leisurely dinner, served in the dining room, we went back to bed, this time to sleep. We both felt exhausted and I don't think either of us had any thoughts of sex. The ache round my pussy would have put paid to that in any case. All the same, my new adornments were settling into place. I was getting used to the feel of them there and beginning to feel excited at the prospects for the future. I'd probably have killed anyone who was even vaguely interested in sex at this particular time, however.

I bathed myself, using Fatso's lotion. It was some herbal concoction and, whatever else it contained, I quickly recognised its healing properties. I turned the rings, making sure they didn't stick and cause infection. James spent much of the Monday on the phone and organising his packing. I lolled around, listless and not wanting to begin to think about working. During the afternoon, Fatso arrived and he and James followed me into the marble bathroom to inspect his work. I lay back on the table, unrestrained this time. I wasn't there for anything other than an inspection to ensure all was well.

'Looking good,' Fatso commented. 'Nice work, eh?' James nodded.

'Show me,' I demanded and James reached for a mirror. The two rows of rings gleamed in the bright lights and looked very well settled. I didn't let either of the men see just how much I was beginning to like them.

'You're my personal property from now on,'

James said with a grin. He held up the mirror again and showed me my pussy. 'My own version of a chastity belt. You once said you'd fantasised about being locked into a chastity belt. Available only to your master. Well, this is it. A purely psychological belt of your own making. Every time you consider being faithless, you will think of the rings. Every man you're intimate with will see my mark. There is no way you can forget your duty – the rings will remind you. I want to keep you just for me, don't I?' His laugh echoed round the bathroom. And I was hugely excited. Something of the slave girl must have surfaced. The thrill of knowing I was locked up tightly, preserved for one man alone by virtue of my own conscience, had me boiling over with lust. Uncomfortably, I walked slowly after James. At the same time, I cursed my big mouth that had ever let him know about this most secret fantasy of mine. My own imagination could never have conjured this version of a chastity belt.

'How do I get out of this, purely as a matter of interest?' I asked.

'When I unlock you,' he replied with a grin. 'Just like the knights of old going away to war. Then your mental allegiance to me will disappear. Now, I must be off or I'll miss my flight. Enjoy your tour and behave. I don't really need to say that, do I?' he dropped a kiss on my cheek and rushed out of the room and the house.

Alone, I stood trying to make some sense of what was happening. Obviously, he wanted to prevent me from having sex with anyone while he was away. Presumably, he was still free to do whatever he chose. What a bastard, I thought. What a complete and utter bastard. What a mind game. If he thought I was going to sit back and let him dictate to me, he'd got another think coming. I'd get the whole lot removed, as soon as I possibly could. And with it any mental loyalty I might feel – because, frighteningly, the idea was making me feel rather wet. Dexi would know what to do. I went to phone my friend.

When Dexi answered, I was suddenly inhibited about asking the question burning on my lips. How on earth did I tell him what I'd allowed to take place and that a man was holding my pussy captive by psychological suggestion alone? It would have made me look a total idiot if I changed my mind. I'd lose any respect he felt for me and that mattered a lot. Though we discussed most things, it did not include my own pre-disposition to bondage games. Fortunately, he prattled on about the arrangements he'd made for us. I needed at least a couple of weeks to get myself back into the peak of fitness and was happy to work out while he organised the final details. He was enthusiastic and full of plans. He'd insisted that anyone booking a bout, filled in a few details about themselves. Though it was hardly fool-proof, at least it meant that I was given good grounds for refusing a fight if they were obviously wrong. If someone claimed to be a hundred and fifty pounds, for example, and turned up looking like Giant Haystacks, I had legitimate reason to refuse him. I was particularly excited by an invitation to fight in Mexico. Dexi was immediately getting carried away by the idea of exotic costumes. Personally, I'd had enough 'exotic' to last me for a while.

I'd still avoided telling Dexi about the embellishments to my anatomy but I knew the time was drawing close when he'd discover them for himself. He must have thought it odd that I didn't request his massages. The rings had actually caused very little problem. They were healing well. Fatso's lotion had been most soothing and, as long as I kept up with the demanding hygiene ritual, all would be well. I plotted my own retribution. I'd find some way of treating him to his own medicine. A cock lock sounded very attractive to me. Even castration entered my mind at some of the more stressful moments. I sat feeling frustrated and so damned hot for relief. How long was it going to be before I got a shag? Masturbation was great, but I wanted bodies. Jesus! It was just a psychological trip. There was no way he was going to keep me from having sex by a mind game alone. Two months before I saw him again, near enough. How could I have got myself into this? Damn James William Travers. He was well ahead in the dominance stakes. At least four–love the scoreboard read.

The day before I was to leave for my tour, Dexi came into the gym as I was finishing my workout.

'Do you want a massage?' he asked, setting up the table.

'I'm not sure,' I stalled. He took no notice and laid out a towel for me. I peeled off my top and kept my pants on. He stared at me.

'You have something to tell me, I gather.' He stood waiting, six foot four of handsome hunk who would be enough to melt any heart, especially if it were a male heart. I looked down and slid myself out of my pants. He stared at my naked and be-ringed pussy. 'Well, well,' he said.

'Oh Dexi ... I don't know what to say. It was James's idea.'

'You surprise me. How on earth did he get you to agree to this lot?'

I looked away. I took a deep breath.

'Helluva turn-on, isn't it?' I admitted. 'You know

the kinkiest thing? They're more of a souvenir. To remind me not to drop my pants for anyone else. Frustrating maybe, but think of our reunion.'

'That's a very clever head trip, I'll say that.' He smiled. 'You'll have to make do with the economy massage. No extras for you, my girl.' He began his ministrations. It seemed an age since I'd felt those familiar hands on my body. I desperately needed some relief. I parted my legs as far as I could and invited him to extend his massage to an upgrade. He pushed fingers into my pussy and moved about. I felt myself softening and beginning the drift towards contentment but, as my lips swelled, the tension grew and I felt myself pulling against my own guilt over being unfaithful. I couldn't believe James could affect me this way. But he was right – the rings were a big, fat, sodding reminder that it was only his will that was keeping me from Dexi's pleasuring. Worse, it was working. I was so turned on. Dexi worked on me, trying so hard, but I simply did not reach the magical point of meltdown, because every time I got near I thought of the rings.

'Bloody man,' I yelled in frustration. 'The shit. Bastard. Where the hell is he? I demand he comes back immediately and unlocks this. It's a fucking head trip.' I may have been willing to go with the piercing but I'd never agreed to the mind game. Well, maybe only because I hadn't known the whole plan. I could see that Dexi was amused but he had the good sense not to comment. He finished my back and slapped my backside.

'Come on. We have an early start. A busy few weeks will make us plenty of dough and then we can think about our future.' I sensed that everything was about to change.

* * *

America was exciting. Everyone seemed so enthusiastic. Our booking system worked smoothly. At one place I stayed, several girls were taking on partners and we even spent a few evenings comparing notes in the hotel bars. Some of the girls were absolutely gorgeous, while others were positive dags. Most of them seemed much more business-like than I felt but when we compared fees, I knew I was a winner.

A girl who fought as Bobby-Lou suggested we did some training together. I said I didn't fight women but she persuaded me. Dexi and her manager came with us to watch. She was as tall as me and a similar build, though her style was very different. My strength was always in my legs and my winning hold, a body scissors, using my strong legs. She specialised in flying tackles, dropping to a cross-press. We fought half-heartedly but, suddenly, something in me knew I needed to beat her. I began to fight to win rather than merely work out. She fought back and soon we had a good match going. We flipped each other over in turn. We rolled on the ground, each trying to get that final hold. At last, I feigned a movement one way and seized her. I got her down on the mat and she was beaten.

'Submit,' she yelled with a laugh. 'You're sure good, honey. We could make a few bucks fighting together. How about a double hander?'

'We're pretty well booked up,' I began to say. 'Besides, I only do private bouts.'

'You must be mad. So am I booked up. But we may be able to take in something together. Where d'ya go next?'

'One week in Phoenix and then we go to Mexico.'

'Couldn't be better,' her manager Brett, chipped in. 'We're doing Mexico in a week, too. We have an exhibition bout. Very, very nice money. We could cut you in on the deal and push for double stakes. What d'ya say?'

Dexi looked at me questioningly.

'How much are we talking about?' he asked.

The figure mentioned left me reeling. Even allowing for the dollar exchange, this was serious money.

'You think they'll cut me in for a similar amount?' I asked thoughtfully.

'Sure do, hon. You seen much of the Mexican style? Lotsa flying kicks and plenty o' pzazz. I can give ya some tips, providing ya don't use 'em all on me and win.'

'If you're sure they'll pay me the same.' Bobby-Lou nodded confidently.

We spent the next couple of days planning, practising. The bouts were all totally choreographed here. I was very disappointed. I'd seen the American men wrestling on TV back home, so I suppose I'd known what it was like. But it seemed so contrived. I knew I'd forget the routine once I got going but maybe I could manage to learn enough to take us through a few bouts. Especially if it was to earn such mega bucks. I could probably afford to take several weeks off after that.

Bobby-Lou joined us in Phoenix, taking a few private clients herself. Dexi seemed to be in a strange mood most of the time. I questioned him but he shrugged me away. He seemed to be getting on well with Bobby-Lou's manager and took to drinking in various bars with him when work was done for the day. Us girls also spent time together, chatting and getting to know each other. I had no girlfriends at all. I hadn't had a girlfriend for years. It felt good to have someone to swap tales with. We got to serious girl-talk and she asked about men in my life. I did admit to James but not quite to everything we did together.

'Ever been in a girl-on-girl relationship?' she asked suddenly one night.

'It's not for me,' I said firmly. 'I'm all hetero. Through and through.'

'You might be surprised. You should try it.' I gulped, a real *Tom and Jerry* gulp. I hated the idea.

'No thanks. I'm strictly for the boys,' I insisted. I really liked this woman but not as a sexual partner. I felt inhibited with her from then on and made up my mind never to get into a lone situation, especially where a bed may be handy.

'Would you be willing to double date?' she asked me. I prayed she wasn't talking four females.

'Maybe. Tell me more,' I said cautiously.

'There's a guy who's been asking me about you. Saw you and me together and asked if we'd take a drink with him and his friend.'

'I guess a drink would be fine,' I agreed and the date was set for the following night. I couldn't help liking the idea of playing away from home, if that's what it was. James, after all, was probably doing all manner of stuff, wherever he was. I couldn't imagine the awful Ramon would be keen on celibacy, not one bit. James surely wouldn't have lost face by refusing whatever was on offer? After all, I could hardly do much with my damned conscience working overtime. All the same, the thought of some male company, even if only for an evening, was enough to invoke several sorts of feeling in me. The sort of men Bobby-Lou was talking about would be expecting a hell of a lot more than a polite drink and chat, I'd have staked my life on it. I felt the now familiar strain against my rings as my pussy lips swelled. Pleasure-pain. I'd really grown to love it.

Some days, I was in a state close to orgasm constantly. I couldn't forget it even if I wanted to.

I dressed myself carefully. I wanted to be a 'look but no touching' sort of woman for the night. My short gold dress was held by the narrowest of straps. My nipples were still surrounded by their gold bands and rubbed against the soft fabric. I wore my entire collection of gold slave bangles. The feeling of slave girl was never too far away and kept my whole body hot with anticipation. I wore tiny gold briefs, which I knew would easily be seen if I bent even slightly. I didn't really want the world to see that I wore rings, though. I brushed my hair and left it hanging loose. Light make-up and a spray of the spicy perfume I liked and I was ready. I knew I looked good, alluring even. I was going to beat the James Travers mind game.

I met Bobby-Lou in the lobby.

'Wow!' she muttered. 'I wonder just what you are expecting this evening.'

We went to the bar and waited for our dates to turn up. I expected to enjoy the evening but didn't have any high hopes for my date. When was a blind date really successful?

Two guys came into the bar and homed in on us. What lookers! They could both have been rivals to most of today's crop of film stars. I could hardly believe our luck – I wasn't bothered which was the one who was supposed to fancy me. Either would do quite nicely. They took us for dinner first. A glorious hotel on the edge of town. The gardens were spectacular and we walked among the fountains, cactus park and sat sipping cocktails as the sun went down. Bobby-Lou and her guy were practically climbing up each other's legs and soon made their excuse to leave us. Tom, as he claimed his name to be, was slower to make his move. To tell the truth, I still wasn't sure what my reply would be, if he did ask for something more. I licked my lips, wishing the keys to my padlocks weren't deep in James's pocket, somewhere in South America.

Chapter Fourteen

'How about a nightcap?' Tom asked, as I was making noises about getting back to my hotel. 'My apartment is on the way. I have some wonderful old cognac you might like to try.' I hesitated and remembered the last cognac I'd drunk was during our orgy, when I needed it to help me through a particular form of delicious torture.

'I'm not sure I should,' I hesitated. 'I ought to get back to my hotel.'

'As you like,' he agreed, disappointingly. We rose and took a cab. 'Change your mind?' he asked. 'I live just off this street.' I took a breath.

'OK. Just a quick drink then.' He leaned forward and instructed the driver. He swerved off at high speed, causing me to fall against Tom in the back. Immediately, he laughed and began to stroke my thighs. His fingers were soft and smooth and pretty soon my rings were reminding me of all the things I couldn't do. I felt myself growing more and more excited. It had been several weeks since I'd had any man anywhere near me, not counting Dexi.

Tom's apartment was large, typically American. I sank back into a huge, white leather sofa and accepted a large balloon glass of cognac. He bent down and slipped off my shoes. Thoughtfully, he stroked my gold ankle bands.

'These look like restraints,' he murmured. He moved to my wrists and the slave bangles on my upper arms. 'D'you go for this sort of thing?'

I licked my lips. I wasn't sure it was at all sensible to allow him access to my peculiar cravings. I had to remain faithful to James. I knew I'd regret it if I didn't. On the other hand, what could I do? I was still searching for an answer when he slipped off my shoulder straps and exposed my tits in their little gold crowns. He stroked them, his eyes firmly on mine. The red buds at the centre of my nipples were engorged already and standing proudly erect. He didn't show any surprise at my adornment and seemed turned on himself at the sight. Hell, so was I.

'Most unusual. Beautiful. It looks painful,' he added.

'Not at all,' I lied. Pleasure-pain was roaring through my body, with my various gold rings, including the hidden ones, being stretched to the limit. It must be the way blood vessels dilate and cause every band around the body to press hard. I was burning with desire and frustration. Tom persisted in caressing my nipples and cupped the whole of my breasts in his hands. He lifted them and began to suck slowly, the very centre of one nipple at a time. What was I doing? I hardly knew the man and here I was, being 'unfaithful'. Sod James, I thought. Why should I always be the one to suffer? I relaxed and allowed the wandering hands to roam over me.

Gradually, Tom worked my dress off. I lay with

my pants stretched over my still hairless pussy. He pushed fingers into the shiny fabric and then stared in surprise. He untied the side ribbons and slipped the pants clear. He stroked my naked mound, and leaned down to kiss it.

'You certainly are an unusual woman,' he whispered. 'Full of surprises.'

'You ain't seen nothing yet,' I muttered, wondering what he would say when he saw the next revelation.

'Let's go to bed,' he said, his voice thick with lust. I rose and knocked back the rest of the brandy. I already felt slightly drunk. I didn't know if it was the alcohol or my mood. I followed him into his room. The bed was enormous but the decor slightly austere. Typical man, I thought. He stood by the bed and I moved to him, sensuously unbuttoning his shirt. I unzipped his flies and his cock sprang out, more than ready for action. He watched as I moved around him, sliding his underclothes away and tossing them to one side. I wasn't in the mood to be a slave tonight. I'd make him be mine. Besides, I was in the mood for the top berth.

I pushed him on to the bed and glanced around for things to use. The bed had a metal frame. I was certain it had been specially chosen. I pulled open a drawer beside the bed. As I'd suspected, handcuffs awaited. I snapped them on to his wrists and hooked them through the bed rails. He didn't protest. I pulled his legs apart and straddled him, fairly gently or I'd have pulled against my rings and probably damaged myself. His cock was standing to attention and I stroked it to get the feel of it. I noticed he'd brought the brandy through with him and I took the stopper out of the decanter. I poured a little over his erect cock. He winced at first because of the cold and then at the slight burning sensation. I was an old hand with neat spirit. I licked it off him and pushed my wet tongue into his mouth so he could taste it too. He smiled.

'I knew you were something special,' he whispered. 'What else are you going to do to me?' Now, if that wasn't an invitation, what was? I lifted myself off him and explored the drawers for more toys. He had a selection of rings and clips. I selected one which I knew would restrict his cock and another for his balls. I remembered James's expression the first time I'd improvised on him. Why did I have to keep thinking of that bastard? I foraged for more goodies. I picked up a shiny metal rod and looked at it. A second piece slipped out and a third. They locked together to make a stretching pole. I found chains to attach to the ends and soon had him fixed to it, his ankles held in chains and his legs wide apart. I pushed it wider and he took a deep breath. This was very much easier than the leg spreads I gave my wrestling opponents. I stood over him, looking down at his poor tight balls. He was suffering beautifully. I watched his eyes as they focussed on my sex, exposed clearly for him to see. He looked at me incredulously.

'Those are lovely rings,' he said, in a voice so husky with lust that I could barely hear.

'Thank you.'

'There's something in my cupboard you could wear, if you like.' I turned to look. What more did he want for heaven's sake? I was almost nude apart from a wide smile and several expensive gold bands. Now he wanted some freaky costume. If I hadn't been so damned kinky myself, I might have slapped him. In fact, when I thought of it, it was a good idea to slap him. I slapped his legs to begin with and then moved up his body. I slapped his face and began to move down his body. As I approached his prick, I continued to slap. He was moaning and rolling around the bed, as far as his tethered arms and legs allowed. I swiped his cock gently. He cried out. I was careful. No use damaging the goods before you've fully inspected them. His long, thin cock was dark, engorged and would have been more than ready to shoot except for my positioning of the locks. I went to his cupboard to see what delights he had waiting. I slipped the black shiny vinyl suit over my limbs and pulled the zip up to the top. I might have guessed it would be black and probably vinyl. It fitted like a glove and seemed to have been made for me. I pulled on high boots and strutted across his room, immediately becoming the madame he craved. My juices were running by now and I wondered how I was going to deal with my own needs. I felt between my legs and realised that there was a second zip which would allow me to be exposed for the full length of my slit and right up to my waist at the back. It left me plenty of choice.

He lay there while I played with him. He moaned and groaned, writhing and twisting in his bonds. The more I hit him, the better he liked it. After a while, I was getting very bored. I knew I needed him inside me but as soon as I released his bound cock, he'd shoot and I'd get nothing. I unzipped the covering over my bum and sat on his still hard cock. I stretched my legs out, gripping my heels against his head. He seemed to like that and moaned even more. I lowered myself right down over him and was just about to tease his slender cock into my wet opening. I hesitated.

I thought of James.

I straightened up.

Dammit.

'Fuck James,' I hissed to myself. If only. 'Bastard, bastard, bastard,' I moaned. Maybe, I thought to myself, moving my position, maybe the rings only signified *pussy* faithfulness. James himself had introduced me to the pleasures of anal sex. Perhaps if I let this one into that narrow, dark place, it wouldn't count. I remembered the time I was filled in every place, when I was James's slave girl. Orgasms? Every movement in every place had sent me soaring. Maybe my bumhole would provide something to satisfy me.

I unfastened his wrists and ankles and knelt before him. He rolled over and knelt behind me.

'Make it good,' I commanded. He massaged the narrow opening and gradually, inserted his fingers to stretch me. He grasped me round the waist and gently eased his long shaft into my rear. He moved slowly at first and then faster. I felt myself beginning to float away as spasms ran through my body. Rivers of fire, weirdly different, stretched my bumhole open to accommodate the full length of his cock. It felt good, but still no climax. To come I had to have my clit attended to. But just as I put my fingers down on the magic spot, I thought of the rings. And I stopped. Jesus Christ! I shuddered and collapsed. He knelt still, looking as if he was about to have a heart attack. Poor sod. I'd completely forgotten what I was doing to him. I leapt up and quickly released the cock lock. He shot his load all over me. I was glad of the vinyl covering. I lay on him and wiped myself clean. He could barely speak. I panicked for a moment or two. I wondered if I could have done him serious damage, but he was now returning to something nearer normal colour. I was relieved. I didn't fancy having to explain a serious medical condition to anyone under these conditions.

'My God,' he panted. 'You're something of a bastard yourself. Or weren't you shouting at me?'

I realised what he was talking about. I'd yelled out at James, as I was unsuccessful in my intent to come properly.

'Not you, buddy. Sorry. I think you've had enough for one night,' I told him, as I released him.

'Thanks, Lili,' he said, nauseatingly. 'I'd like to play again sometime. I never even asked what you charge.' I stared at him in horror. What the hell did he think I was? It clicked soon enough. Tempting as it was, I was hardly about to let him buy me. That way, he'd expect to pay for my services whenever he wanted. No way.

'I did that because I wanted to. Not for you. Now, where's your bathroom?' I left as soon as I was decent again. That night, I wanked myself into a frenzy. Maybe the stupid chastity thing was working, after all. Maybe it was orgasms themselves that were being denied to me – or at least orgasms in the presence of other human beings.

A couple of days later, we all flew down to Mexico. Bobby-Lou and Brett, Dexi and me. We laughed a lot, designing wilder and wilder costumes. I had the rough outline of what was expected. We planned to buy masks and the more outlandish gear once we'd landed. Before the evening's entertainment began, all the fighters paraded round the venue, a huge auditorium filled with screaming fans. The wilder the costume, the more the crowds yelled. I planned that mine would be the most exotic.

The first morning in Mexico City, Dexi and I set out to find my crazy gear. A mask was essential. In a back-street store, away from the main tourist run, I found a man who produced the most ingenious masks I had ever seen. They were built in layers, and parts could be removed, leaving the wearer still anonymous. I selected a creation that was a couple of feet in height, over all. It was a painted face in the middle with scarlet feathers, gold beads and a mass of woven braids. It fastened over the head with straps, attached to a close-fitting hood. When the main part was removed, the fine silk lining remained, a smaller version of the intricate patterns. I bought it, together with a long cloak, scarlet silk, to match the feathers.

'I'll have to get something new for underneath,' I muttered. 'I haven't got anything suitable, have I?'

'Nope,' Dexi replied. He was still showing a remarkable lack of interest.

The Mexican sent us to another address, off the beaten track. This time, a huge woman was running the shop. She laughed at nothing most of the time. It was infectious and soon even Dexi's mood was lifting. I showed her the mask and cloak and she nodded, going to a storeroom and returning with a bale of shiny red fabric that looked like vinyl. I shook my head.

'I need a fabric that won't split.'

'This won't split, senorita,' she promised.

I felt it. It was as shiny as vinyl but was indeed a stretch fabric. It was perfect.

'But I need it tomorrow,' I said doubtfully.

'No problem. I make, plenty time.'

I described what I needed. Long trousers, skin-tight and some sort of top. I could have nothing loose that could be grasped or pulled away. Most female matches involve one or the other pulling off their oponent's bra top to reveal the tits. It was all part of the scene I'd fought to escape. Why was I doing it again? I remembered. Money. Mega money. I told the woman that I needed something foolproof and she promised to have something ready for me to try on that evening. She even promised to bring it to the hotel, so what more could I ask?

Dexi and I went on a short sight-seeing trip. We'd neither of us been here before and we had to grab a spot of culture. We were meeting Bobby-Lou and Brett later in the afternoon for a rehearsal in the stadium. We discussed our costumes and decided we'd look good together. She was wearing white and, with me in scarlet, we'd make a striking pair.

'And what's Dexi wearing?' asked Bobby-Lou.

'Dexi?' I echoed. 'What's he got to do with it?'

'It's customary for the man to be led into the ring as well. He's your slave figure. He must be there. A good-looking man is just as important as everything else.'

I looked at my friend and secretary-come-manager. He never went on show. He looked slightly worried, but then he grinned.

'OK. If that's what it takes.'

'Great. You should complement her outfit. Scarlet, you said? No problem. Brett can kit you out. You'll need a mask of course, but the rest is a series of straps, basically.' I could have hugged Dexi. He barely flinched. He is never an exhibitionist in public places. If he does do kinky gear, it's always in his own time and space.

'You sure, Dexi?' I asked.

'As long as this is purely a one-off. I'm getting well paid, after all.'

Bobby-Lou and I played out our roles. We were to have two bouts over the two nights and each would win one. The first, she would be determined to beat this pretender to her throne, from Britain. The second bout, I would be seeking revenge and would win. The whole thing was orchestrated. I couldn't bear the lack of freedom. The audience expected all the razmataz, glitz and glamour but seemed happy to accept that the whole thing was rigged from the start. Still, was I going to miss out on the chance of such a generous purse? Not likely.

We took a limo to the venue. It was a huge arena, filled to capacity with a noisy crowd. Music blared out and I peered at the audience from the dressing room. Banners were being waved everywhere and huge great cut-outs of the favoured players were held up everywhere. No one had heard of Madame Lili, nor much of Bobby-Lou, but the crowd was ready to shout or boo at anything. We watched some of the huge men lumbering round and the acrobatic skills of some others. We changed into our exotic costumes and waited. I admit to having more than a little nervous tension. My outfit was perfect. Skin-tight red shiny fabric that looked as if it had been painted on. I added high laced silver boots and finally a traditional hooded mask, also red. The huge feathered mask was added at the end, just as an extra show, along with my all-enfolding cloak. Dexi wore scarlet briefs and a sort of strange harness, provided by Brett. It seemed that the few women wrestlers on the programme always had their studs in tow. I felt uncomfortable with the idea, mostly for Dexi's sake. It seemed demeaning for a friend to be treated this way. My fears were unfounded. Dexi seemed to have taken to the idea in a big way. Some deep-seated exhibitionism had risen to the surface and he was positively relishing the idea of his role.

The fanfare sounded and the Master of Ceremonies whipped up the fervour. He gave both of us a huge build up, until the crowd were roaring our names. Talk about mass hysteria! The hype was like something I'd never experienced. Maybe there was something in this public arena stuff after all. Feeling like the star that had been created for me, I strutted out into the arena. I gulped at the sheer numbers waiting for us. Nerves? Like never before. The crowd chanted names and music crashed around us everywhere. I strode along in my fantastic mask, my cloak trailing behind me like a brilliant flame. I leapt into the ring and Bobby-Lou raced across to throw a punch at me. I snarled back at her, as we'd rehearsed. Brett jabbed at Dexi and he threw up an elbow to deflect the blow. The crowd roared its approval. Dexi came to take my cloak and there were loud whistles as the crowd appreciated my figure. I felt like a film star and revelled in the whole show. My huge mask came off and I was left with the hooded, close-fitting mask that matched the rest of my outfit. Dexi kissed my hand as he left the ring, carrying my gear. Meanwhile, Bobby-Lou and Brett had been doing their own bit in their corner. She was clad entirely in white, though, with looks like hers, virginal did not spring to mind.

We danced around briefly and I began to play the bad girl role we'd rehearsed. I pulled her hair, tried to rip off the mask and bra top and threw her to the ground. I dropped on top of her, cross-pressing and eventually gaining an early lead. We had to make it last for at least twenty minutes, so she could have a long period to fight back. The fanfare blared out in triumph. Bobby-Lou hurled herself at me in a drop kick to my shoulder. I went down quickly, to avoid anything in the way of actual contact. All the same, I clutched at my shoulder, pretending to hurt really badly. I shook my fist at her and she winked back.

Though it was all too contrived to be real to me, I could see the absolute showmanship that kept the sport at the top of the popularity ratings. The careful choreography paid off and the crowd loved us both. We were well matched for weight and height and it was just a matter of entertaining the audience. There was certainly a grace with most of the moves and there was a balletic fluidity to the performance.

Before I could believe it, we were through. It was all over and Bobby-Lou had taken our first bout. The referee came over to each of us and did a live interview for the crowd. This was where we sold seats for the following night. I shook my fist at her and promised revenge. She yelled that she was never going to give in. I said she was a coward if she was scared to fight me again. She ran over to me and dragged my mask and hood away. She'd made several unsuccessful attempts before. I pretended to hide my face. She yanked at my top and managed to expose one of my gold tipped breasts. She stared in fascination. I feigned horror and tried to escape from the ring. Dexi rushed forward with my cloak and flung it round me. Safely hidden, I attacked Bobby-Lou and pulled her mask off. The crowd, booed, cheered and generally went wild.

'Can we go now?' I whispered to Dexi. 'I've had my fill of all this.'

'Think of the dollars, honey,' he intoned.

At last we were done. We paraded out of the ring and back to the dressing rooms. I blew kisses as we went. I reckoned the crowd were around fifty-fifty in their support by now.

'Wow,' Bobby-Lou called out as we flopped down. 'You're really something. You sure you have to go back home? I guess you really know how to work the crowd. We could make a bomb if we went on working together. Think about it, will you?'

'I couldn't face it,' I replied. 'It's fine for a one-off but I couldn't do all the stuff for long.'

'Say, where d'ya get the nipple gear? It's so whacky. You wear them all the time?'

'More or less. They are semi-permanent. I can have them removed but not easily.'

Bobby-Lou licked her lips and came over to inspect my adornment. She fingered the tight pink bud that was exposed and bent down to lick it. It responded to her ministrations. She cupped both my breasts in her hands and bent to nuzzle them. I sat so still that I could hear my own breathing. I felt a mixture of discomfort and desire. She stroked the rest of my naked top and her hands moved down to caress my shiny, red-covered thighs. I sighed as she moved between my legs and began to rub against my crotch. She stopped, feeling my rings firmly locked into place. She looked at me quizzically, one eyebrow raised.

'I don't go with women,' I whispered huskily. I felt strangely turned-on. I'd always hated the thought of another woman touching my bare skin but I was in a state of euphoria after the show.

'Let me see your pussy.'

'I . . . I . . .'

'Come on, lovely. I am dying of curiosity.'

'Please,' I managed to stammer. 'I can't.'

'Just a peek, honey. Maybe it's something I should investigate, if it's what I think it is. I'm not looking for a relationship. Just some fun. I like men too. Obviously.'

I remembered the matching pair of handmaidens who'd attended me in that fantasy, which now seemed like years ago. I'd had a very gentle orgasm then, quite unexpectedly. Bobby-Lou was peeling off my pants and pushed me down against the wall. She prised my legs apart and bent down to get the full picture. She stared at my rings and then touched them gently.

'You're very brave. It must have hurt like hell.'

'Not really,' I said with a smile. 'I actually found the pain quite erotic. They – the rings – are sort of a memento.'

'A memento of what?' she asked.

I pursed my lips. 'Maybe I just look forward to meeting my lover again.'

Her eyes fixed on my own. Her hands explored my pussy, still completely devoid of hair. She flicked very gently at the rings and I winced slightly. Pleasure-pain was seeping through my entire body as I swelled to acknowledge my needs. My breasts became aware of their own bands of gold. Down below, I could feel the juices, waiting, wet in their dark tunnel. Bobby-Lou's fingers probed, stroked and pushed their way inside me and I lay back, letting her do as she wanted. It was gentle, a feeling of comfort, almost. None of the soaring excitement that I was used to. But then, she wasn't touching my clit. Maybe I could ask her to – I opened my mouth, but for some reason I thought of James and I clamped it shut again. I lay back, the pulses beating through me, even if they did not lead to what I'd call satisfaction. I couldn't ask her to touch my clit. I couldn't touch it myself. I couldn't touch her, or bring her to orgasm or even feel her body, magnificent as it was. I couldn't do any of this, because all I could think of was those fucking rings – and James himself.

She seemed to understand, because slowly she withdrew and licked her wet fingers. Always, her eyes were firmly fixed on mine. She slipped her fingers into her own cleft and began to rub herself. She was obviously well-practised and soon showed every sign of impending orgasm. She lolled back against her chair and allowed herself to come with violent shudders of pleasure. I was jealous. Not that she'd done it to herself, but that I couldn't do the same. Once again, I cursed the rotten sod who'd imprisoned my sex this way, however willing I may have been at the time.

'You must love him a lot to let him leave a memento like those rings,' Bobby-Lou said.

'Love him? I hate the bastard.' I almost meant it at that moment. 'He's fixed me good and proper.'

'Get 'em taken out then.'

'I don't know. I sort of like them. They turn me on. They make me feel like I'm someone's possession. Maybe that seems odd to you.'

Evidently it did. She shook her head and went to her side of the room to change. As she stripped, I saw that she carried several tattoos. Something else I've never been turned on by.

'OK for tomorrow? I guess we've got the whole audience roaring and ready for the rematch.'

'Fine. Look, I'm sorry if . . . well, you know.'

'It's OK, honey. It's cool. You should think about things though. Don't be too hasty. You're maybe missing something good.'

I felt exhaustion taking me over. All I wanted was a long cool bath and to sink into my queen-size bed. Alone. My brain was teeming with conflicting ideas. Last night I'd been with a man and I'd got very little pleasure from it. Tonight, another woman had tried to bring me off. I desperately needed to get at my own pleasure centre. James, damn him, had effectively locked it away from me. How could I possibly let anyone control me like that? My thoughts swung from love to hatred for the bastard. Meantime, I'd just have to use any men I wanted, for whatever I wanted. I planned my revenge on the entire male population of the world. I could beat most of them to a pulp in the wrestling ring. I would too, I thought.

Chapter Fifteen

The following night, I had my contrived rematch with Bobby-Lou. At the end, she tried to whip up the crowd to fever pitch, demanding another bout. I snatched the mike away from her and yelled that I was through. I knew I was the stronger and called for my stud to bring my cloak. Bobby-Lou got the crowd yelling for more. She bellowed, 'You too scared to fight a deciding bout? Best of three. Come on bitch!'

'No way. I'm too good for you!'

The banter went on. I suddenly felt totally drained. I wrapped myself in my cloak, put on my huge mask and strode from the ring and the arena. The crowd roared and chanted but I was deaf to their voices. The first night had been good and I'd enjoyed the whole spectacle. This second night had finally proved to me that I didn't want to be a part of this scene any more. Whatever the purse, I couldn't live this way.

'Can we go home now?' I asked Dexi.

'I guess so. It's time, isn't it?'

Bobby-Lou was furious when she came back to the dressing room.

'You're a crazy bitch. That crowd lapped us up. We could have made a real killing on the circuits. Enough to retire on. For heaven's sakes, honey. You can't do this.'

'I'm sorry. I just can't do it any more. It was great. Terrific fun but I just don't want this sort of life.'

'A couple of years, tops. One year if you like. I've never had such a well-matched partner. Please, just think about it.'

'I have. Sorry. It's been great but I have to move on.'

'Back to your bastard keeper. The one who makes you feel guilty if you have a little fun on your own. I'd never let any man do that to me.'

'Maybe you haven't found a man willing to do it to you.'

I thought for a moment she was about to hit me. But she took a deep breath and went over to her own changing area. Quickly she put on her street clothes, shovelled everything into a suitcase and turned to leave.

'It's OK honey. I do understand. Keep in touch, hey?' To my shocked amazement, she came over to me, put her arms round me and planted one of the most erotic kisses I've ever experienced, right on my open mouth. 'Don't you dare forget me,' she said softly and swept out of the room.

'OK,' I whispered to the shadow of her presence. It really was time I went home.

Dexi dropped his own little bombshell during our flight back.

'I've finally decided to give it a go with Joel,' he announced. 'The extra money we pulled in Mexico has made all the difference. I've e-mailed him to tell him I agree to everything. We're going to buy a restaurant.'

'What?' I said stupidly. 'A restaurant? How the hell will you manage that?'

'Joel is a first-class chef.'

'I never knew that.'

'Did you ever think to ask? I think I can do a good job as front of house. I've had the experience, after all.'

I thought about it. He was certainly good at managing my affairs and had a good personality. As for Joel, I admitted, I'd never even wondered what he did for a living. Ironic. Buying a restaurant had been my ambition once. Why had I never discussed it with Dexi?

'I'll miss you. In fact, I don't know how I'll ever cope without you.'

'I think you'll soon be giving up the fighting business. James is going to want you all to himself. Then, I'd be out of a job anyway.'

I nodded, thoughtfully. I found my usual stomach-churning excitement when I thought of James. With any luck, my rings would soon be removed and I could get back to some decent, or preferably indecent sex. Dexi looked at me and laughed.

'I know just what you're thinking. I can read you like a book,' he said, and he lay back against his seat and closed his eyes.

We landed in Manchester at some ungodly hour of the morning. Dexi could hardly wait to get back to Joel and discuss their future. We parted company at the airport. I felt tearful. We'd been together for several years and I was about to miss him like hell.

'Be lucky,' I whispered to him, a boulder-sized lump in my throat.

'Hey, this isn't goodbye, you know. I'll always be around for you. Besides, I expect you to be one of my major customers in the new establishment.'

'Sure,' I replied. 'Give my love to Joel and don't forget my invite to the opening night.'

I waved him off. Having nowhere else to go, I took a cab to James's mansion. I had no idea of my reception there or whether James was even back in the country. I needn't have worried. He'd been back a couple of days and was already trying to find out where I was. He welcomed me with enthusiasm and champagne. I was relieved. Everything was going to be all right.

'I have a few calls to make,' James announced once we had finished the wine and swapped a few traveller's tales. 'Let's have a late lunch and a long, sexy afternoon and evening.'

'Sounds good to me.' I suddenly remembered our last time together and our week-long orgy. I was more than ready to enjoy some proper sex again and thrilled at the prospect of his ministrations. There was no one who turned me on the way he did. He was a beautiful, crazy bastard but I wanted to be with him. No one else would do. Whatever may have happened in South America, he'd come back to me, hadn't he? I spent the rest of the morning soaking in a beautifully perfumed bath. I unpacked and hung my exotic mask on the wall. Maybe, one day, I'd give the whole costume a re-run for James's benefit.

It was almost two by the time he returned to find me. We went down for lunch in the dining room. It felt so weird. The last time we'd eaten here, I was hurting badly from the newly installed rings in my pierced pussy. I remembered the mixture of hate and thrill that had filled me. Now, the wretched, erotic rings were a part of me. The healing process was complete and my body ready to enjoy them, once they were undone. I shivered at the prospect of feeling James releasing me from my 'vow' of chastity and wondered whether the rings would add even greater pleasure.

He led me upstairs to the room we called our playroom. It was back to its usual self. All traces of the exotic Arabian Nights had gone. The wrestling mat was laid out. So, it was to be a domination session, was it? Me on top. I could handle that.

'Your clothes are in there,' James told me, indicating the bathroom.

To my amazement, I saw my own gold dress, the one I'd worn in Phoenix. The same tiny gold triangle that counted as panties was also there, as were my collection of slave bangles. I was puzzled. I slipped the bangles on to my arms, ankles and wrists and pulled on the pants. The gold stilettos were new. I couldn't remember what shoes I'd worn in Phoenix. What was the guy's name? Tom? Whatever, this outfit didn't exactly look like one for wrestling. What did James have in mind? Confused, I slipped on the shoes and tottered back into the playroom.

James stood waiting, gold trunks and bare torso. I faced him, not walking on to the mat in case the spiky heels damaged it. He walked over to me and, with one movement, ripped the dress away. His eyes were hard. He untied the strings at the side of my panties and flung them over his shoulder. I said nothing. Several hundred dollars worth of clothes were now lying in ruins. I wondered briefly why he'd wanted me to dress, if all he wanted was to drag the clothes off me. Part of his complex sex games, I suddenly realised. I felt anxious.

'Shoes,' he gestured. I slipped them off obediently. I stood clad in my slave bangles and nothing else. What was he expecting? I almost dared to step forward and make a shot at a hold, but something held me back. His green eyes ranged over my nakedness.

'Have you something to tell me?' he asked.

'What do you want me to say?'

He dragged me to a chair and bent me over the back. I may have been hot for him without the preamble, but there was something missing here.

'I'm sorry if I failed to please you, my master.' If he wanted slave girl, he could have her. Just as long as slave girl got some decent sex out of her master. I licked my lips, suggestively, provocatively.

'Slut.'

I looked down again. I suddenly twigged. The gold dress and panties. I'd worn them to go out with Tom. Instincts told me that James had somehow managed to spy on me.

'I think you know exactly what I'm getting at.'

'Tom?' I whispered.

'The very same. You couldn't resist, could you?'

'I bet you didn't practise celibacy while you were away.'

'I think the answer would surprise you. However, that's my business.'

'Then, surely, so is whatever I choose to do.'

'I thought I'd made it clear that I wanted you to be mine. Exclusively. The rings don't actually prevent you having sex.'

'They're pretty effective,' I countered.

'They are symbolic. You knew what I wanted.'

'Symbolic or not, they certainly prevented me

from having sex. Do you even begin to understand what it's like for someone like me? I couldn't even have a decent orgasm. Just a half-hearted roll around.'

'It didn't stop you, though.'

'Can't you get it into your head? I can't have sex with these rings in place. Oh yes, I can be fucked. I can touch my clit. But the most important pleasure centre is simply not available. I can't get at my mind, damn you.'

'But you were willing to try.' I stared at him, my mouth gaping like a wet haddock. 'Oh it's all right. Tom's clean. Otherwise I'd never have used him.'

I stared at him in horror.

'Used him? You mean he was a plant? A test?' He nodded and grinned.

'I needed to know if I could trust you. Oh, believe me, you got an excellent report: wild; wacky; uninhibited; willing to try anything. He also liked the body jewellery. It is unique, so there was never any case of mistaken identity.'

'But how on earth did you organise it? I'm sorry. I didn't realise you felt this way. I thought that possessing me the way you do was enough. I never had a proper orgasm at any time. That's in your hands.'

'I know, sweetheart. I know you're a lusty, kinky gal, Lili – that's what I love about you. Tom didn't confirm anything I didn't already know. It's just that . . . even though it was all part of the game, it made me feel . . . strange.' I suddenly realised something. He was plain jealous. Sophisticated, confident James William Travers was jealous.

I noticed his crotch was bulging and hoped he was still going to come my way. I wanted to make it up to him. Quickly he pulled several cushions over and shoved me down on to them. He lifted my legs on to his shoulders and slipped off his trunks. I saw the familiar sight of his glorious cock and felt myself becoming ready for him, anticipating the feel of it sliding into me, filling me as only he could. My pussy was already being stretched tight, as my desire drove me forward. It was the greatest turn-on ever. And then, with no warning, I thought of the rings. Even with *James*, the thought of them still worked like a frigging chastity belt. The last laugh was on him – and me, too.

'For heaven's sake,' I yelled, 'take them out!'

He drew back and I could see the surprise on his face. I think he realised, right then, that he couldn't own me, not entirely. I decided to take action. It was quite therapeutic. Our eyes met first, though, and he winked to let me know he was up for the game.

So I flung myself at his back and knocked him to the ground. I seized his head in an arm lock and he tried to twist away. I looped my legs round his torso and squeezed. I felt him sag, as he accepted that he was beaten. I released him and he rolled over. I made a flying leap at him and pulled him down again. This time, I gave him a body scissors, clamping my legs tight round his middle. He braced against it and I could see his prick rising as he got turned on by his favourite hold. This time, I was about to gain dominance over him. I grasped his shaft and squeezed until he groaned, part ecstacy and part pain. I moved until I could get his balls with my other hand and squeezed them too. I felt merciless.

'Get the pliers,' I demanded.

'What do you need pliers for?'

'What do you think? You've surely proved to your own satisfaction that I'm totally screwed. Or should

I say, the precise opposite. You were just plain jealous, weren't you?' He nodded. 'It's your own fault. You were adamant that I couldn't come with you.' I squeezed him harder and he winced again.

'I'm sorry.'

'Louder,' I demanded. Amazing how confident one can be when in my position.

'I'm sorry. I fucked up. I admit it. I was jealous and I shouldn't have tried to test you.' I grinned in satisfaction.

'Now, are you going to get those damned pliers or do I break your balls?' He nodded. Silently, I let him go and he picked up the trunks he'd been wearing earlier. From a tiny inside pocket, he brought out a pair of pliers and indicated that I should lie back. Those four clicks of the rings being prised apart were the most welcome sound I'd heard in a long time. He removed them and placed them on a nearby table. I felt released. I felt as if my choices were my own again. I also knew that if I had chosen to remove them myself, I wouldn't have felt this sensation of pure liberation. I lay quietly, waiting. I wasn't at all sure what he was going to do. I waited for what seemed a lifetime and just as I was about to get up, he put a hand on my legs.

He smoothed back the flesh and seized the tiny bud of my clit. Gently, he touched it into life and wiped his moist cock over it. I felt the pulses starting to sweep through me, instantly. It was the most glorious sensation. I felt more like myself and completely forgot my frustrations, anger and hurt, as I waited for the most welcome of orgasms to take me over completely. High on my cloud of pleasure, I saw my torturer as the bringer of pleasure once more. I know I'm weird but it's part of me. Maso-chism or something.

'Thank you,' I gasped when he finally rolled away from me. He glared for a moment, then his expression softened.

'Let's give each other a second chance,' he muttered. 'I want you to have sex only with me.' My heart leapt. It wasn't too late.

'I . . . I guess so.' With the sort of sex we had, why wouldn't I promise? I was his obedient slave again. I wanted him, more than ever, the bastard.

'Go and bathe,' he ordered. I rose and went into the bathroom and stepped into the bath that was awaiting me. The warm bubbles caressed me and my fingers ran riot over the exposed slit that had been denied me for so long – at least in psychologi-cal terms. He came in and joined me in the huge bath. He handed me a glass of cold wine that had appeared from somewhere. He pulled my hand away from my ministrations and his own long, sensitive fingers took its place. He nuzzled my breasts. I felt myself drifting away again as his relentless fingers worked on me. I lost track of the time we were lying in the water and the number of times I came. I felt drowsy, detached from the earth and wafted along by rivers of fire and pleasure. When I was sated, he pulled me out of the water and began to dry me. I felt like a child again, cosseted and loved. I realised I'd rarely felt cosseted and loved as a child and laughed gently.

'Happy again?' he murmured softly.

'I reckon,' I replied.

'Good. I didn't want to lose you.' I felt a glow envelop me. 'You're very special,' he continued. This was the nearest thing I'd ever got to a one-man relationship. He laid me down on a fresh, dry towel and dried between my legs. I was too mellow and relaxed to realise what he was doing, until he reinserted the rings and clipped them together again, smiling gently. 'Safely locked away for me,' he whispered. I even managed to smile back. As long as I was unlocked reasonably often, I could cope. I didn't think I'd have that 'chastity' feeling whilst having sex with him in the future, either. I was free to choose. I was in control, and so was he. I felt again the thrill of being possessed, being owned by someone who evidently cared enough to go to such lengths.

For several weeks, everything seemed to be back to normal ... normal for us. In fact, it seemed like being married, or what I imagine that felt like. He went off to work each day and I did things like shopping, meeting the occasional friend and exercising at the gym I'd joined. The rooms we'd set up for me to use in town had now been let to someone else. Without Dexi, I no longer had a business. With James around, I no longer needed it. In the evenings, we sometimes went out for dinner and often wrestled. Sex was frequent and satisfying.

One evening, he arrived home with a couple of men in tow. Business colleagues, he told me. He'd managed to tell Mrs Davis to cook dinner but had neglected to tell me.

'Put on something sexy,' he ordered. 'Something sexy but sophisticated.' He opened the wardrobe and rifled through my clothes. Obviously, I couldn't be trusted to choose the correct outfit. He selected a low necked, very short black dress. 'No knickers. Stockings and suspenders. High black stilettos. Oh, and all the gold bangles.' He nodded to me as he left the bedroom.

'Yessir, certainly, sir,' I muttered to the closed

door. Obviously, I was expected to play some special role this evening. I dressed myself as instructed and went downstairs. The men were drinking and sharing in-jokes. They looked at me lasciviously, undressing me with their eyes. Once we'd finished eating, we went into the drawing room. I felt ill at ease, knowing there were undercurrents flowing. One of the men patted the sofa, encouraging me to sit next to him. I glanced at James, who nodded. Instantly, hands began wandering along my thighs, slipping into the tops of my stockings. I gently but firmly removed the hand, only to find it was then placed along the back of the sofa, from where it began to stroke the back of my neck and down my back. If I was supposed to sit and take it, James could think again. I'm choosy about the men I allow to fondle me.

'I'll pour coffee,' I announced, removing myself from octopus man. James frowned at me. I took no notice. I passed the cups to the three men. As I reached James, he casually let the spoon drop from his saucer. It was quite deliberate, as was his request that I should pick it up. I knew exactly why he'd done it. As I bent down, the other two men would get a full view of my be-ringed pussy. No wonder he'd told me not to wear knickers. I assumed he was demonstrating my obedience. He knew I couldn't resist the chance of getting men turned on, even if they couldn't touch.

'These two gentlemen are very interested in wrestling,' he told me. 'I suggested you might fight a bout with them. You don't mind do you, darling?' I glared. Of course I minded. I'd agreed to be James's exclusive partner. I was finished with taking on just anyone. 'Lili, I asked you a question.' He was looking at me carefully. He'd probably punish me later if I disobeyed. I grew hot at the thought of it. It was worth the risk. I licked my lips and allowed myself to imagine what he might do to me. I still hadn't replied. With a thunderous expression, he rose to his feet and grabbed my wrist. He dragged me out of the room. 'You'll do it,' he told me. 'What's the big deal? Go and change and get yourself ready to fight. I'm proud of you. I want to show you off.'

Sulkily, I turned and walked away. I was fighting my own battle inside. I adored my life and didn't want to lose it, or James. Was it really such a big deal? I'd fought enough strangers before, and always won. Maybe being James's slave had become something more private to me. I shrugged my shoulders and went up to the playroom. In the changing room, he'd put out a costume for me. A cobweb-fine stretch suit in silver grey. It had long sleeves and legs and seemed fairly modest, in that nothing was exposed. When I put it on and pulled the zip down from the top, I realised that it finished well before the crotch. There was a gap that stretched from just below my stomach through to my bum. Great, I thought, just when he has visitors, he allows me to fight with total pussy exposure. If that's what he wants, fine, I thought. I was getting mad. In fact, so mad that I'd have taken them both on at once and probably insisted that they both fucked me senseless afterwards. Maybe that's what he intended. Doubtless he'd watch and even take films of me doing it. I tugged on the silver wrestling boots and laced them tight. I surveyed myself in the mirror. Various parts of my body showed through the filmy fabric, especially where it was stretched. My gold nipple covers showed clearly, the centres exposed and standing proud.

I clipped on the slave bangles, as if to make a

point, and went into the playroom to await my opponents. This was all about James getting carried away with one of those men things. Childish boasting, as far as I could see. James had led them through another door and they came into the room ready changed into shorts. They both watched me as I moved on to the mat.

'Nice outfit,' one of them said. 'Pity we're not wrestling in water. Wet that costume and nothing's left to the imagination.'

'You're right.' James leered. 'Go and take a shower, Lili, without removing the clothes, of course.' He moved towards me. I held up my hand in mock surrender and went to soak myself under the shower. I dripped back, leaving a trail over the floor. Well, I did exactly what I'd been told. He said nothing.

'Can we have some of these lights on?' number two asked. James obliged, turning the spotlight to illuminate me so that nothing was left to the imagination. I gritted my teeth and smiled. I decided to forget my irritation and realised that I could enjoy it, if I only allowed myself to relax. I'd got three men all drooling over me, for heaven's sake. I stood tall. I may have been treated as a slave by James but I was determined that I would soon be in control of this particular fight. I knew I could easily get them all turned on. In fact, bulges were already evident in the fronts of both pairs of shorts. And besides, my chastity belt was still in place, wasn't it? Why should I worry about showing off my body? It was a very good example of a body. Obviously, James wasn't going to be jealous, not when he was in total control. I suppose he was turned on by wanting to share part of me. I'd show him all about control, later, I promised myself.

I stood poised and ready for action. Red Shorts came at me first. He'd obviously wrestled somewhere before and knew a few moves. I could see he was reasonably fit and prepared myself to counter his attack. It was almost too easy. He went down heavily as I caught him off balance. I clamped my legs round his middle and squeezed. Body scissors. Never fails. He lay gasping for breath and tried to move every which way. Eventually, I relented and allowed him to wriggle free, only to turn him over the next second and clamp his head between my thighs. He reached up and cupped my breasts, both of them, pinching hard as he did so. I felt the metal bands constrict and let go of my hold. I pulled myself free of his clutching hands and stood up, beckoning him to get up as well. He rolled to one side of the mat and nodded at his friend. He joined us and I quickly threw him over one shoulder. Before he knew what had hit him, I dropped on to his prostrate body and caught him in a cross-press. He was helpless and I laughed out loud. I felt a pair of hands grip my ankles and my legs being spread apart. My pussy rings were being tugged at a bit and I yelled out, 'Let me go, bastards!'

My arms were gripped and I was dragged off my opponent. James towered over me, while Blue Shorts rolled away from my hold. Red Shorts leered at me, still clutching my ankles.

'How do you like being on the losing end?' he asked.

'Three on one is hardly a fair fight.' I wriggled furiously, kicking out with both feet so that Red Shorts lost his grip.

'Vixen,' he yelled, rubbing his arms where my second kick had caught him. I yanked my arms free and did a quick roll. No one was going to catch me

234

again. I'd show the lot of them. I was a spitting ball of frenzied activity. I took flying kicks, sharp jabs and didn't much mind where they landed. Both pairs of shorts went down and I hoped I'd hurt them enough to respect me in future. James had stood back, watching in some surprise. When he stepped forward to catch me, I thrust a kick at his nether regions, for once not caring if I hurt him or not.

For several minutes, I condensed my hostility towards the whole race of men into this fight with the trio in the playroom. I was undoubtedly the victor. I didn't intentionally hurt anyone, seriously I mean, but I knew they'd all have more than a few bruises to show the next morning. I wiped my hands together in a gesture of a job well done. I left the room and went to take a shower. I turned the pressure up high and the temperature down low. The jet of water washed away my anger.

I'd gone along with James just so far before the bubble burst. What had he expected? I'd just lie back and think of Britain? Bullshit. I'm happy to fight when the fight is fair. As my temper flowed away, I wondered what I was in for later, when they had left the house. James would certainly not be best pleased that his slave had rebelled. Maybe I'd get punished. Maybe not. I flung on a robe and went into the room that had been given to me for my own use. I lay on the bed. I closed my eyes, trying to hear what was happening, but the doors were thick and soundproof. I must have dozed, as I was jolted awake by James. I opened my eyes to see him standing over me. Before I could even react, he'd slipped a pair of cuffs on my wrists and was dragging me back to the playroom. He stuck my wrists over a hook on the wall, one of the many. He ripped my robe away. He turned and picked up one of his thinnest whips. The swish cut the air but didn't touch me.

'Stop right there,' I yelled.

'You need punishing,' he said, watching me closely. 'I asked you to fight. You tried to make a fool of me.'

'Hold on there a minute. What the hell did you expect me to do? I was being attacked by three at once. What the hell would have happened if I hadn't fought back? You will never do that to me again. Damned men. Your mouths run away without thought at times. Bollock-driven, the lot of you.'

'Don't forget, you wear my rings,' he said softly. 'You'll always wear my rings.' Was I imagining the tears in his eyes?

'OK, James. You've made your point. We'll need to talk about this. Let me go.' Silently, he released me and went out of the room.

Sadly, I went into my own room and began to pack. Fortunately, I still had savings. Mexico had ensured my future, for a while at least. By the time I'd finished packing, I had managed to convert my sadness to anger. He had gone too far. Much too far. I was only his whore in our fantasy games. I no longer had the comfort of *any* control. I stuck my head in the air and picked up one of the cases. The rest of my things I'd send for when I found somewhere I wanted to be.

It was near midnight as I reached the city centre. I found a hotel and checked in. Now the only pain I felt was loss. We both needed time to cool off.

I pushed my fingers down and began to move in towards the centre of my sex, needing comfort. How could I possibly have forgotten? The neat set of rings was still in place. They were locked firm and the bastard I'd just walked out on had the pliers. Oh he'd like that one all right. Never mind, I tried to comfort myself, there's bound to be a good DIY shop somewhere around. I could pick up a pair of pliers myself and remove them in a jiffy.

'Let's face it,' I told my reflection, 'there aren't too many people I can actually ask to do it for me.' Even Dexi was no longer around. I flopped back on the bed, totally exhausted. I fell into a deep sleep and was oblivious until late the next morning.

For the best part of a couple of weeks, I drifted around. I couldn't face the prospect of starting my wrestling business again but, if I had to, I knew I was probably good for a few more years. Maybe after that I could begin to look for the dream that plain, ordinary Penny Jackson had once held: my own restaurant. I glanced through my bank statement. It looked healthy enough for ordinary living. With the rise in property prices, I'd be lucky to afford a small hot dog stand. I knew that I wanted to be with James more than anything. I wouldn't quite admit to loving him, but I suppose it was a pretty close thing. Would he ever regain my trust? Would I want him to? I thought of my rings again. I must find a DIY shop, I told myself for the umpteenth time. I still hadn't worked out how I could tackle the problem.

Chapter Sixteen

'*S*urprise!' I said into the phone.

'Lili?' Dexi replied happily. 'Where are you?'

'In Manchester. How's it going?'

'Great. We're opening in a couple of days. We hope you're both coming to eat.'

'Sure are. Well, I am. I think James and I have just parted company.' I tried hard to keep my voice sounding light and cheerful. I evidently failed.

'Oh, Lili, I'm so sorry. Are you all right? What are you going to do?'

'I'm sorry too but it was never going to be for long. Maybe I could turn waiter for a while?'

'Get your sassy little butt down here. Immediately. Understand? You may not be my ideal choice of waiter but we'll find something for you to do.'

A few hours later, I arrived in Birmingham, where 'Mussels' was about to make its mark. I was greeted like the long-lost friend I undoubtedly was.

'Oh, Dexi, I've missed you,' I said from the middle of a big hug. I noticed Joel standing in the background. 'Joel, hi!'

'Hello, Lili. You OK?'

'Sort of. Good to see you again.' Joel smiled but it was only his mouth that smiled, not his eyes. Despite everything, I knew that he still resented me.

'Come and look around,' invited Dexi. 'We've just about finished everything now. Once the menus are back from the printers, I think we're ready to start cooking on gas.'

'Great,' I said as enthusiastically as I could. It was a pretty ordinary city restaurant, from what I could see so far. 'It's very blue,' I said without thinking.

'Ocean's the theme. We shall specialise in fish dishes. TV cookery has done wonders for the image. Joel knows several people who can supply us, so we've taken the theme for the decor as well.'

I wandered through to the dining area. It was remarkable what had been achieved. This time I didn't need to pretend enthusiasm. It was gorgeous. Way-out lighting, and seaweed fronds, artificial of course, hanging from anywhere and everywhere. It looked like a scene from a movie. Huge fish tanks full of bright fish suddenly reminded me of diving in the Seychelles. Could that really have been only a few months ago? It seemed like a lifetime. I missed James. I was still missing him, every second.

Fortunately, there was plenty to do. For the next couple of days, we all worked like crazy to get everything exactly right. There was to be a freebie for the first night. Local and national press members were invited and various food critics from the major magazines.

'I suppose you'd like me to dress up as a mermaid?' I suggested to relieve the tension the night before the opening.

'Hey, that's brilliant,' Joel said. I thought for a moment he meant it. I settled for a long blue velvet number. I was going to drift around handing out Joel's clever snacks but mostly listening for comments.

By the time everyone was suitably filled with good food and wine, I was ready to throw up. My face ached from smiling but, undoubtedly, it was a success. There should be no stopping Mussels and its two owners.

For the next few weeks, I worked at anything they asked me to. I had a tiny room above the restaurant, tucked away somewhere at the back. Joel and Dexi had the only decent-sized room and there was a small, private sitting room besides. It was hard to get away from each other during our few rest periods. After a month, I really felt in the way. Dexi and I got on as we always had done but I could see that Joel resented me. I sensed that he was jealous. Dexi and I knew each other too well and he felt left out. I knew it was time to move on. The trouble was, I had nowhere to move to. I began to accept dates from some of the customers. I had no real interest in it and whenever anyone wanted to follow it up, I was 'too busy'. I couldn't be bothered. It was boring. Amazingly, I'd gone off sex for the first time in my life. Maybe it was a subconscious thing, a fear that one of the men may have been sent by James. He might well have been testing me. Why did I still feel anything for him? Why did I care? I kept asking myself. There was no logic in me.

'You're not happy, are you, Lili?' Dexi asked one morning.

'Not really. I just feel I'm in the way here. And I'm not doing anything with my life. I've totally lost my way,' I ended sadly.

'You could always get in touch with Bobby-Lou

again. There's plenty of money to be made in the States.'

'I don't think so. It isn't what I want any more.'

'If it's money you need, it seems to me that you should think about what you do best. Remember how much we made, even on the road.'

'I can't go back to all that. Really I can't.'

'Only you can make up your mind. What do you really want, Lili?'

'James William Travers,' I said finally. 'I want James. Whatever went wrong, ultimately I know he's what I want.' I fled upstairs and locked my door. I was shaking. It was partly the shock of coming out with the statement. I had actually admitted to wanting James. I really wanted him. I wanted the excitement of him. His very unpredictability had me enthralled. What we did together fulfilled my every fantasy. How often in life can one man come along, so perfectly willing to do all the things I wanted to do? After all, it was only the once he'd lost his temper in all the months we'd been together. Once we could establish some new ground rules, a cut-off signal if either of us thought we were going too far, everything would be all right. I had walked away that dreadful evening. There would always be that reminder but I knew I had to – wanted to – give us another chance. Being me, I had to do it spectacularly.

I began to do some serious thinking. I'd heard nothing from James since I'd walked. If he'd wanted to find me, he would have done. It surely wouldn't take much imagination for him to realise where I'd go. I wondered if he was still interested in wrestling. He had been something of a fanatic and I knew he still would be. Maybe he'd already got himself a new partner. Maybe not. I thought carefully and planned my campaign.

With the help of another of Dexi's friends, I set up a website, a special secure page, only open to someone who had the code. It cost serious money, but I hoped it would prove worth it. There were a series of animations ... a long-legged woman wrestler, squeezing men the way men seemed to like it. I knew that James especially liked it. She claimed to be an American and offered exclusive, very expensive bouts with selected men, in a hotel near the airport. I'd seen several similar websites and mine had to look good. Convincing.

I called myself the Avenging Angel. The picture, one of my publicity shots I'd never used before, showed me completely covered by a hood and full-face mask. I knew that he might recognise my shape or something about me, but I had to risk that. I added a few fictional letters of recommendation to the site and I was ready. I got a friend to send an anonymous e-mail to James, drawing his attention to the website, complete with the code. I then had to find some way of occupying myself while I waited.

After almost a week, my friend received a reply. It had to be James. No one else had access to the website. The last-name anagram was also a bit of a giveaway. He claimed to be Will Strevar and said he was interested in arranging a bout with the Angel. I leapt around joyfully, delighted that he had taken the bait. I didn't even pause to consider that he was obviously on the lookout for a replacement for me. I wasn't about to let him get the chance of finding anyone else. I sent back my terms and a couple of dates for him to choose. I wondered if I had made the price too exorbitant, but I was determined to enhance my reputation. I was high class, a high earner, and I meant him to know it. As soon as I got his positive reply, I went into action.

I booked the hotel suite and made suitable arrangements. I had the costume made and everything else I thought I might need was ready, in place. I had no secretary or minder this time. I knew exactly how I wanted to manage Mr Will Strevar. If nothing else, at least I'd get the opportunity to demand that he and he alone remove the rings. Because once again, they were like a mental chastity belt – keeping me pure, keeping me faithful to him. I was really hung up on him! I needed to be back in control of myself, every last part of me.

I felt strangely nervous as I prepared for his arrival. I'd arranged the room pretty much as I had done in the past. The large wrestling mat, white this time, filled the floor area. I'd put out towels and drinks and various piles of signed photographs of myself, disguised as the Avenging Angel. I'd had a giggly afternoon in a studio in Birmingham a couple of weeks ago. Joel and Dexi had provided me with a couple of their friends to act as my opponents for the pictures. There was no way that James would recognise them. I went into the bedroom to get ready.

I poured myself into the skintight white leather suit. The hidden zip pulled it close to my bare skin. I've always loved the feel of soft leather on bare skin. The sleeves were very long, finishing in points attached to two rings over my middle fingers. I twisted my hair into a soft pleat and clipped it down. The hood was also close fitting, zipping down the back to cover every inch of my face except my eyes and mouth. I'd even contemplated wearing tinted lenses in case he recognised my eyes but decided that was going too far. I wanted him to accept me as a stranger until I was quite ready to reveal myself. I finished the outfit with a pair of ultra-high boots. I wouldn't wear them for wrestling of course, but they created the first impression I wanted. I looked sinister but alluring. I'd applied a slash of bright red lipstick that was visible through the hood. I felt incredibly sexy, even though my entire body was completely hidden. The familiar tug against my locks began, as my sex was getting itself prepared for whatever was about to happen. The lower part of my abdomen was beginning to boil. The phone rang and I picked it up.

'You have a visitor madame. Is it OK to give him your room number?'

'Fine. I'm expecting him.' I dropped the phone. This was it. Probably the most important fight of my life. I heard the lift swish to a halt and seconds later my doorbell rang. I took a deep breath and went to let him in.

'Hello, er … Angel, I suppose. Do you have another name?'

'Angel does fine,' I said in my pseudo American accent. 'Glad to meet you.' I hoped he didn't notice how my hand was trembling. He looked devastatingly gorgeous. I thought he may have lost a pound or two. His casual muddy-green slacks and silk shirt were a perfect match, to each other and his eyes. He carried a sports bag.

'I'm a little out of practice,' he began. I smiled. I was glad. It meant he may not have been seeking too many other women after all. On the other hand, he probably wanted me to think he was less strong than he really was. I remembered being caught that way before.

'You wanna change through there?' I asked, pointing at the bathroom.

'Right. Well, OK. Won't be long.' He disappeared and I had the distinct feeling that he felt ill at ease. So he should be. Maybe he was just acting. I didn't care. I was about to prove my superiority. If nothing else, I'd make him realise what he'd been missing. Once I'd got him beaten and finally showed myself, I'd be the one making the terms and conditions. If, of course, I still decided he was worth fighting for. My gut was telling me he was. He came back into the room wearing a pair of silk boxers. Black ones.

'Pardon me,' I said loftily. 'I left something out for you to wear. It's my particular preference. Go get it on, please.' I examined my red nails with interest. He gave a shrug and came back holding the leather thong I'd put out for him.

'This?' he said incredulously.

'Sure. It covers the essentials.' It was soft white leather, matching my suit exactly. 'I like my men to be co-ordinated with me.' I grabbed his boxers and ripped them off. He looked surprised. He stood with his legs parted, making sure I saw his large, smooth cock. He covered it carefully with the white leather and hooked up the straps of the posing pouch at the back. I waved my hand for him to turn round. The thong slipped neatly between his buttocks, emphasising the roundness of his lovely tight arse.

'Nice,' I said, slapping it gently. 'Now get my boots.' He stared at me, about to say something, but he stopped. I stuck out a leg in front of him and he knelt down. He unzipped the boots and peeled them down. My suit went right to my ankles.

'Hang on. I want to see your legs. I like legs. Naked legs. Please take that lot off and let me have your legs bare.'

'Nope,' I replied. 'Fighting boots now.' I stretched

my foot out imperiously and he laced on my wrestling boot. The second one was the same. I wasn't even about to ask him what he wanted me to do. This was my show and I was running it, even if he did think he was paying for it.

There was no polite preamble on this occasion. I got right down to it. I grabbed him in a neck hold and pushed my knee into his back. He buckled and sank to the ground. I pounced on him and soon had him in a powerful leg-lock. He was sweating. Both he and I knew he'd met his match. I'd kept myself pretty fit and he was obviously less exercised than me. I let him go and immediately he tried to grab me in a new hold. Easily, I twisted away. A flying drop-kick and he went down again. It may have been called erotic wrestling but there was nothing erotic in what I was doing. He tapped my back to make me release my new hold and I complied immediately. I had to take pity on him. He looked quite shattered suddenly. I needed to lift the pressure slightly. I rolled him on to the ground and gave him my leg-scissors. He groaned with pleasure and I saw his cock rising, filling the pouch delightfully. I felt myself wanting him. That dick was always too much for me to resist.

'If only you'd let me have your bare legs,' he moaned.

'Shut it, slob,' I said in my strong southern accent. 'It's my party here today.'

'But I'm paying through the nose for you.'

'Not yet you don't. But you won't leave without paying handsomely. If you get my drift.' I squeezed even harder and he braced against me. He was totally powerless. I dominated every moment of the fight. Move after move, he lost. Any time his erection looked like spilling over, I let him go again. I wasn't about to give him any relief. I didn't want him calling a halt to the fight until I was good and ready.

'Bitch,' he hissed the third or fourth time I stopped him coming. I laughed. He snatched at my hood. It was too well fitting for him to make any impression. Several times he made the attempt but I was always too quick for him. I clamped him down again and he panted, waiting for me to release him just before he was about to come. He was learning.

'Haven't you got a guard out there?' he panted suddenly.

'No. Do I look like I need a guard?'

'It's usual, I believe.'

'I don't think I need anyone, do you? I don't like sharing my dough.'

James made a huge effort and toppled me over in a moment of lapsing concentration. He held me down and pulled the zip at the back of my hood. I fought him off but he managed to rip it away.

'I knew it was you!' he exclaimed.

'Liar.'

'That leg hold you do is unique. Nobody does it quite like you.' He lay back on the mat, laughing softly. Unable to resist, I dropped on top of him, pressing his abdomen hard against the mat. He groaned once more.

'Enough,' he managed to gasp. I let him go. I sat over him, resting back on my heels.

'So, you're in the market for a new partner, are you?' I asked.

'Only because you dumped me. You were the one who walked out, remember.'

'And you well know why.'

'I'm sorry. I was mad. You'd made me look a fool in front of clients.'

'You shouldn't have assumed I'd fight,' I replied

carefully. 'Not without asking. You made me feel like a whore. I didn't want to think of you as a pimp. I was only ever your whore in fantasy land. When I wanted it too. When it was exciting.'

'You were right. I was carried away by the challenge. I had been boasting about you and I didn't treat you with respect. I am truly sorry.' I was beginning to get fidgety.

'I expected your memory to go away, but it didn't. I couldn't get you out of my mind.'

I lay beside him, quietly. I didn't know what to say. I wasn't used to hearing him apologise.

'How's it going?' he asked. 'You must be raking in the dough. Doubled your prices. And no Dexi to pay. Sorry. Maybe I'm outstaying my welcome. You've probably got your next client waiting.'

'James ... I'm not back in business. This was a special, a one-off just for you. I set you up. I didn't know how else to see you again.' His eyebrow rose slightly and he rose, propping himself on one elbow.

'I see. And sex?'

'I don't do sex any more. Your rings are still in place. And they're still a very potent reminder to keep myself for one man alone.'

'That's hard to believe.'

'Maybe. But true, nevertheless. If you remember, the mental method is pretty foolproof.'

'You surprise me. I'd have thought you'd have removed them.'

'Every time I entered a DIY shop, I could never decide on a pair of pliers. The wrong size, the wrong colour, the wrong brand. And then finally I decided, maybe what was wrong was the act of taking them off. Maybe I wasn't the person meant to remove them. They're symbolic, after all. As you yourself once said.'

He roared with laughter. 'You're priceless. Good job I always carry the pliers with me, isn't it?' He sprang to his feet and went into the bathroom. He came back with the said pair of pliers. He dropped them on top of me and disappeared back into the bathroom. I waited but he did not come back. I felt deflated. At the very least I'd expected some ceremonial unlocking before we copulated. I'd got this far and expected – wanted – so much more. I waited for what seemed like hours. He didn't return. I pushed open the door to see what he was doing.

'Pour me some wine, wench,' he demanded. He was lying in my bath, surrounded by my bubbles. My expensive bubbles. 'Where the hell have you been? I nearly drowned in here several times. Aren't you a trifle overdressed?' He reached over and pulled me into the water.

'Stop it,' I yelled, as my very expensive leather suit was ruined forever. 'This gear cost me an arm and a leg.'

'I'll buy you another. Several. I never expected you to walk out. I'm sorry. I didn't realise I was pushing you too far.'

I stared at him. Another apology. The mighty James William Travers had actually apologised to me, twice. I was confused.

'You know now,' I said shakily.

'I was angry with you. I went too far. I let the slave thing get out of hand. Maybe I was allowing our fantasy into real life.'

'Those two jerks were out of order. You should have talked to me first. I may have agreed to fight your friends, if you'd asked properly. And a clean fight. Not the way it was going.'

'I boasted about you one night when I'd probably had too much to drink.'

'I'm not an erotic sex object,' I said softly. 'Not all the time.'

'I realise. But I thought it was part of the game. Come back, Lili,' he begged.

'Can I trust you?' I asked him. God, how I wanted him. I was hot, wet and juicy. I could feel my rings pulling, pulling at me, reminding me of my desire for him. The chemistry between us had to be something very special.

'I've learned my lesson. Now, are you going to allow me to remove that wet leather from your glorious body?'

I totally surrendered, as he and I both knew I would, eventually. He unzipped the soft white leather and tried to peel it away. It was difficult, wet and constrained by the bathtub. We laughed at our ineptitude. Happy laughter, almost like two lovers coming together after a long break. We gave up the futile task and climbed out of the water. He stood in front of me and removed the garment. It slid to the ground, wet, slippery, like a sloughed skin. I stood still, watching his movements reflected in the mirrors surrounding us. He stroked my naked, damp body. He lifted my breasts, his thumb outlining the rosy dark nipples, still in their circlets of gold. They were hard, erect, screaming for him to suck them. He caressed them and tweaked them just hard enough to make me squeak with pleasure-pain. I felt the familiar surges of need between my legs. I was swelling, straining. I parted my legs, hoping he would be directed to release me. I wanted that feeling of pure liberation – almost as exhilarating as enslavement, in its own way. He well knew what I wanted but he was teasing me. Playing with me.

'Lie down,' he ordered. I sank to the ground, trying to tug at the towels, to relieve the hard, cold marble of the floor. He pulled them away and began to dry me. He used the roughness of the towel to rub my skin to a rosy pink, wiping, teasing me to a point of need that was becoming unbearable.

'The pliers,' I gasped. 'In the other room.' He stood over me, smiling, shaking his head. 'Bastard,' I muttered. Suddenly, he pulled me to my feet and led me into the main room: the room where the huge wrestling mat was still in place. I bent to reach the precious pliers but he held my hand out of reach. I looked at him, longingly. I pleaded. He kicked the pliers out of my reach and lay down on top of me. I could feel his hard prick pressing against the rings on my pussy, pushing against the metal hoops. I was giddy with longing and desire. He rolled on to his back, pulling me over him. I leaned back, stretching my legs out beside him. He could see how ready I was.

He rolled me on to my back again and parted my legs. He stroked my rings, shifting them very slightly, just enough to allow me to feel the movement. I was so very nearly coming, I almost yelled. He flicked the rings again, shooting pleasure-pain through my entire body. He took his cock in his hand and played it round the whole area. He lay back and stretched an idle hand towards the pliers. He sat up, pushing my legs away from his. He held the pliers in his hand. I waited for the moment. I was still waiting as he bent his head over me. His tongue played round the edges of my rings, his warm, moist tongue sending jets of fire surging through me. I wanted him, God how I wanted him inside me. I was still confined behind his wretched locks. He toyed with the rings using his exciting tongue and began to lap at the juices in my deep cleft. I was limp, hot with longing and impatient for action. He leaned back and grinned at me. He was enjoying the suspense. I was nearly crazy for him.

I reached out to take the pliers. I knew it wasn't the same thing, symbolically, if I undid them myself, but I had to regain some control. I put the pliers in his hand and lay quietly waiting. At last, he sat up and moved to look again into my sex. He gently took the rings and unclipped them, then gently removed them. Now I was free again. If I was giving myself to him, it was because I wanted to, not because of a mind game. I lay back, opening myself as wide as I could, waiting, waiting for his touch on my sex bud. He touched it lightly, so lightly that it made me want to scream. His hands felt cool against my inner flesh. Maybe it was just me who was hot. He licked me, sending me straight to the dizzy heights of an instant orgasm. It took no effort to make me come and come. Bliss.

He thrust his hips forward, pushing deep, deep inside me. The familiar feeling of him filling me was total heaven. We rolled over together until I was on top. I sat up straight, gasping as I felt his length pulsing against me. I rode him, feeling his every thrust. I rode him hard. Panting. Gasping. Loving every fucking minute of it. When he finally came, I allowed myself to crest with him, my fingers working frantically on my clit. I fell back, panting.

Before long, he rolled me over and began to massage my anus. I felt muscles contracting and opening to his movements. Using our own mixed fluids, he moistened the narrow opening and coaxed it to widen. I could make no sound as I lay in anticipation. I felt him pushing against me. His cock was already stiff and ready to go. Gently, he slid it into my lubricated passage and I gasped once more as he filled me so completely. I hardly dared move in case I tore my flesh. His fingers slid beneath me, seeking my hidden bud. I could have wept with frustration as he came so close to it, without touching it. He was driving me wild all over again. He rubbed gently around everywhere but the vital spot. As he pushed into me, his rhythm increased. Then the ecstasy reached me, as he scraped his nails against the very spot I needed him to. By now, I was so stretched and lubricated that every slightest movement felt wonderful. Another gut-wrenching orgasm shot through me, leaving me yelling, totally incoherently. He pulled out and fell back on the mat. He lay panting for several minutes, his body soaked in sweat. I was slick with my own moisture and lay beside him, sliding against him to feel the full length of his beautiful body.

'Now, isn't it worth the deprivation just for this?' he croaked. I was too busy to reply. The instant he removed his fingers, my own fingers sought out my clit. He laughed softly. 'You're a very greedy thing, aren't you?' I saw that, yet again, he was stiff and ready. He pushed himself into me. 'Nice feeling,' he said huskily. I had to agree. Again, I felt that soaring, ringless liberation. I ground myself against his pubic bone, pulling him closer and tighter to maximise the effect of being unfettered. I pushed one finger into my cleft and found the spot. He kissed me at the same time, his tongue filling my mouth and his fingers stretching to probe my bumhole. Every slightest movement was erotic, passionate and deeply satisfying. Because we had already reached our highs a number of times, this particular coupling lasted for a blissfully long time. As we both relaxed, pausing for breath, a sense of euphoria overtook us. We became one single organism, striving for the ultimate in sensuous pleasure. We achieved it.

Chapter Seventeen

'*A*re you coming back home with me?' James asked the next morning. We'd made love, yes, I do mean love – early in the morning when we first awoke.

'It depends,' I said coolly. *Of course I am*, my senses screamed.

'On what?'

'On the terms.'

'Name them.'

I thought for a few moments. I knew exactly what I wanted him to promise, but it's not an easy task to tell someone like James William Travers what to do. I drew a deep breath and began. To give him his due, he did listen. I finished my list of terms.

'I'm not giving up anything,' he said with amazement.

'I'm not asking you to. I love our games just as much as you do.'

'And making you dress up is a part of it, even when you seem to hate what I do to humiliate you. It's a part of the ritual.' He reached over to my legs and pushed them apart with his own. I was about to protest that I wanted to establish our rules first, when he dived down beneath the covers and began to lick me. I knew I couldn't speak, not for several minutes. I lay back and enjoyed his ministrations. I drifted away for the umpteenth time on a cloud of sheer physical pleasure. I almost didn't notice as he reinserted the rings and pressed them into place once more. He emerged from the covers and grinned.

'Whatever else, I do retain charge of your intimate places.'

'All right,' I said, mollified.

'You know, these rings are so successful, I wonder if we shouldn't consider other piercings. I'm told that there are many more intimate places that can improve the satisfaction for both of us. What do you think? Do you think you'd feel just as beholden? Just as faithful?' He rubbed the exposed tips of my nipples. The metal clamps tightened, as they always do, as my breasts swelled to the stimulation.

'I'll think about it.'

'You must admit, it gives a real edge, for both of us. I can see you're turned on by your rings. Admit it.'

I remained silent. He was right. I did like them. I was very turned on by them. I did feel it gave me an edge. It was unusual, but he was right. But I insisted that I would be the one who chose when and if I was going to be adorned with more rings – or partake in any subsequent mind game.

'Of course, I should organise something for you,' I said with a grin. 'Maybe a permanent cock lock would be a good idea.'

'Don't even think of it. I shall have to think of new ways to use what is in place already. There must be lots of ways I could use the rings to our mutual satisfaction.' He was silent for a moment and then he grinned.

'I agree to your conditions. I won't promise never to treat you as my slave in the bedroom though. A beautiful body slave will always be needed. Are you interested in the post?'

'I guess so.' I knew that I couldn't resist his games. Pinning him down to too many restrictions would take away all spontaneity.

'Let's get back to our playroom. I've got some ideas to try. Get up, slave. Order me some breakfast and then we can get driving.' He reached for his mobile on the bedside locker and dialled a number. 'Davis? We'll be ready to drive back in an hour. I need some fine chains. Pick some up, will you?'

I listened as he specified various sizes and lengths. It sounded exciting. I couldn't wait to see what he had in mind. Using my existing rings, he'd said. I began to imagine various ways he could use the chains to pull at my rings ... damn the man. He'd got me captivated, well and truly. I could hardly wait. I clipped on my beloved slave bangles and awaited my master's instructions.

It would take a long time to explore all the possibilities. I certainly hoped so.

'What exactly are you planning to do with the chains?' I asked James.

'Use your imagination,' he said.

'No need,' I replied. His imagination was quite enough to keep me satisfied for most of the time.

'Lawnmower,' I said suddenly. He stared at me as if I'd gone suddenly mad.

'Lawnmower,' I repeated. 'If either of us wants to stop any game for whatever reason, we say *lawn-*

mower. It's a safety thing. We must both swear to obey it.'

'Why lawnmower?' he asked, looking totally puzzled.

'It's so far removed from everything we do, we're never likely to say it unless we're serious.' He looked at me strangely and then grinned.

'OK. If it makes you happy.'

'You make me happy, James. I really missed you.'

Maybe it will all end one day but for the near future, I know we're going to have fun and plenty of sex!

BLACK LACE NEW BOOKS

Published in April

HOTBED
Portia Da Costa
£6.99

Disaffected journalist Natalie is on the trail of an exposé. Her quest for a juicy story leads her to discover that her staid academic hometown has become a hotbed of sleaze and hidden perversity. Quickly drawn in, Natalie soon falls under the spell of Stella Fontayne – a glittering drag queen at the centre of an erotic underworld. Her sister and rival Patti is in on the action, too, and nobody is quite who or what they seem in this world where transgressing sexual boundaries is the norm.

ISBN 0 352 33614 5

WICKED WORDS 4
Ed. Kerri Sharp
£6.99

Black Lace short story collections are a showcase of the finest contemporary women's erotica anywhere in the world. With contributions from the UK, USA and Australia, the settings and stories are deliciously daring. Fresh, cheeky and upbeat, only the most arousing fiction makes it into a *Wicked Words* anthology.

ISBN 0 352 33603 X

THE CAPTIVATION
Natasha Rostova
£6.99

In 1917, war-torn Russia is on the brink of the Revolution and Princess Katya Leskovna and her relatives are forced to flee their palace. Katya ends up in the encampment of a rebel Cossack army. The men haven't seen a woman for weeks and sexual tensions are running high.
This is a Black Lace special reprint full of danger, sexual tension and men in uniform!

ISBN 0 352 33234 4

PLAYING HARD
Tina Troy
£6.99

Lili wrestles men for money. And they pay well. She's the best in the business and her powerful body and stunning looks have her gentlemen visitors begging for more rough treatment. Her golden rule is never to date a client, but when James Travers starts using her services she relents and accepts a date.

An unusual and powerfully sexy story of male/female wrestling.

IBSN 0 352 33617 X

HIGHLAND FLING
Jane Justine
£6.99

Writer Charlotte Harvey is researching the mysterious legend of the Highland Ruby pendant for an antiques magazine – a ruby that is said to sexually enslave any woman to the man who places the pendant round her neck. Charlotte's quest leads her to a remote Scottish island where the pendant's owner – the dark and charismatic Andrew Alexander – is keen to test its powers on his guest.

A cracking tale of wild sex in the Highlands of Scotland.

ISBN 0 352 33616 1

CIRCO EROTICA
Mercedes Kelley
£6.99

Floradora is a lion-tamer in a Mexican circus. She inhabits a curious and colourful world of trapeze artists, snake charmers and hypnotists. When her father dies owing a lot of money to the circus owner, the dastardly Lorenzo, Flora's life is set to change. Lorenzo and his accomplice – the perverse Salome – share a powerful sexual hunger, a taste for bizarre adult fun and an interest in Flora.

This is a Black Lace special reprint of one of our most unusual and perverse titles!

IBSN 0 352 33257 3

To be published in June

SUMMER FEVER
Anna Ricci
£6.99

Lara McIntyre has lusted after artist Jake Fitzgerald for almost two decades. As a warm, dazzling summer unfolds, she makes the journey back to her student summer house where they first met, determined to satisfy her physical craving somehow. And then, ensconced in the old beach house once more, she discovers her true sexual self – but not without complications.

Beautifully written story of extreme passion.

ISBN 0 352 33625 0

STRICTLY CONFIDENTIAL
Alison Tyler
£6.99

Carolyn Winters is a smooth-talking disc jockey at a hip LA radio station. Although known for her sexy banter over the airwaves, she leads a reclusive life, despite the urging of her flirtatious roommate, Dahlia. Carolyn grows dependent on living vicariously through Dahlia, eavesdropping and then covertly watching as her roommate's sexual behaviour becomes more and more bizarre. But then Dahlia is murdered, and Carolyn must overcome her fears in order to bring the killer to justice.

A tense dark thriller for those who like their erotica on the forbidden side.

ISBN 0 352 33624 2

CONTINUUM
Portia Da Costa
£6.99

Joanna Darrell is something in the city. When she takes a break from her high-powered job she is drawn into a continuum of strange experiences and bizarre coincidences. Like Alice in a decadent Wonderland, she enters a parallel world of perversity and unusual pleasure. She's attracted to fetishism and discipline and her new friends make sure she gets more than a taste of erotic punishment.

This is a reprint of one of our best-selling and kinkiest titles ever!

ISBN 0 352 33120 8

If you would like a complete list of plot summaries of Black Lace titles, or would like to receive information on other publications available, please send a stamped addressed envelope to:

Black Lace, Thames Wharf Studios,
Rainville Road, London W6 9HA

BLACK LACE BOOKLIST

Information is correct at time of printing. To check availability go to www.blacklace-books.co.uk

All books are priced £5.99 unless another price is given.

Black Lace books with a contemporary setting

THE TOP OF HER GAME	Emma Holly ISBN 0 352 33337 5	☐
LIKE MOTHER, LIKE DAUGHTER	Georgina Brown ISBN 0 352 33422 3	☐
THE TIES THAT BIND	Tesni Morgan ISBN 0 352 33438 X	☐
IN THE FLESH	Emma Holly ISBN 0 352 33498 3	☐
SHAMELESS	Stella Black ISBN 0 352 33485 1	☐
TONGUE IN CHEEK	Tabitha Flyte ISBN 0 352 33484 3	☐
FIRE AND ICE	Laura Hamilton ISBN 0 352 33486 X	☐
SAUCE FOR THE GOOSE	Mary Rose Maxwell ISBN 0 352 33492 4	☐
INTENSE BLUE	Lyn Wood ISBN 0 352 33496 7	☐
THE NAKED TRUTH	Natasha Rostova ISBN 0 352 33497 5	☐
A SPORTING CHANCE	Susie Raymond ISBN 0 352 33501 7	☐
TAKING LIBERTIES	Susie Raymond ISBN 0 352 33357 X	☐
A SCANDALOUS AFFAIR	Holly Graham ISBN 0 352 33523 8	☐
THE NAKED FLAME	Crystalle Valentino ISBN 0 352 33528 9	☐
CRASH COURSE	Juliet Hastings ISBN 0 352 33018 X	☐

ANIMAL PASSIONS	Martine Marquand ISBN 0 352 33499 1	☐
ON THE EDGE	Laura Hamilton ISBN 0 352 33534 3	☐
LURED BY LUST	Tania Picarda ISBN 0 352 33533 5	☐
LEARNING TO LOVE IT	Alison Tyler ISBN 0 352 33535 1	☐
THE HOTTEST PLACE	Tabitha Flyte ISBN 0 352 33536 X	☐
THE NINETY DAYS OF GENEVIEVE	Lucinda Carrington ISBN 0 352 33070 8	☐
EARTHY DELIGHTS	Tesni Morgan ISBN 0 352 33548 3	☐
MAN HUNT £6.99	Cathleen Ross ISBN 0 352 33583 1	☐
MÉNAGE £6.99	Emma Holly ISBN 0 352 33231 X	☐
DREAMING SPIRES £6.99	Juliet Hastings ISBN 0 352 33584 X	☐
THE TRANSFORMATION £6.99	Natasha Rostova ISBN 0 352 33311 1	☐
STELLA DOES HOLLYWOOD £6.99	Stella Black ISBN 0 352 33588 2	☐
UP TO NO GOOD £6.99	Karen S. Smith ISBN 0 352 33589 0	☐
SIN.NET £6.99	Helena Ravenscroft ISBN 0 352 33598 X	☐
HOTBED £6.99	Portia Da Costa ISBN 0 352 33614 5	☐
TWO WEEKS IN TANGIER £6.99	Annabel Lee ISBN 0 352 33599 8	☐
HIGHLAND FLING £6.99	Jane Justine ISBN 0 352 33616 1	☐

Black Lace books with an historical setting

INVITATION TO SIN £6.99	Charlotte Royal ISBN 0 352 33217 4	☐
PRIMAL SKIN	Leona Benkt Rhys ISBN 0 352 33500 9	☐
DEVIL'S FIRE	Melissa MacNeal ISBN 0 352 33527 0	☐
WILD KINGDOM	Deanna Ashford ISBN 0 352 33549 1	☐

DARKER THAN LOVE	Kristina Lloyd ISBN 0 352 33279 4	☐
STAND AND DELIVER	Helena Ravenscroft ISBN 0 352 33340 5	☐
THE CAPTIVATION £6.99	Natasha Rostova ISBN 0 352 33234 4	☐
CIRCO EROTICA £6.99	Mercedes Kelley ISBN 0 352 33257 3	☐

Black Lace anthologies

SUGAR AND SPICE £7.99	Various ISBN 0 352 33227 1	☐
CRUEL ENCHANTMENT Erotic Fairy Stories	Janine Ashbless ISBN 0 352 33483 5	☐
MORE WICKED WORDS	Various ISBN 0 352 33487 8	☐
WICKED WORDS 3	Various ISBN 0 352 33522 X	☐
WICKED WORDS 4	Various ISBN 0 352 33603 X	☐

Black Lace non-fiction

| THE BLACK LACE BOOK OF
   WOMEN'S SEXUAL
   FANTASIES | Ed. Kerri Sharp
ISBN 0 352 33346 4 | ☐ |

Please send me the books I have ticked above.

Name ....

Address ....

....

....

.... Post Code ....

Send to: **Cash Sales, Black Lace Books, Thames Wharf Studios, Rainville Road, London W6 9HA.**

US customers: for prices and details of how to order books for delivery by mail, call 1-800-805-1083.

Please enclose a cheque or postal order, made payable to **Virgin Publishing Ltd**, to the value of the books you have ordered plus postage and packing costs as follows:
    UK and BFPO – £1.00 for the first book, 50p for each subsequent book.
    Overseas (including Republic of Ireland) – £2.00 for the first book, £1.00 for each subsequent book.

If you would prefer to pay by VISA, ACCESS/MASTER-CARD, DINERS CLUB, AMEX or SWITCH, please write your card number and expiry date here:

....

Please allow up to 28 days for delivery.

Signature ....